Reckless abandon

Book cover design by Y'All That Graphic
Formatting by Classic Interior Design
Professionally edited by Silla Webb
Proofreading by Tiffany Hernandez

Reckless abandon

Prologue

BRYNLEE

I NEVER IMAGINED MY WEDDING DAY AND HIGH SCHOOL graduation falling within weeks of each other. My cap and gown hung next to my hastily purchased wedding dress in the closet of my bedroom in my parents' house. I always dreamed of my big day being this grand affair with all my college friends mingling with my family and the girls from my high school cheer squad who I managed to keep in touch with. It was supposed to be years from now, something I planned over the course of several months, not weeks. A spring event at a ritzy venue with waiters in bow ties carrying trays of hors d'oeuvres and flutes of champagne, the aisle lined with bundles of lilies and tulips, tables draped in fine linens with meticulously designed centerpieces adorning them. But a trip to the local pharmacy and two blue lines changed all that.

Sean stared at me when I broke the news to him, his mouth opened in shock, the boutonniere pinned to the lapel of his tuxedo hanging askew. His hair was disheveled and he smelled of cheap beer, but my life-changing confession sobered him up.

"Are you sure?" he asked once he found his voice.

"Positive." I winced at my choice of words, but I was positive, just like the three pregnancy tests I'd taken two days earlier. That was how long it took me to work up the nerve to tell my eighteen-year-old boyfriend he was about to be a dad. I probably shouldn't have told him at senior prom, but I'd been irritated with him. He started drinking with his buddies before we arrived, taking sips from the flask hidden in the pocket of his tuxedo jacket. Normally it wouldn't have bothered me, but his reckless behavior compounded my anxiety over being pregnant. We'd both have to grow up and grow up fast.

He ended up puking on me later that night. Instead of talking to me and figuring out what we were going to do, he got black-out drunk and ruined my dress. The next morning, he had to face both our parents with a vicious hangover. My mama cried, and his daddy cussed. He at least held my hand through it all, offering more comfort than he had the night before. My father sat stoically, his fingers steepled beneath his chin.

"Sweetheart," he said, finally breaking his silence, and turned to my mother. "Why don't you take

Brynlee into the kitchen and help her get cleaned up." He motioned to my tear-stained face and snotty nose. "Get her something to drink while you're at it," he added, surreptitiously requesting a moment of privacy with Sean. "There's a fresh pitcher of lemonade in the fridge." His tight smile was the only sign of the undercurrent of rage boiling just below the surface.

"I can help her." Sean shot to his feet, eager to be out of my father's reach.

"Sit down, son. You and I need to have a talk, man to man," my father instructed. Sean sank back onto the couch, swallowing hard. Like a coward, I jumped at the opportunity to leave. I had a pretty good idea of how the conversation would go, but I didn't want to be a witness to it.

Twenty minutes later, my father and Sean emerged from the den. Daddy's large hand clamped over my boyfriend's shoulder. The gesture was meant to be assuring, comforting even, but it was also a warning.

Do right by my daughter or face my wrath.

There was never really a proposal or an acceptance of an offer to get married. There was simply an understanding that I needed to have his last name before I started to show. My mom and future mother-in-law drove into the city to a bridal boutique where we could buy a gown right off the rack and take it home. I tried them on in a daze, wondering what life would be like now. How would all my plans and dreams be affected? Would I still be able to go to college in the fall? I had a full ride scholarship that would get me through all four years. Would I have to forfeit it if I needed to take a break from school? So many unanswered questions swam in my head. I barely noticed my mother's gasp and gentle praise.

When I finally lifted my gaze to her, tears welled in her eyes, and one hand covered her mouth to shield her sudden show of emotion.

"You look beautiful, sweetie." I glanced at the mirror, struck by how perfectly the dress fit and how beautiful it was. Finally snapping out of my stupor, I faced the mirror fully before turning from side to side. The silhouette was romantic and the bead work exquisite with a modest train and sheer back with lace embroidery.

I didn't hesitate to make my decision. "This is the one."

"Looks pretty good," Janet, my future mother-in-law crowed. "Just make sure you watch what you eat over the next few weeks," she tsked, planting a hand on her bony hip, her willowy frame and hollow cheeks a stark contrast to my ample curves. I'd never been ultra-thin like some of my friends. My legs were toned but thick with muscle from years of gymnastics, and my hips kept me from being able to borrow pants from the other girls I hung out with. "You don't want to put on too much weight and not be able to fit into this beautiful dress." My face flamed red. Surely she was just trying to be helpful, but not only was she addressing the elephant in the room—the fact Sean and I were getting married so soon because of my pregnancy—but she also just chipped away at my biggest insecurity: my weight. My hands went to my stomach, already feeling self-conscious about the changes my body was about to go through.

"I wouldn't worry too much about that, honey. Your baby is only about the size of a grape right now." My mother's eyes softened, and my chin quivered a bit. She was doing her best to soften the blow Janet had landed without making a scene.

I backed away from the mirrors to escape to the dressing room, quickly slipping off the dress. Tears coursed down my face as I gently replaced the white fabric onto the sturdy hanger. Lowering myself to the bench, I curled into a ball, hugging my knees. It was all too much. Graduating, getting married, having a baby. I was hardly ready for one of those, but all three were barreling toward me full speed ahead.

When the tears finally stopped, I wiped my face and got dressed. Mom was waiting for me when I stepped out of the dressing room. "Ready to go?" she asked. I nodded and followed her outside where Janet was waiting with the car. Judging by the tense silence between the two women, I could only assume my mother had said something to her about the remark on my weight. I smiled to myself, assured that she was still the same protective mama bear even though I was an adult about to enter the real world at lightning speed.

The day of the wedding my eyes were dry, wrung out completely from the previous week. I loved Sean and was certain he was the one, but I'd wanted to do this on our terms and in our own time. Now it was a rush to the altar so we wouldn't have a child out of wedlock. Never mind that everyone would know in approximately six months that I was pregnant before the wedding. No one would dare say anything to me, but they wouldn't hesitate to whisper about it behind my back.

I was all dressed in white and ready to go, poking a dainty, pearl earring through my lobe. The jewelry was my something old— a family heirloom passed down from my great grandmother. Every woman in my family had worn them on their wedding day, and now it was my turn.

Two quick taps sounded on the door and without hesitation, I called out to the person on the other side. "Come in." The door slowly creeped open as I gave myself one final look over.

Macon, Sean's best friend, tentatively stepped inside and pulled the door shut behind him.

"Hey, Macon!" I greeted him with a friendly smile and walked over to him, arms outstretched. He was the best man and all around the best guy I knew. He and Sean were complete opposites, but they'd been close since elementary school. Macon was quiet where Sean was boisterous. They were both athletic, but Macon was much more studious. Sean partied and made average grades, but Macon was a dedicated student with a perfect GPA.

Sean's easy-going personality and sense of humor was what won everyone over. He was charming and funny with a smile that made girls melt at his feet. I'd been one of those girls. The day he'd asked me to be his date to the winter formal after sophomore English, I was a goner. A year later, I gladly offered up my virginity because I knew he was the one. He was my first and my last, and despite the distance between us the past several weeks, I knew he loved me. We were both coping with the sudden changes in our own ways.

"Hey, Bryn." Macon hugged me gently, careful not to muss my hair or smear my makeup. When I stepped back, my smile fell a little. He looked tense, his jaw tight and his usually broad smile absent. Before I could ask what was wrong, he shoved a piece of paper at me. "Sean asked me to give this to you," he announced, and a bit of my excitement returned. He wasn't the type to write me love letters, but it looked like he made an exception for our special day.

I hastily unfolded the page, my heart fluttering in anticipation.

Brynlee, it began, and I nearly squealed.

I'm sorry I couldn't do this in person. It's just too much. I can't stand the thought of seeing the tears in your eyes when I tell you I can't go through with it. I'm just not ready to get married.

Pain sliced through my chest, and a sob broke free. I covered my mouth with a shaky hand and continued to read, needing to know why he was doing this.

I still love you. I hope you know that. I hope that one day we can make this work, but for now, I have to go. I can't stay in this town and watch everybody judge me. It will be better for both of us if I'm not around for a while.

7

Please don't try to find me. I just need to be alone right now.

My knees buckled, and I braced for impact with the floor, but it never came. Macon wrapped his arms around me, and I lost control, my emotions slamming into me like a freight train. I thought I'd run out of tears, but I was wrong. So very wrong.

BRYNLEE

LITTLE FEET SLAPPED AGAINST THE FLOOR, AND I pinched my eyes shut as a smile curved my lips. I braced for impact, ready for the morning attack. Giggles erupted a second before a tiny wiggling body landed on top of me. The covers were yanked below my chin, revealing my face stretched in faux surprise as though this didn't happen every Saturday morning.

"Mornin', Sweet Pea."

Seafoam green eyes peered at me through a mess of soft blonde curls. "Mornin' Mommy." Harper's arms wrapped around my neck, and I blew raspberries against her cheek as she hugged me close.

These mornings were my favorite. I didn't have to slip out of the house before she awoke to head to class or my part-time job. My shift didn't start until two, so I wouldn't have to drop her off to my mother until this afternoon. Mom got to spend as much time with my daughter as I did, and I tried not to resent that. I was lucky. I knew that. I had parents who helped me so I wouldn't have to choose between school and work. They provided my daughter and me a modest house that I only had to pay utilities on so that my child and I could have a home of our own. My college was mostly paid for with scholarships, and I had a job that let me work around my class schedule. I was very lucky.

Yet...

I was still on my own, and I hated Sean McEntire for that. The hurt of him abandoning me on our wedding day three years ago had begun to dissipate, but the anger still simmered like a pot that could boil over any minute. God help that boy if he ever rolled back into town. I supposed I should be grateful, even to him. A lot of young, single moms didn't have the support I did.

Six months after Sean left, he began sending money. But that was it. No note, no explanation, no physical address, just a PO box in North Carolina. What he was doing there, I didn't know. All I knew was he had an uncle who lived there.

If he had just told me he didn't want to get married, we could've worked something out. We could've made the decision together to call off the wedding. He didn't have to make me the laughing stock of our small town. Nobody would say it to my face, but I could feel their judgmental gazes on my back and hear their pitying remarks whispered behind their hands, as though that somehow made them less hurtful.

I pushed those feelings aside so I could focus on my daughter. She cackled as she flopped down next to me, landing in an angel pose atop my duvet. I popped up and turned so I was leaning over her. Squeals of laughter echoed through the room as I tickled her belly and tiny feet.

Getting our morning routine started, I set Harper up with her juice and some cereal and threw a load of laundry into the washing machine before starting on breakfast. Macon was bringing my car back after changing the oil and fixing the brakes. They went out on me a couple days ago on my way home from class. Luckily, Harper wasn't in the car with me. I was scared enough as it was. After nearly crashing into the local Wal-Mart and crying hysterically for nearly ten minutes, I pulled myself together and called Macon.

At one time, Macon Lewis had been Sean's best friend. As far as I knew, they didn't keep in touch after my ex split, but I never asked. I didn't want to know. I was afraid the answer would change the way I felt about Macon, and those feelings had already become far more complicated than I cared to admit.

Macon was the one who held me together when I fell apart after Sean left. I think he felt responsible somehow because he was the messenger who delivered the bad news. For a solid month, he checked on me every day to make sure I was alright. He brought me my favorite snacks—how he knew what those were, I'll never know—and made me leave the house for something fun at least once a week. When he left for college that fall, I broke down all over again. I'd been leaning on him hard. Even though I still had my close girlfriends, he'd become my *best* friend. He was there for me when nobody else was.

Part of me felt like I'd kept him so close, clung to him so tightly because he was my only link to Sean and the only person who had any insight into why he did what he did. But when I asked him, he said he didn't know and that Sean never confided in him that he'd planned to leave. He was just as surprised as I was and almost as angry.

A knock at the door startled me, and I dropped my spatula into the skillet of bacon frying on the stove. Hot grease splashed across my knuckles, sizzling my skin as I let out a low curse. Thankfully, Harper didn't hear or she'd likely be repeating it at Sunday School.

I brought the back of my hand to my mouth and sucked on the tender skin in an attempt to soothe the burn as I pulled open the door. Macon waited just over the threshold with a friendly smile plastered over his face. It dropped when he saw me, registering the pain in my expression.

"What's wrong?" he asked in his deep drawl, stepping into my space and reaching for my hand.

"Bacon popped me," I answered, letting him inspect my reddening skin. His fingers gripped me gently, but the pressure was enough to make my body react, just like it had every time he touched me lately. My stomach dipped and my chest tightened at the contact, but he seemed completely unfazed.

I didn't remember exactly when I began to see him in a different light. All I knew for sure was once I finally gave up hope that Sean would come back and that I was no longer in love with him, things began to shift between Macon and me. It started out slowly, subtle changes that I didn't even realize were happening at first.

The only problem: I was the only one who noticed. Nothing changed on his end, and I didn't want to risk ruining our friendship by making my feelings known. But it was so hard when he was this close and being so caring and gentle with me. Not to mention, how much Harper adored him, and he adored her. She even called him Uncle Macon. He doted on her. He had since the day she was born.

He was seriously perfect.

He was also taken.

Macon met Reece six months ago when they became lab partners in Chemistry. A spike of jealousy hit me right in the chest when he called me after their first date, but I had no right to say anything. I was seeing someone at the time too, and Macon had been supportive of my relationship. It was only right that I support him as well.

Reece was always cordial with me when she came to visit, but I could tell she didn't like how close Macon and I were. More than once, I caught her looking me up and down like she was sizing me up. Anytime Macon and I were engaged in conversation, she'd find a reason to touch him. A hand on his arm, her arm around his waist. Sometimes she'd step into his side and nudge him, knowing he'd pull her in with an arm around her shoulder. It was like she was rubbing it in, letting me know he was hers. Or maybe it was all in my head. Maybe it was just my subconscious worrying that someone would notice I'd developed feelings for my best friend.

"You got any vanilla extract?" My gaze snapped to Macon in surprise. Why on earth would he ask me that? Was he thinking about baking cookies at a time like this?

"Um, yeah," I replied, my brow furrowing in confusion.

His responding grin sent flutters to my belly. "Come on." He closed the door and motioned for me to follow him. At his request, I located the vanilla. He took it from my hands and pulled me to the sink, holding my burned hand over it. Flipping the cap open, he carefully poured a little over my burn. The relief was instant. I let out a sigh, my shoulders sagging.

"Better?" he asked.

"Yes."

"Have a seat. I'll finish the cooking."

"You don't have to do that. Besides, I was going to make gravy for the biscuits in the oven."

He scoffed at my response, sending me an exasperated look. "I'll handle the gravy. Mine's better anyway."

He was taunting me. He knew I took great pride in my cooking. I learned from the best, and you never challenged a Southern woman's cooking skills. I stood defiantly with my hand on my hip.

"I beg to differ. You don't put nearly enough pepper in your gravy."

"No way. Yours is too thick. You definitely need to add more milk."

"Macon Lewis, are you insulting my cooking while standing in *my* kitchen? Now I know your mama taught you better than that." He was getting me fired up, and his amused smirk was only adding fuel to the fire.

"You're right," he acquiesced, scooping the bacon from the pan and placing it on a paper towel-lined plate. "This is your show, and I don't want to steal your thunder."

My mouth opened, ready to deliver my retort, when he stepped in close and pressed a chaste kiss to the top of my head. Words caught in my throat as he quickly stepped away and took a seat at my table. It wasn't the first time he'd done that, but it was the first time it felt like it was all too much and not nearly enough at the same time.

My heart squeezed in my chest as I finished up breakfast, listening to Macon interact with my daughter. I chanced the occasional glance over my shoulder, and it made my chest ache even more. Harper would probably never know her father, but I was incredibly thankful for Macon's presence in her life.

As Macon dug into his fourth buttermilk biscuit smothered in gravy—too thick, my ass—I rinsed my plate and went to the laundry room to transfer my freshly washed clothes to the dryer.

"What the hell?" I exclaimed when I stepped in a puddle of water in front of the washer.

"Everything okay in there?" Macon asked from the next room.

"I'm not sure. There's a bunch of water on the floor." The legs of his chair scraped against the floor as he pushed away from the table. A moment later, he stood next to me, inspecting the mess in front of the appliance.

"Uh, oh," he murmured, and my happy mood instantly disintegrated.

Two

"What do you mean 'uh oh?' Is this really bad?"

"Ah, I don't know yet. I'm gonna have to pull the washer out and take a look. Could be the pump or could just be a hose."

"Macon," I began, not wanting to make this his problem. It was the weekend, and I was sure he had other plans. I didn't want him to have to fix something else for me. "You don't need to worry about this. I can call my dad." But he was already in fix-it mode.

"Where's that tool kit I bought you?" He opened the washer and started pulling out damp garments and depositing them into the dryer. My cheeks flamed as he removed a handful of my underwear. He turned to me, eyebrow quirked, a mischievous grin tipping up one side of his lips. My face grew hotter as he held out one blood red thong.

"Who you wearing these fancy draws for?"

"Who says I gotta have someone to wear them for? Maybe I just want to feel sexy and empowered." I jutted out my chin in defiance.

His eyes flitted down my body briefly. It was almost too quick to notice, but I did, and my breath caught. The tiny laundry room suddenly felt even smaller, and his large body—which had always dominated any room—suddenly felt suffocating. Or maybe that was the sexual tension.

He turned from me, the look of longing that flashed momentarily in his eyes gone in a heartbeat. Back was his playful smirk.

"At least they're clean I guess."

"Macon," I gasped and swatted his arm. "You rascal. Get outta here, and let me take care of the rest of my laundry."

"No need," he replied, shutting the door to the dryer and turning it on. "All done."

He exited, and I finally felt like I could draw a deep breath. Letting out a long sigh, my shoulders sagged in defeat. First it was my car, now the washing machine. I stopped myself from asking what else could go wrong, knowing better than to send that question out into the universe.

I cleaned Harper up and then turned on her favorite cartoon while Macon retrieved the tools needed to fix the washer. As soon as she heard the opening theme song, she nestled into her spot on the couch and watched in rapt attention. I was mildly convinced this show had some kind of mind control over young children, but it was educational and allowed me to get things done around the house.

Retrieving my cosmetics bag, I settled into my favorite spot at the kitchen table where the natural light was just right for applying my makeup. This was my routine and had been ever since Harper became mobile. I could better keep an eye on her out here in the open.

As I applied a dab of concealer under my eyes to hide how tired I was, I paused with my beauty sponge halfway to my face at the low murmur of a deep male voice. Macon was on the phone, and although I knew I shouldn't be eavesdropping, I couldn't help but listen. When I heard him apologize and insist, "It's not her fault," I knew immediately who he was talking to. *Reece*. Jealousy and guilt flooded me as I realized he must've had plans with her, and fixing my problems once again was ruining their day. I quickly finished my makeup and went to the laundry room to remedy the situation.

Three

MACON

MY STOMACH KNOTTED WITH DREAD AS I TAPPED ON Reece's name in my phone's contact list, knowing she'd be pissed that I was pushing back our plans for the day. It couldn't be avoided, though, and I prayed she'd understand. I couldn't leave Brynlee without a washing machine, and who knew how long it would take to get a repairman out there to look at it.

"Hey, baby," she crooned when she picked up.

"Hey, Reecey cup." I used her favorite nickname in the hope that it would

soften the blow a little bit.

"You miss me already?" she asked sweetly. I'd spoken to her once already this morning and was supposed to meet up with her in a couple hours.

"Of course I do. I may be a bit late getting to you, though. Something's come up."

"Oh no. What happened?" she asked, her voice filled with concern.

"I brought Brynlee's car back to her this morning, and her washer started leaking all over the floor. I'm taking a look at it now. I think it's going to need a hose replaced."

"Well, uh," she huffed, clearly irritated now. "Can't her daddy help her with that? We've had these plans for weeks. It's all my mom has talked about." We were supposed to drive up to her parents and spend the afternoon with them. They were nice folks, and her mom treated me like the son she never had.

"I'm sorry, baby. He won't have time to look at it today." Not to mention, he wasn't great with machines. He was a smart man and good with numbers, but give him something mechanical to work on, and he could tinker with it for hours and never manage to fix it. "Hopefully it won't take too long to get the replacement part and install it."

"I know you don't want to hear this because she's your friend, but that girl takes advantage of you. You fix everything for her."

"It's not her fault. She can't help it that her brakes went out or her washer's broke." I did my best to clamp down my irritation and tried to see things from Reece's point of view. She didn't know Bryn like I did. She didn't know that she was independent and begrudgingly accepted help only when she absolutely had to. Reece didn't see how hard Bryn had worked to get to where she was so she could provide a good life for herself and her daughter. If I could save her several hundred dollars by helping her fix a few things now and then, I was more than willing to do it. Lord knew Sean wasn't going to help. He probably didn't even know where she lived now (he still sent money for Harper to Bryn's parents' house). He'd never met his daughter nor had he spoken to Brynlee since the night before he was supposed to marry her.

She let out a long, defeated sigh. "I know that. I'm not trying to be mean or insensitive," she began, and I relaxed a little. Sometimes Reece could be just that: insensitive. She didn't completely lack compassion, but she also didn't like to be inconvenienced. "I just don't see why it's always *your* job to fix her problems." A spike of anger pinged in my gut, and I gritted my teeth. I didn't like the direction in which this conversation was going. It was time to hang up.

"Look, I gotta go. There's water everywhere. I'll make it up to you."

"Alright," she agreed. "I'll talk to you later."

We said our goodbyes, and I slipped my phone into my back pocket before grabbing the screwdriver out of the tool kit I'd bought Brynlee when she first moved in.

"If you have other plans today, I can call my dad." Bryn's voice startled me, and I nearly dropped my tool. I turned to look at her. She stood in the doorway, one arm crossed over her abdomen as she watched me with trepidation. My chest tightened at the sheepish way she wouldn't meet my eye. She must've heard me on the phone with Reece.

"It's no big deal. I don't think it will take long to fix."

"But this shouldn't be your problem. You're always fixing everything.

I'm not your responsibility." She echoed Reece's sentiments.

"I know that. But what kind of friend would I be if I had the skills and means to help you and just left you high and dry?" She winced, the space between her brows creasing. "Who knows, maybe one day I'll need your help with something," I added with a shrug.

"Oh yeah? What could I possibly help *you* with?" she asked, one taupe eyebrow lifting in intrigue. Her question might have been innocent, but it sounded suggestive, and I was suddenly fighting the urge to let my eyes roam down her body at the curve of her breasts showing just above the neckline of her tank top and the tiny little shorts framing her long, lean legs.

I swallowed thickly as sweat beaded on my forehead. "I may get sick or hurt one day and need someone to cut my grass," I joked, knowing damn well that was her least favorite chore. She claimed it was the bane of her existence but was too stubborn and budget conscious to hire someone to do it.

She scowled before rolling her eyes and crossing her arms over her chest, pushing her breasts even higher.

Don't look down. Don't look down. Don't look down.

She's your best friend and will slap you if you gawk at her.

"I'm being serious," she rebutted.

"So am I." She knew I wasn't, but this was how I distracted her. If I could make her laugh, she swatted me playfully and walked off, muttering under her breath about what a pain in the ass I was. Every time she did that, I wanted to pull her into my arms and kiss her smiling lips.

But that couldn't happen.

I was taken, and she was still hung up on Sean. She denied still having feelings for him, but any time his name came up, she got red faced and madder than a hornet. You don't react that way over someone you don't have feelings for still. She also never stayed in a new relationship for long, claiming some deficiency or another when she inevitably broke up with the poor guy.

When she turned and walked out the door, I finally let my gaze drop, but I didn't let it linger. I needed to remember I had a girlfriend.

And that Brynlee only thought of me as a friend.

A COUPLE HOURS LATER, I WAS SECURING THE LAST screw into place on Brynlee's washing machine when she brought me a tall glass of iced tea. The local hardware store had thankfully had the hose I needed in stock, so it was a fairly quick fix once I found the problem.

"All done," I announced as I stood and wiped my hands on a spare towel. Brynlee handed me the glass, and I thanked her before taking a long draw from it. Bryn was dressed in her typical work uniform, and her hair was tied back neatly, soft blonde waves gathered at her neck.

"You're a lifesaver," she appraised and stood on her tiptoes to kiss my cheek. "I don't know what I'd do without you."

Ditto.

"Glad I could help." I shot her one of my signature crooked grins and for just a moment, I thought I saw something in her eyes that resembled longing when they flashed to my mouth. Maybe I imagined it. She would never think about kissing me.

Would she?

"Are you heading out soon?"

"Yeah, just as soon as I get Harper loaded into the car."

"Mind dropping me off at home on your way to your parents' house?" I needed a ride since I drove her car over here this morning after finishing it up late last night. Yet another reason Reece was cross with me.

"Not at all. That was my plan."

I finished cleaning up the tools and made sure the floor was dry while she got Harper buckled into her car seat. We made the short trip to my house, and Harper cried when I got out. I leaned in and gave her a quick kiss to the top of her head and promised to see her later.

"Be good for your mamaw, and I'll bring you a toy next time I see you."

"O-tay," she sniffled, the big, fat tears glistening on her cheeks tugging at my heartstrings.

"Thanks again for fixing my brakes and my washing machine," Brynlee called out the window, leaning over the passenger seat.

"Anytime," I assured her before waving goodbye.

And I meant it.

Four

BRYNLEE

After dropping Macon off, I headed to my parents' house where my mother was waiting on the front porch. Harper's tears dried instantly when she saw Mom. She couldn't get out of her car seat fast enough.

"There's my baby girl," Mom said, scooping my little one up and cradling her to her chest. She pressed a kiss to her cheek and propped her on her hip. I had wonderful parents. Growing up, they treated me and my little sister, Blake, like gold. Still, nothing could've prepared me for how amazing they would become as grandparents. They both doted on my daughter, and it warmed my heart every time I watched them together.

"How's my other baby girl?" Mom asked, wrapping

her free arm around me and giving me a gentle squeeze.

"I'm good. Glad to have my car back."

"Was Macon able to fix it?"

"Yes, he dropped it off this morning. Thankfully he was still there when my washer decided to spring a leak."

"Oh no. What was wrong with it?"

"Just needed a new hose, I guess." I shrugged. My knowledge of appliances was little to none. All I knew was Macon ran to the hardware store and came back with a new hose and viola, my washer was fixed.

"He's such a nice boy. I'm glad you have him in your life."

"Me too." I smiled, hoping she wouldn't see that it didn't reach my eyes.

I lifted my gaze to find her watching me quizzically. Her head tilted to one side, and I knew I was in trouble.

"You know," she began, and I instantly dreaded what was coming. "You and Macon are such good friends, and he's quite handsome. Have you ever considered—"

"He has a girlfriend." I cut her off before she could go any farther.

"Oh," she said, her shoulders sagging in disappointment. Then she looked at my face and must've read the feelings I'd failed to mask. "Oh!" Her eyes widened, and she took a step toward me. "How long have you had feelings for him?"

"I don't know. It's been a gradual thing."

"Does he know?"

"Heavens no. And it needs to stay that way. I don't want to ruin our friendship."

"But—" she began, but I held up my hand to stop her.

"He has a girlfriend," I reminded her.

She frowned. My mother frowned like a child who was told they couldn't have a piece of candy after finishing their dinner.

Thankfully, she dropped the subject and went into the kitchen, handing me a paper bag. "I packed you dinner so you'd eat something other than a granola bar while you're at work."

I didn't tell her that I usually didn't eat anything during my six hour shift every other Saturday, but that would've sent her into a tizzy. Instead, I smiled and thanked her before heading to work.

The bookstore was bustling when I arrived for my shift, but it finally slowed down a couple hours later. I slipped my name badge off and took my break, leaving the other associate, Mina, on the floor to help customers. Settling into one of the oversized chairs in the very back corner of the store, I opened the paperback I'd started the last day I worked and nibbled on the turkey and avocado sandwich my mom had made me. My cheeks began to flush as the hero and heroine began to remove each other's clothes as though anyone who walked by would somehow know what I was reading.

I sank further into the cushions, lifting the book to hide my reddened face. The scene progressed, the writing becoming more explicit as my skin grew hot. My breathing became more rapid as each party grew closer to release.

And then I was there, within the scene of this steamy book. I imagined it was Macon growling my name, his hand fisting in my hair. My body reacted to the vivid scene playing out in my imagination. I could see his eyes darkening as he looked down at me, his body hovering just above mine. Before I could let myself dream of what it would feel like as he slid slowly into me just like the couple on the page, I slammed the book shut and stood, not allowing myself another moment to fantasize about something that would never happen.

I was hot and bothered throughout the rest of my shift, and I couldn't wait to finish the book. Normally, I didn't allow myself the luxury of buying the books from the store, opting instead for borrowing from the library, but I *had* to have this one. I would finish it tonight.

THE NEXT WEEKEND, I WAS COMPLETELY FREE. HAVING finished my last final on Wednesday, there was no more studying left to do, and since I'd worked the last two days, I was ready to spend some quality time with my baby girl.

With a cooler full of ice, drinks, and sandwiches, I packed a bag with our beach towels and a change of clothes and loaded up my car. It was too hot to do anything other than spend the day at the lake.

It was still early when we arrived, so we had the beach nearly to ourselves. I spread out our oversized towels, grabbed Harper's floaties, and lathered us both in sunscreen.

Harper was splashing in the shallow water when a familiar voice called out my name. I looked up to find Macon standing on the shore, his hand shielding his eyes. Harper's head snapped up, and she skipped out of the water.

"Macon," she squealed and crashed into his legs, wrapping her tiny arms around his calves.

"Hey, Half Pint." He bent to pick her up, and before I could warn him that her bathing suit was soaked, she was propped on his hip, both of them wearing big, goofy grins. I finally took a moment to look around and saw the group that was with him. Reece stood at his side, looking like the picture of elegance in her floppy hat, oversized sunglasses, and designer sandals with a sarong tied around her svelte figure. I suddenly felt self conscious about my body and crossed my arms over my midriff, trying to hide the bare skin on my stomach. My stretch marks weren't terrible, but out here in the harsh, bright late morning sun, they'd be much more noticeable.

Besides Macon and Reece, there were two other couples: Haley and Jonah, the duo everyone considered the power couple of our graduating class, and Shayla with her on again, off again boyfriend Calvin who'd attended a rival school. Shayla and I had been close once, but we didn't see much of each other these days. We were both busy with school, and I had Harper to take care of. Still, we kept in touch through text and social media, but rarely got to hang out anymore.

I swallowed hard as a lump formed in my throat and a spike of jealousy hit me square in the chest. I told myself it was because of Sean. He should've been here with me. It could've been us hanging out with our friends at the lake on the weekend. Instead, I was rarely invited on trips like this. It wasn't their fault. For nearly three years, I'd said no. After all, I was either pregnant or had a small child to take care of. I couldn't just drop what I was doing or come and go as I pleased. I had responsibilities that they couldn't even begin to understand.

A pang of guilt speared through me with those thoughts. My daughter was my whole world, and I wouldn't have traded her for anything even if it meant missing out on my youth.

I tried to convince myself that my jealousy had nothing to do with Macon and the fact that he had another woman hanging on his arm. Nope, nothing at all.

"Reece, how are you?" I plastered on a smile and greeted everyone in turn. Reece offered one delicate hand for a gentle shake, but the rest of the group greeted me with hugs. These were my friends, and I was excited to catch up with them.

"Let's just set up here," Macon announced to the group. They voiced their agreement and started setting down their supplies. Ten minutes later, they had a canopy set up and a few chairs for lounging. A couple of large floats were placed into the water, and the guys began dragging their dates out into the lake.

Except for Macon. He was helping Harper build a sandcastle while Reece lounged in the shade. She didn't have much to say, but she didn't look happy about being here. Maybe the lake simply wasn't her scene. Or maybe she was upset that Macon was playing with my daughter instead of talking to her.

Macon and Harper finished their sandcastle and Macon looked up, seeming to suddenly remember his girlfriend was here. He stood and brushed sand from his board shorts and walked up to her. He ducked under the canopy and leaned down to kiss her. I turned away quickly but not before she puckered up, meeting his lips halfway.

When I looked up again, he was coaxing her from her shaded perch, his hands clasping hers. A genuine smile curved her lips as he gently pulled her to her feet.

"Okay, okay, I'll get in the water. But if anything touches my leg, I'm out," she warned playfully.

He laughed and wrapped her in his strong arms. "Don't worry. I'll keep you safe," he promised.

I turned away, unable to look on as the happy couple walked into the water hand in hand. A deep ache settled into my chest. I wanted to be the one holding his hand, the one he picked up and carried into the deeper water as I squirmed and clung to his broad shoulders.

A tug on my hand drew my attention away from the group as they waded in chest-deep water. Harper was ready for lunch, so we went to our cooler and plopped down on our towels. I unwrapped her PB&J first before grabbing my turkey sandwich.

"Are you having fun?" I asked, and she nodded vigorously, her mouth full of food.

"Did you save any for me?" Macon walked toward us, his skin glistening in the sunlight. My breath caught at the sight of his muscled chest and rippling abs. His shorts hung just low enough I could see the deep V cut into his hips. I couldn't speak as he knelt in front of my daughter. She offered him an animal cracker, and he took it gratefully, popping it into his mouth and giving her the biggest, cheesiest grin as he did so.

Macon turned to look at me, and his face fell. "What's wrong?"

I shook myself from my haze and quickly answered, "Nothing. I think it's just the heat getting to me."

His brow knitted with concern. "Why don't you lie down under the canopy, get out of the sun for a bit. I'll keep an eye on Harper."

"No, no that's okay. I'll be fine after I drink some cold water. Besides, you have a date to entertain." He turned and followed my gaze out to the shallow water where Reece stood. She was turned to the side, not directly facing us, but she could see us from her peripheral vision. I was certain she'd been watching our exchange. That was probably what I would do if I were in her position.

"Reece doesn't need to be entertained. She's having a great time and would understand." I couldn't put my finger on it, but I could feel it in my bones that he was wrong. She most definitely wouldn't understand if he babysat my daughter instead of paying attention to her.

I took a long swing of my water and replaced the cap. "I'm fine. Really. I think I'm gonna get back in the water."

"Are you sure?" he asked skeptically.

"Positive."

I had just enough time to slather another coat of sunscreen onto Harper's skin before she chased Macon back to the water. He picked her up and twirled her, sending droplets of water flying in all directions. I laughed as the spray landed on my face and arms. Reece didn't look quite as happy about it. She smiled, but it didn't reach her eyes. I knew then that Macon was wrong about Reece not needing to be entertained.

Five

MACON

"BRYN, YOU ARE ABSOLUTELY FRIED." JONAH announced as we packed up our things. I turned and caught sight of Brynlee's back and shoulders. Sure enough, her skin was an angry pink that blanched when he pressed a finger to it. She hissed, the pain causing her face to contort. I went to her without hesitation.

"I must've forgotten to reapply sunscreen." She immediately bent to examine Harper. "Thank goodness I didn't forget to put more on her." She turned her daughter, checking her front and back before cupping her hands on each side of Harper's face. She had a few freckles peppering her nose and cheeks that had become more noticeable after her day in the sun but no sunburn.

Brynlee never ceased to amaze me. She was such a

good mother, even though she did it all on her own and was barely out of childhood herself when her baby came into the world. Even with the severe discomfort she must've been in, her main focus was making sure her daughter was okay.

"I have some aloe," Reece said, reaching into her bag. "Here, put this on," she instructed, handing the bottle to Brynlee.

"Thank you," Bryn said, taking it from Reece. She squirted some onto her palm and rubbed it into her shoulders, air hissing through her teeth with the contact.

"Here, let me," I said as she struggled to reach the space between her shoulder blades. Taking the bottle from her, I deposited a glob of blue goop onto my fingers and tentatively pressed them to her back. She sucked in another sharp breath, and I winced, knowing it must've hurt.

"Sorry."

"It's okay," she assured me and pulled her shirt over her head.

"Are you going to be okay to drive home?"

"I'll be fine. I'll just have to keep my back off the seat."

I passed the aloe to Reece who hastily shoved it in her bag and folded her arms across her chest. Her lips pressed into a thin, flat line, an expression I knew all too well. She was irritated. Before I could ask her what was wrong, Jonah spoke up, drawing my attention away from Reece's vexed glare.

"You should also take an anti-inflammatory when you get home," he instructed.

"Not even accepted into med school yet, and you're already giving out medical advice," Calvin taunted, and Shayla snickered.

"That's not medical advice. That's common sense, dickweed," Haley, Jonah's girlfriend replied.

"Easy, there are little ears present," I warned, tilting my head toward Harper.

"Oops, my bad." Haley winced and covered her mouth.

Brynlee chuckled. "It's okay. She's not paying attention." She was instead playing in the sand again. Bryn sighed. She'd just cleaned her up, and now she was covered again.

"Come here, Half Pint," I said, scooping her up. She squealed and kicked but started to giggle when I turned her upside down and tickled her belly. "I've got her," I assured Brynlee.

We made our way back to the parking lot, splitting off from our friends so I could follow Brynlee to her car. I deposited our chairs on the black top while balancing Harper on the opposite hip and dug my keys from my pocket. "Do you want to grab my truck and pull it around?" I asked Reece, reaching out to give her my keys. We both had our hands full, and it would be easier if we set everything down and she brought the vehicle to us. I knew she had to be tired from the sun and swimming, so I didn't want her to have to carry anything to the truck.

Her gaze slid briefly to Brynlee and back to me as

unease clouded her features. It was gone in an instant and she smiled, taking the keys from me. "Sure," she replied as I took our bag from her and placed it next to the car. I helped Brynlee load up her supplies while she buckled her little girl into her car seat.

"Thank you," she sighed, relieved to have that task taken care of. A spark of anger shot through me at my former best friend. He should've been here to help. He should've been part of the family he helped create instead of running off and shirking his responsibilities. I didn't give a damn that he sent her money every month. It didn't make up for his absence. I was sure Brynlee and Harper would rather have him in their lives.

I pulled her into my arms and immediately regretted it when she gasped, and I remembered her sunburn. "Sorry," I said, releasing her. Instead, I pressed a kiss to the top of her head like I had a hundred times before. When I pulled back, her eyes were closed and a grin tugged at the corners of her mouth. I swallowed hard, fighting back emotions I had no right to feel. "Drive safe," I muttered and hurried away.

My truck's engine roared as Reece pulled into the spot across from Brynlee's car. The windows were rolled down and the air conditioner was turned on full blast since it always took several minutes to cool down the spacious cab. I tossed everything in the bed, then I slid into the driver's seat. Reece sat quietly with her elbow propped on the passenger side door, her eyes trained on the window as lush green trees passed by in a blur. It wasn't like her. She was usually perched next to me on the bench seat with her hand in mine or on my leg. This distance was unusual for her, and it unsettled me.

"Everything okay over there?" I asked after several minutes of silence.

"Yeah," she replied, unconvincingly.

"Reece, what's wrong?" I probed, knowing something was bothering her.

She sighed and propped her cheek on her closed fist. "Nothing."

She was lying. Something was definitely wrong.

I swung my truck into an abandoned lot of an old warehouse and put it in park, turning to face her. "Talk to me, Reece. I can tell something is bothering you."

She stayed quiet for a few heartbeats, then took a deep breath and turned to me. "Is there something going on between you and Brynlee?"

Stunned, I drew back like she'd struck me. "What?" I blurted out. "Why would you think that?"

"You just spend a lot of time with her, and it seemed like you were in an awfully big hurry to get rid of me earlier." Her chin wobbled as tears filled her eyes, and my gut twisted with guilt.

I slid across the seat and pulled her into my arms. It hadn't occurred to me that was how my actions could be perceived. I thought she understood my friendship with Bryn, but I guess I hadn't made that clear. It was time to remedy that.

"It's not like that," I assured her, smoothing a hand over her hair. "She's my best friend."

"You treat that little girl like your own." She sniffled, her voice laced with accusation. "She's not really yours; is she?"

I pulled back and framed her slender shoulders with my hands, urging her to look at me. "That baby is not mine," I promised, even though it made my chest ache to say it. Sometimes I wished she was mine, but I didn't let myself entertain those fantasies for long.

"Are you sure?" Annoyance flared inside me. How could she think that?

"Reece, I need you to listen to me. Brynlee and I are just friends, and that's all we've ever been. There is zero chance of Harper being mine." I gave her a pointed look, hoping she wouldn't make me say it, that she wouldn't force me to tell her I'd never slept with Brynlee.

She watched my face for a moment, her eyes darting back and forth between mine, searching for any hint of a lie. Finally relaxing into my touch, she decided I was telling the truth.

"I'm sorry. I guess I just felt insecure and let my imagination run wild. I shouldn't have doubted you." She cupped my face, her eyes brimming with unshed tears.

"It's alright," I assured her, and before I could say anything else, her lips were on mine. She kissed me fiercely, almost apologetic as her hands roamed up my chest and over my shoulders. Her fingers laced together behind my neck as she pressed her body into mine.

"Take me home," she whispered, her heated gaze full of promise. I rushed home, letting her take the lead when the bedroom door shut behind her. She was gorgeous, one of the sexiest women I'd ever laid eyes on. Still, I had to fight the urge not to imagine she was someone else when I closed my eyes.

Six

BRYNLEE

SUMMERS IN OUR SMALL VIRGINIA TOWN BROUGHT about two things: sports camps and wedding season. Jonah and Haley were gearing up for their upcoming nuptials, and Macon was helping out with our local high school's football camp. His cousin was one of the coaches, and since Macon had been one hell of a left tackle back in the day, helping to keep Sean protected while he executed plays as our starting quarterback, Coach Lewis asked if he wanted to help.

That's right, Sean and I had been the head cheer-leader and the QB. We were a walking cliche back then, and despite every teen movie I'd ever watched, you couldn't have convinced me that our relationship would end in heartache.

Blake's voice pulled me back to the present as she prattled on about the new volleyball coach. I was dropping her off at the school for conditioning since my mom had an appointment and Blake still didn't have her driver's license despite being seventeen. She'd been dragging her feet when it came to taking her driver's test—claiming she'd been too busy with school, sports, and cheerleading—but promised to do it this summer.

We passed by the football field on our way to the gym, and Harper spotted Macon's truck.

"I see Macon truck!" she announced from the back seat. She craned her neck around to keep it in sight, but began to cry when she could no longer see it.

I stopped to let Blake out just outside the gym's entrance. She reached back and gave Harper's cheek a playful squeeze, and my daughter giggled, forgetting how upset she'd been a moment ago.

"Later, Harpy," Blake said and slung her bag over her shoulder, thanking me before slipping out of the passenger seat.

I turned my car around and headed back the way we came. As soon as Macon's truck came into view, Harper started asking to see him again.

"Baby, he's busy right now." Harper's cries filled the small space inside the car, and I winced. The closer we got, the harder she sobbed, begging to stop and see Uncle Macon. There were some parents and a couple of the coaches wives hanging out around the field, ready to hand out drinks when the time came to take a break. I decided we could blend in with the small crowd gathered in the bleachers.

Harper squirmed in her seat as I undid her straps.

The kids were finishing up a drill when I settled onto the bottom row of the bleachers with Harper perched on my knee. Some of the parents would clap when one of the players caught a difficult pass or dodged a tackle. Harper joined them, clapping excitedly each time.

Macon was midway across the field working with one of the younger kids on his stance when he glanced up and caught sight of us. A slow smile crept over his cheeks, and he gave us a little wave. I watched as he worked with kids of different ages. He was so patient and attentive with them just like he was with Harper. He was going to be an excellent father one day.

The shrill sound of a whistle echoed across the field and all the activity slowed, eventually coming to stop. Players began to trickle out, and I realized they were done for the day. I glanced down at my watch and was surprised to see we'd been there for nearly forty minutes. Macon was probably starving after hours out in the sun, so I decided to stick around and ask him to grab lunch with us. As he neared the gate to the fence surrounding the field, Harper caught sight of him and bounced up and down. I expected him to come straight to us, but he climbed up the far side of the bleachers and leaned down to a dark-haired woman I hadn't noticed before. I realized the moment he pressed his lips to hers that it was Reece.

My stomach dipped, and my shoulders sagged as disappointment took root inside my chest. If she was here, he definitely wouldn't want to hang out with me and Harper.

"Macon!" Harper called. He turned our way and gripped Reece's hand to lead her down the steps.

"Hey, Half Pint." Harper practically dove out of my arms and into his. He kissed her cheek, and she hugged her tiny arms around his neck. "What are you guys doing here?" Reece sidled up next to him with an expression that said "I was wondering the same thing." She schooled her features quickly and flashed a tight smile.

"Harper saw your truck when we dropped Blake off at volleyball and wanted to stop by and see you. She wouldn't stop crying until I parked the car and got her out."

"Is that true?" he asked, and she nodded. He chuckled, and the sound did funny things to my belly. "Well, I'm glad you guys stopped by." Warmth bloomed in my chest at his genuine smile. He looked truly happy to see us. Reece, on the other hand…

"We were going to grab something to eat before we head out for the concert. You guys wanna come?" Reece stiffened beside him, and her nostrils flared. Large, dark shades hid her eyes, but I could still feel her staring daggers through me. I'd forgotten Macon had tickets to see one of his favorite bands. The show had been sold out, but Reece had connections and was able to score two VIP tickets with backstage passes for the two of them.

It was far more than I could ever give him. I was a single mom trying to make a living and take care of my daughter. She was a gorgeous future millionaire with a trust fund and membership at a country club. Why would he even look my way when he had that right in front of him?

I stuffed down those feelings as deep as they would go and offered him a regretful smile. "I don't think I have time before I need to drop her off at Mom's," I replied, nodding toward Harper. It was a lie. My shift didn't start for another two hours, but it was the only excuse I had. "Thanks anyway."

Macon tried to hand Harper back to me, but she wouldn't let go of him. "We need to get going, baby. Mamaw's waiting on us," I implored, reaching for her again. She wouldn't budge.

"I'll make you a deal," Macon said, and she looked up at him. "I'll carry you all the way to your mama's car, but you gotta get in your seat and put your seat belt on. Okay?"

"Okay," she agreed.

Macon and Reece followed me to my car, and as promised, Harper let Macon strap her in. He placed a kiss on the top of her head and shut the door. Before I could slip behind the wheel, he pulled me into a hug, and my breath caught. It wasn't unusual for him to hug me goodbye, but these days his embrace felt different. It stirred something inside me I didn't want to explore when he belonged to someone else. And this time, he did it in front of his girlfriend, a woman I was positive already hated me. I didn't look her way, but I didn't need to. Her eyes bored into me like a laser beam ready to burn me from the inside out.

"I'll see you later," Macon said and stepped back, pulling my door open as he did. I bid them both goodbye and watched as Macon laced his fingers with Reece's. She spared me one last glance before turning to walk away. She tried to hide it, but I could sense her suspicion in the set of her jaw and the hurt in her downturned mouth. She could sense I had feelings for him, and she wasn't happy about it.

OVER THE NEXT COUPLE WEEKS, I WAS ABLE TO ENJOY Macon's company without Reece's looming presence. I didn't have to feel her staring daggers at me when my back was turned only to find the fake smile she forced whenever I faced her. Macon joined Harper and me for a trip to the park one day and took us out for ice cream one evening after work. Everything was as it had always been.

Except for my growing attraction to him and the fluttering in my chest and stomach every time he was near.

Other than that, we talked most days and spent time together doing things friends did with each other all while I yearned for more. I ached for his touch, for some sign that he wanted me just as badly as I wanted him. Guilt clawed its way up my throat, knowing that he wasn't free for me to pine after. No wonder Reece hated me. Women's intuition was a strong entity, and she could sense that I had feelings for him.

On the night of Macon's parents' twenty-fifth anniversary party, I applied my makeup and curled my hair all while praying Reece wouldn't be there. Deep down, I knew she would. There was no way he'd leave her out of this celebration. I'd honestly been a little surprised when he'd invited me, but it was going to be quite the party with his entire family and many of the Lewis' friends.

Some of the guests were already there sipping from flutes of Champagne and nibbling on hor' dourves when I arrived. Macon's mom greeted me first, pulling me in for a hug.

"Brynlee," she crooned, squeezing me tight. "I'm so glad you could make it."

"Congratulations on twenty-five years. That's truly amazing," I replied as she pulled away and held me there by my arms.

"It hasn't always been easy, but it's certainly been worth it." She glanced toward the living room, and I followed her gaze. It settled on Macon and Reece as they stood talking with Macon's sister and brother-in-law. She sighed. "I just hope Macon finds the same kind of love one day."

"Me too," I mumbled, unable to tear my eyes from him. He wore a nice button-down with the sleeves rolled up to his elbows, his muscular, tan forearms on full display. His hair was smoothed down, not sticking out under a baseball cap like I usually saw it. He laughed at something his brother-in-law said, and my insides curled deliciously at the sight of his smile.

When I turned back to his mom, she was watching

me with a curious tilt to her head. Had she caught me ogling her son? Could she tell that I was falling for him? My cheeks heated, and I muttered my excuses before moving deeper into the house. I found Macon's dad and wished him a happy anniversary. He too pulled me in for a hug, his large frame nearly swallowing me whole in his embrace.

When I couldn't put it off any longer, I headed to the living room to greet Macon. Savannah, Macon's sister, spotted me first, excitement glittering in her eyes as she placed her hands in mine.

"Brynlee, it's so good to see you," she gushed, kissing my cheek.

"It's good to see you too." Savannah had been a senior when we were freshman, and although I didn't know her well back then, we clicked instantly when Macon and I became best friends. Her husband, Jace, shook my hand as we exchanged a friendly greeting. I'd only met him a handful of times, but he seemed like a great guy. He was clearly head over heels for his wife which was so incredibly sweet it caused an ache to settle in my chest. I wanted what they had. I just happened to want it with someone I couldn't have.

Macon's hug was expected but still threw me off balance. His scent surrounded me, and I let my eyes fall closed for the briefest moment as I savored the feel of his body pressed against mine. As soon as he released me, it felt like I was crashing back to earth. I didn't dare move for fear of toppling over.

I looked to Reece, prepared to give her a friendly greeting despite sensing that she wished I wasn't here.

She looped her arm through Macon's and pressed against his side, flashing me a friendly, albeit fake, smile.

"Brynlee, how are you?" she asked in the sweetest voice she could muster.

"I'm well. How are you?"

"Wonderful," she purred, glancing up at Macon, and I fought to keep my face impassive. "It's so nice to see two people still in love after twenty-five years together. They're truly an inspiration." Macon peered down at her and returned her smile. Pain lanced through me at the look he gave her, but I pretended like it didn't kill me to see the love shining in their eyes. I swallowed thickly and forced myself to smile through the pain.

"Where's Harper this evening?" Savannah asked, pulling my attention away.

"She's with my parents."

"I'm not going to lie, I was low key hoping you'd bring her with you. I haven't seen her in forever."

"She's gotten so big," Macon joined in, his face lighting up as he spoke of my daughter. "She talks so well and is already potty trained." His voice was laced with pride, and that warmed my heart.

"That's amazing! We'll have to get together next time I'm in town," Savannah announced.

"I'd love that."

We continued to make small talk for a few more minutes before I excused myself. I slipped up the stairs to use the restroom and took a moment to catch my breath.

When I stepped out of the bathroom at the end of the hall, Reece was waiting just outside the door. Her fake smile was gone and her eyes were narrowed into slits.

"Excuse me," I said and tried to side step her, but she blocked my path. What the hell?

"Why are you here?" she growled, her voice low and full of venom.

Her question took me by surprise. She'd never shown so much open hostility toward me before. I sputtered in response, unsure what to say in the face of such blatant aggression.

"It's not like you're part of the family. I'm his girlfriend. I belong here. You don't."

"I-I'm his best friend."

She scoffed, looking down her nose at me like I was a stray dog begging for scraps. "That's only because he feels sorry for you. He told me how pathetic you were after Sean left. He felt bad that his *real* best friend abandoned you after knocking you up." My chin wobbled as her vile words hit their mark. I'd always wondered if that was why Macon had been so persistent and kept coming around: out of pity and guilt for being the one who delivered the bad news.

"What the fuck, Reece?" Macon's voice boomed from the opposite end of the hall.

Her eyes grew wide, and she whipped around to face him. "Macon, I—" He held up a hand to stop her, his eyes a raging inferno of barely contained fury. Then his gaze shifted to me and softened. She turned back to me one last time, hatred filling her eyes. "You knew he was there, didn't you?" she hissed, her voice laced with accusation.

I shook my head as tears threatened to spill over. I hadn't been able to see him come around the corner past her tall frame, but it was clear she thought I'd purposely let her get caught in the act. That wasn't the case, but I was glad he got the chance to see her for who she really was. We were all getting a glimpse of the real Reece.

He stalked toward us, and Reece shrank back, crowding me even further into the corner. I didn't know why. He wouldn't hurt her, but boy did he look pissed.

"Come on," he growled, taking her gently by the elbow. "I'm taking you home." Guiding her in front of him, he turned to me once she'd disappeared around the corner. His mouth opened, then shut again like he didn't know what to say to me. Finally he settled on, "I'm sorry," and my heart sank. It landed in the pit of my stomach like an anchor tossed into the churning sea. With that, he turned and followed his girlfriend down the stairs and presumably out of the house while I picked up the pieces of my shattered heart.

Seven

MACON

I DIDN'T THINK I'D EVER BEEN THAT ANGRY IN MY entire life. Reece's words sliced through me like a hot knife through butter. The awful things she said to Brynlee made my stomach churn and my chest ache. Who was this woman? I never would have dreamed that she could be so cruel. I knew she was insecure and had initially felt threatened by my friendship with Bryn, but I never expected *this*. "Let's go," I barked as she stalled by the front door.

"Can I at least tell your parents goodbye?" she asked, trying to peek into the house over my shoulder. I almost laughed. It wouldn't matter. She would never see them again. I couldn't be with someone who treated anyone like that, especially someone who meant as much to me as Brynlee.

"No," I replied stoically and gently prodded her

forward. She stalked toward my truck but didn't argue as I shut the door behind us. Opening her door, I waited for her to climb in, my jaw set in a hard line.

"Macon," she said softly, lifting her hand to cup my face. I moved back, turning away from her touch, and her eyes filled with tears. They were probably fake, just like she had been to my face so many times before. I hated that she'd hurt Brynlee, but I was glad I finally saw her for who she was.

Brynlee.

My chest tightened at the thought of her standing in my hallway, unshed tears filling her eyes. Surely she knew none of it was true. I hadn't heard all of what Reece said, but I'd heard enough. Yes, I felt awful for Bryn when Sean left like he did, but I never pitied her. We didn't suddenly become friends then. We'd always been friends, just not as close as we were now. Maybe I did feel a little guilt over being the one who'd delivered that devastating letter to her that day, but that wasn't why we'd grown so close.

Our connection blossomed in Sean's absence. He was no longer there to overshadow everything and everyone. He wasn't vying to be the center of attention anymore, and if I was being honest with myself, it was kind of a relief. He might have been my best friend at one time, but now I saw how toxic he was. He was too lazy to do his homework half the time and demanded to copy off mine. When he broke my mom's favorite snow globe, he convinced me to take the fall, claiming he wouldn't be allowed to come over anymore if I didn't. I ended up grounded for two weeks and missed the winter formal, the dance where he and Bryn officially became a couple. I never told him, but I'd been planning to ask her to the dance. I'd had a crush on her for nearly a year at that point but hadn't gotten up the nerve to ask her out. He beat me to the punch and on the day of the dance, he sealed the deal with a kiss during a slow dance to Rascal Flatts. I was so disappointed and angry with him for causing me to miss the dance. Looking back, it didn't make sense. It's not like I could've stopped it. But still, I'd wanted to be the one slow dancing with her and wrapping my arms around her waist to pull her in for a kiss, even though I probably would've been too chicken shit to make the first move.

"Can you please just talk to me?" Reece's voice pulled me from my thoughts, and I shook away the memories.

"I don't have anything to say to you," I answered honestly. As far as I was concerned, our relationship was over, and there was nothing she could say to change that.

"Please just let me explain," she pleaded.

"Explain what?" I snapped. "How you cornered my best friend and told her I was only friends with her because I felt sorry for her? That seems pretty straightforward to me." My patience was wearing thin, and my anger threatened to boil over. Did she think I was stupid or that she could somehow justify what she'd said?

"I'm sorry, okay!" she screeched, crying in earnest now. "I know it sounds silly, but I got jealous. Every time she's around, it's like I'm invisible! It's not right. I'm your girlfriend, and you're spending more time with another woman. How do you think that makes me feel?"

"Are you kidding me? You got jealous so you purposely tried to hurt someone I care about?"

"Are you admitting that you spent more time with her?" She stuck her chin out defiantly, triumph gleaming in her eyes.

"That's what you got from this? You're unbeliev-able, Reece. I saw her for maybe five minutes tops, but you never left my side. How can you say I spent more time with her, then use that to justify your cruelty? Who *are* you?"

"I'm your girlfriend," she claimed, echoing her earlier argument.

"Not anymore," I informed her through gritted teeth, my knuckles turning white on the steering wheel. We couldn't get to her parents' house fast enough. I didn't know how much longer I could stand her being in my truck.

She gasped, turning toward me in her seat. "You're breaking up with me?" she screeched, her mouth morphing into a gaping oval of shock.

"Yes," I replied, surprised that she didn't see this coming.

"What? No! You can't break up with me."

"I can, Reece. And I just did. It's over," I declared, leaving no room for argument. That didn't stop her, though. The rest of the drive, she tried to convince me not to end things with her, making promises to change and do better. She even offered to apologize to Brynlee.

"You *should* apologize to Bryn. But it won't change anything. You're not the person I thought you were. I can't be with you anymore."

Her face turned red, and she crossed her arms over her chest. When we finally pulled into her driveway, she jerked open her door and stormed out. I let out a pent-up breath, and my shoulders sagged in relief.

Pulling my phone from my pocket, I noticed a few texts from my family, but I ignored them and went straight to Brynlee's name and tapped out a quick message.

Me: Are you still at the house?

It was several minutes before my phone dinged again.

Brynlee: No.
Me: Where are you?

She never responded, and I found out from my sister that she'd left only minutes after me, claiming she didn't feel well, but her eyes were red and puffy. Guilt sliced through me, knowing the cause of her tears. I wanted to go to her, to make sure she was okay. Tapping on her name, I pressed my phone to my ear and listened to it ring. And ring. And ring. When her voicemail came on, I ended the call.

Why wasn't she answering? I need to check on her. I had to know she was okay and didn't think that anything Reece said was true. Surely she knew that.

I tried her number again, but this time it didn't even ring. Straight to voicemail. I hadn't wanted to give merit to my suspicions, but now I knew for sure she was avoiding me. Maybe she just needed space. I'd give her some time, then try to get a hold of her again.

Eight

BRYNLEE

I EXPECTED TO HEAR FROM MACON THE NEXT DAY. HE tried calling a couple times the night before, but I couldn't bring myself to answer the phone. I felt like an idiot and was determined not to be his charity case anymore.

Still, it hurt when he didn't call again the next day or the day after that. I kept waiting, but the call never came.

A few days later, he sent me a text.

Macon: I'm in town with Dad. Wanna grab lunch?

I was relieved to finally hear from him but hated myself for the butterflies that took flight in my stomach at the sight of his name on my phone.

Me: I can't. I had to go into work early today.

It was true. They needed someone to open since our early person called in sick, so I picked up the extra hours. Mom was happy to have the extra time with Harper, and I needed the money. But it also gave me an excuse to avoid Macon. I wasn't ready to see him yet. I was too hurt, too embarrassed. What Reece had said struck a nerve, and although I didn't want to believe it, deep down, I suspected it was true. Macon hadn't tried to deny it. I saw the truth of her claims in his eyes when he said, "I'm sorry."

My stomach knotted at the thought, wishing I could erase the sadness on his face from my memory. My phone buzzed again, and I opened up the new text.

Macon: No worries. I'll catch up with you later.

I released a heavy sigh, feeling like I'd dodged a bullet. I knew I couldn't avoid him forever and would eventually have to face the music, but I didn't have to do it today.

Nine

MACON

SHE WAS AVOIDING ME. AT FIRST, IT JUST SEEMED LIKE she needed some space, but now it was obvious what she was doing. I hadn't seen her in nearly two weeks and had only gotten a handful of texts from her, and they were all responses to messages I'd initiated. She never answered my calls, so I hadn't even heard her voice. And I missed it. I missed her. Everything about her was like a sunny day. Her bright smile and contagious laughter, the warmth of her touch and her honey rich voice. The soft pale curls that fell down her back and the way her eyes lit up every time her little girl smiled. She was good and bright and full of life. Even when life knocked her down, she got back up and approached her next challenge with love and positivity.

I missed her the way I should've missed Reece. The

truth was I'd hardly thought about my ex but couldn't get Brynlee off my mind. She was the one who'd gotten hurt after all. I was worried about her. At least, that was what I told myself.

Every time I was in town, I fought the urge to stop by the bookstore where she worked. I knew she'd picked up some extra shifts and was working more days than not. But it felt invasive to just show up there. I wouldn't be that guy who tracked a girl down when she wouldn't return his calls. I was desperate, but I wasn't *that* desperate.

Reluctantly, I avoided calling or texting her for another week. It was the longest we'd ever gone without communication. I didn't know what was going on with her or Harper, and it was killing me.

Imagine my surprise when she walked into the bar Saturday night for Haley's birthday celebration. I knew she'd been invited but doubted she would come. She rarely joined our group of friends on outings like this since she didn't like to be away from Harper. I was glad she decided to this time because I knew she needed a break.

Her eyes scanned the space until they landed on our group sitting at a raised table, and she smiled, waving in our direction as she strode toward us. I took a moment to drink her in. The flowy yellow tank she wore accentuated her sun-kissed skin and dipped low enough to show off her ample cleavage. The dark denim of her shorts molded to her curves like a second skin and showed off muscular legs sculpted by years of gymnastics and cheerleading. Blonde waves fell down her back, and those green-blue eyes glittered beneath thick black lashes. She was absolutely stunning.

Her step faltered when she caught sight of me, and she averted her gaze. My chest tightened, and I yearned to pull her in for a hug. Reece's insults must've still stung. I just prayed she knew they weren't true. She knew me better than anybody. Surely she knew that what Reece said was absolute BS.

She glanced around the table for an empty seat and smiled tightly when she found the only one.

Directly across from me. It was right next to Shayla who squealed and pulled her in for a hug.

"I'm so glad you came! I didn't know if you were going to make it." Brynlee returned the embrace and slid into the tall wooden chair.

"Is Harper with your parents?" Haley asked before sticking her straw in her mouth and taking a huge gulp of some blue concoction Jonah brought her from the bar.

"Yeah. They practically begged to keep her tonight. I couldn't say no." She smiled, and it lit up her whole face. I was glad she had the parents that she did. They were wonderful people who adored their granddaughter. Harper had at least one set of grandparents to spoil her and make her feel special. Sean's parents were as worthless as he was, maybe even more so. At least Sean sent money. His parents wouldn't even show up for Harper's birthday party. They didn't call or send a gift. Nothing. They'd only seen their grandchild a couple times, and it was mostly at Brynlee's insistence. She finally stopped trying last Christmas after they flaked on the visit they'd planned. As far as I knew, Sean didn't keep in touch with them either after he'd left. At least that was what they claimed when Bryn asked about him.

I was dying to talk to her, but not in front of our friends. I hadn't told anyone about what had happened at my parents' anniversary party, and I was certain she hadn't either. Although, everyone most likely knew about my split with Reece since I'd told Jonah, and he had the biggest mouth in town.

"Hey, Bryn," I greeted, the affection in my voice evident.

"Hey, Macon," came her soft reply. She met my eyes briefly but wouldn't hold my gaze.

"How ya been? I haven't talked to you in a while."

My subtle call out had its desired effect. Her shoulders stiffened, and she slowly returned her focus to me. With a tight smile, she replied, "Good. Just working a lot. How about you?"

I longed to tell her the truth, that I missed her and yearned to talk to her. She'd been absent from my life for weeks, and it was like part of myself was missing. But I couldn't say that. She'd only returned my question to be polite.

"Pretty good," I replied instead. "Been keeping busy working with Dad." My father was a successful contractor and had taught me many skills of the trade growing up. Now I worked for him during the summer when business was at its peak.

"I heard you guys finished up the Madisons' house this week. It looks beautiful."

"Thank you."

Brynlee seemed to relax after that, and we fell into a natural conversation with the rest of our friends. There were eight of us in total. In addition to Jonah, Haley, and Shayla, we were joined by our friends Cameron and Delilah—who were both home from college for the summer—and Delilah's boyfriend, Chad. Cam and Delilah had been part of our group for years, but Chad was a new addition. Immediately, I got a weird vibe from him. It wasn't just because he was arrogant and pretentious—although those attributes didn't play in his favor—but there was something darker in him, almost ... sinister. He seemed very possessive over Lilah and watched her with an almost predatory gaze. I would have to keep my eye on him. Something in my gut told me not to trust this guy.

The sight of our friends laughing and enjoying each other's company was refreshing and nostalgic. There hadn't been this many of us together in one place for a long time. Only two people were notably absent: Sean, whom no one had heard from in years, and Liam. The latter, who had gotten himself into some trouble with the law our senior year, rarely came back to town, despite still having family in the area. We stayed in touch through social media, but I hadn't seen him face-to-face since the day they led him out of Calculus in handcuffs.

Brynlee and Shayla giggled as they slipped from their seats, bringing my attention back to the present.

They headed for the bar, and I fought the urge to watch Bryn walk away, but I lost as my eyes dropped to her ass. Swallowing hard, I looked away, hoping that nobody saw me check her out. It was wrong. I knew that. I shouldn't have thought about her like that. She was my best friend. She thought of me like a brother, and if that was *all* she ever felt toward me, I would take it. I just wanted to be part of her life. After everything blew over with Reece, I hoped we could go back to the way things were. Before everything became awkward between us and she looked at me like I'd let her down completely. The disappointment in her face was like a knife to the heart.

An hour later, the girls were all giggling and sipping colorful drinks except for Bryn who favored spiced rum and diet cola. They were catching up after a long absence.

"Calvin and I broke up again. This time for good," Shayla declared.

"Oh, I'm so sorry," Bryn said, rubbing a hand over her friend's back.

"Don't be. It was long overdue. I don't know why we kept trying to make it work." She rolled her eyes, clearly exasperated with herself.

"He was kind of a douche," Jonah added.

"He kind of was," Shayla agreed with a wince, making everyone around us laugh.

Ten

BRYNLEE

"WHERE'S REECE TONIGHT?" SHAYLA ASKED, AND I instinctively took another swig of my drink. It was strong and burned as it went down, but I'd need the alcohol to tolerate hearing about Macon's girlfriend.

"Didn't you know?" Jonah butted in before Macon could answer. "They broke up." All the air was sucked from my lungs, and I nearly choked.

"No, I didn't know that," Shayla said on a gasp, as though it was a juicy piece of gossip. I guessed technically it was. It just so happened that the subject of the gossip was sitting right there. "When did *that* happen?"

I pointedly avoided Macon's gaze. I could feel the heat of his stare on my face, but I couldn't look at him. The distance that had grown between us the last few weeks settled in my chest like a cold I couldn't shake. Things were suddenly awkward between us, and I hated it.

"A few weeks ago," he replied, taking a sip of his beer. "The night of my parents' anniversary party," he added and let his gaze settle on me. That addition was solely for my benefit since no one else understood the significance.

My chest heaved as I tried to catch my breath. This was news to me, and to the others apparently. There were gasps and murmurs all around the table. Shayla squirmed in her seat next to me, leaning forward to listen closely. She was hoping for more details, but if I knew Macon, he wouldn't reveal what had really happened. But *I* knew. Deep in my gut, I knew it was because she'd been cruel to me and had finally shown her true colors.

I drained the rest of my drink and pushed away from the table, swaying a bit as I stood. "You okay, Bryn?" Haley asked, and I waved her off as I headed to the restroom. I was tipsy, probably almost as drunk as I'd been the time I passed out in the field after one of Sean's football games. He'd given me moonshine, and it hadn't taken much for me to start seeing double.

Bracing my hands on the sink, I couldn't bring myself to look in the mirror for several long seconds. One minute turned into two, and finally I lifted my gaze. The edges of my vision were a little hazy, but I could tell that my hair and makeup were still intact. I didn't look too bad. Maybe this was a sign. Maybe this was the chance I'd been waiting for. But how could I make a move on my best friend after going weeks with hardly any communication.

Ugh, maybe it wasn't the right time. After all, he and Reece had been broken up less than a month, and quite frankly, I didn't feel like being his rebound.

I wadded up some paper towels and ran them under the cold water, pressing them to my chest and the back of my neck. I needed to get back out there before someone came looking for me.

Macon's eyes found me as soon as the table came into view, and his brow furrowed. Whatever his concerns, he mercifully kept them to himself. Instead of sitting in the chair I'd vacated earlier, I went straight to the bar and ordered another drink. I felt the press of a warm body against my side, and the clean scent of Macon's soap filled my nostrils.

"You okay?" he asked, leaning against the lacquered top.

"Yeah, I'm fine. I think the question is, are *you* okay? I'm sorry about you and Reece."

"Don't be," he replied, and my eyebrows shot to my hairline in surprise. Just then the pretty, redheaded bartender came to take his order as she deposited my drink in front of me without a second glance. After some painfully obvious flirting on her end, she left to grab the bottles of beer and water he requested. "It wasn't meant to be," he continued when we were alone again. "I could never be with someone who would treat my friends or family that way. I knew she had her reservations about our relationship," he said, motioning between the two of us, and my heart began to flutter. *Our relationship.* "But I thought she understood. I never dreamed she'd act the way she did or thought of you that way. I'm sorry I didn't see it sooner and that you had to go through that."

"You have nothing to be sorry for," I assured him, squeezing his forearm. The contact sent a tingle up my arm that landed low in my belly. Now that I knew about the breakup, I felt guilty for avoiding him for so long.

"You know what she said wasn't true, right?" I looked away, still feeling the sting of her words and tried hard not to believe them. There was a part of me that feared she was right.

He reached for me, slipping a finger beneath my chin and tilting my face up to meet his stare. "Right?" he asked, gentle yet forceful at the same time. My brain went fuzzy, and all I could think about was how much I wanted to kiss him and how good it felt having him hold my face.

"Uh huh," I replied absently, unsure what I was even agreeing to. Before I could lean in, the bartender was back, sliding Macon's drinks across the bar. She made sure to brush her fingers against his when she handed his card back. I fought the urge to roll my eyes at her blatant flirtation and took a long draw from my drink. With each sip I took, the burn became less and less noticeable. By now, I barely felt it. The heavy knot that had formed in my stomach the moment Macon announced he'd broken up with Reece was finally starting to unravel. The alcohol was loosening the tension that was built up in my body.

We returned to our table and reclaimed our seats. Our friends' laughter and conversation filled the air around us as Macon passed around the beer and water he'd collected at the bar. He unscrewed the lid from a plastic bottle and drank deeply. If my memory could be trusted, he'd only had one beer since he arrived nearly two hours ago, so he was completely sober.

When I got up to go to the restroom again—this time to actually use the facilities and not just to get away from Macon and the rush of emotions I felt from learning about him and Reece breaking up—I wobbled, nearly crashing into a nearby table. Those drinks had been stronger than I realized, and since I'd had nothing but a few chicken wings and some celery sticks, it hit me harder than expected.

Macon was waiting just outside the restrooms when I came out, his forehead creased with concern. "Are you okay?" he asked, reaching for my shoulders to steady me as I took a step toward him.

"I'm fine. I think I just over did it."

"You think?" He chuckled. I nodded, a little embarrassed at myself. I hadn't been drunk in a long time, since before I got pregnant with Harper. "Do you want me to take you home?"

My pulse accelerated at his suggestion, and I nodded again, unable to speak. I wanted nothing more than to be alone with him in his truck. Maybe with all the liquid courage flowing through my veins, I'd finally get up the nerve to tell him how I felt.

We said goodbye to our friends, and I followed him outside. He opened the passenger side door for me and helped me into his truck. If it hadn't been for the surge of electricity coursing through my body at the sensation of his hands on my hips, I would've fallen into the seat in a fit of giggles, but his touch had momentarily sobered me. And I wanted more of it.

Once he climbed inside and settled behind the wheel, I slid over next to him and rested my head on his shoulder. I closed my eyes and basked in his clean scent. He didn't need cologne or suffocating body sprays to smell good. I fought the urge to lean up and run my tongue up his neck to get a taste. He was driving after all.

Eventually, he lifted his arm and draped it around my shoulders. I snuggled in closer, leaning harder on him. "Tired?" he asked, and I shrugged. I was too wound up. There was no way I'd be able to fall asleep anytime soon.

As we turned onto my street, I realized it was now or never. I needed to make my move, but I couldn't just jump his bones, so I lifted my hand and let my open palm rest on his jean-clad leg. He sucked in a sharp breath, but his eyes never strayed from the road. He wiggled in his seat a bit, subtly clearing his throat.

I couldn't be imagining it. There was something on his end too. It wasn't just me.

I snuggled in closer, and he gave my shoulders a

squeeze. It felt like encouragement, a granting of permission to keep going. I was prepared to do more as soon as he put his truck in park.

He pulled into the driveway, his lights illuminating my front door momentarily before he cut the engine. He turned to me, eyes hooded, and his gaze dropped to my mouth.

I took my chance and leaned up to kiss him, just a soft peck at first. When he didn't pull away, I placed my hand on his chest and went in for a deeper kiss. His lips parted, and I tasted the cinnamon gum he always chewed. Funny, I never much cared for the flavor, but on his tongue, it tasted like heaven.

His arm tightened around me, and I let go of all my reservations. He wanted this too. Without thinking, I swung my leg around and climbed onto his lap. My knees bracketed his hips, and his hands fell to my waist. I cupped his face in my hands, my tongue probing inside his hot mouth. He groaned and opened his palms, splaying them over my ass. I instinctively flexed my hips, wanting to feel more of him. And boy did I get my wish.

His body responded, his growing arousal pressing hot and hard against my core. His lips moved to my neck, his hot tongue sweeping over the sensitive skin there. I let out a soft sigh, reveling in the feel of his body against mine. My hips surged forward, grinding against him as he found my mouth again.

Suddenly, he wrenched away, tearing his lips from mine. I clung to him desperately, trying to get back to his mouth. It had tasted so good.

In a split second, I was pressed flat on my back across the bench seat with Macon hovering above me. My legs snaked around his back, and his eyes fell closed as he dropped his forehead to mine.

"Bryn," he groaned, and the sound of my name on his lips shot a bolt of arousal straight to my center. I rolled my hips, my thighs clamping down on his sides. His head shot up and his eyes burned, the golden flecks surrounding his irises glowing like embers. His scorching gaze sent a shiver down my spine.

I reached for him, but he gripped my wrists before I could wrap my arms around his neck. He brought my hands above my head and pinned them to the seat. "Bryn, you're drunk," he said, his voice laced with concern. I wanted to argue with him, but he was right. However, my brain struggled to find the significance in that statement. "I'm not going to take advantage of you in this state."

"I'm not *that* drunk," I argued.

"You are," he countered. "And you're my best friend. I would never do that to you." Pain lanced through me at his words. I fought back the tears that burned the backs of my eyes.

Oh my God, I'd just thrown myself at him. He was just being nice and taking care of me, and I took it as him showing interest in me. I was such an idiot.

I swallowed hard, pushing down the emotion threatening to break loose like a flood gate fighting off a tidal wave. "Oh," I muttered pathetically and slipped out of his grasp. Ducking to the side, I slid from beneath him. We sat up in unison, an awkward tension filling the space between us.

"Thanks for bringing me home," I said and quickly slid across the seat to open my door. He called my name gently, but I couldn't look at him. I was too mortified.

Eleven

BRYNLEE

WHEN I AWOKE THE NEXT MORNING, THERE WAS sunlight poking around the edges of my blinds and a dull ache throbbing in my temples. The events from the night before were momentarily forgotten as I stretched and reached for my phone on the night-stand. My hand froze at the sight of a sports drink and bottle of over-the-counter pain relievers sitting next to it.

Memories from last night came crashing back, and I fell against my pillow.

Macon pushing me away.

Macon saying he'd never do *that* to me.

Despite my protestations, he'd insisted on walking me to my door and making sure I got inside safely. I left him standing in my living room, the need to escape to my bedroom stronger than my sense of hospitality. He knew his way out and would surely lock up when he left.

Silent tears dampened my pillow as the sound of him rummaging in my kitchen drifted down the hall. When his heavy footsteps sounded just outside my room, I turned my back to the door and covered most of my face with the blanket. He hesitated next to my bed before leaning down to press a gentle kiss to my hair. I pretended to be asleep, doing my best to regulate my breathing. He must've bought it because he quietly exited my bedroom and shut the door behind him. Muffled sobs wracked my body, but I waited until the engine of his old Chevy roared to life before I let it all out.

How could I face him again after practically throwing myself at him? Would he feel uncomfortable around me? Did he still want to be friends? Maybe if he didn't bring it up, I could pretend like I didn't remember. I decided that was my best course of action. If he believed I was drunk and not in my right mind, maybe he wouldn't hold it against me, and we could go on like it never happened. We could restore our strained friendship, going back to the way things were before Reece came into the picture.

I finally braved a peek at the clock on my phone and realized it was almost ten. My mom would wonder where I was if she didn't hear from me soon. I never went this long without seeing or talking to Harper.

An aching void filled my chest. I missed my daughter and needed to hold her. I rarely left her overnight, even though I knew my parents were perfectly capable of taking care of her. Still, it always left me feeling a little anxious, and I never slept well when she wasn't home with me, unnecessary worry gnawing at my conscience every time I drifted off to sleep.

Dialing my parents' number, I pressed the phone to my ear and took in my reflection in the full-length mirror. I looked rough. Black smudges darkened my eyes, and my hair was a matted mess. A shower was an immediate necessity.

"Good mornin', sleepy head," my mother's cheery voice greeted me on the other end of the line.

"Mornin', Mama."

"I trust you slept well," came her knowing reply.

"I did."

She snickered. "I figured. Otherwise you would've been calling at the crack of dawn." I rolled my eyes even though I knew she was right. "I take it you had a good time?" That was her way of asking if I drank a little too much last night.

I winced and nodded as though she could see me. She couldn't, of course, so I quickly responded with a simple, "I did." Pinching the bridge of my nose, I continued. "So good in fact that I'm going to need you to come get me and take me to my car. I had to leave it there last night."

"No problem," she assured me, her voice laced

with understanding. "Harper and I will head over in about an hour." We hung up, and I went straight to the shower. I'd just finished blow drying my hair when my mom pulled in the driveway.

"So, who all was there?" she asked as we headed to the restaurant where I'd hung out with my friends the night before. She was a tad bit nosy and wanted to know all the tea. I indulged her, listing the names of everyone who came out to celebrate Haley's birthday, saving Macon's name for last.

"Speaking of Macon," she began, a mischievous lilt to her voice, "I heard he broke up with that girl he was seeing. Did you know?"

"Not until last night. I hadn't seen him in a few weeks." I admitted, a little ashamed of myself for letting my pride and hurt feelings keep me away from my best friend.

"Hmm," she said, the simple sound a few octaves higher than her normal voice. I didn't like the sound of that. It meant the wheels were turning. She was cooking up something I wasn't gonna like.

"You know," she began, and I could sense trouble was coming, "now that he's single—"

"Mama, don't," I pleaded, cutting her off. "We're friends. He doesn't think of me like that."

"Well, how do you know? Did you ask him?"

"Trust me. I just know." I needed her to drop the subject. The sting of his rejection was still fresh. I wasn't interested in having salt rubbed into that wound. Mercifully, we arrived at our destination before she could probe any further. Hopping out of her car, I retrieved Harper from the backseat and transferred her to my vehicle. I thanked my mom and bid her goodbye, hoping she got any notion of Macon and I becoming more than friends out of her mind.

Twelve

MACON

MY PHONE BUZZED IN MY POCKET, BUT I IGNORED IT. I knew who it was. Reece was persistent. I'd give her that. She gave me all of one week before she started calling and begging for forgiveness. In her mind, I'd come around and forgive her once I had some time to cool down. She was wrong. Her words had been like a punch in the gut. My heart broke at the sight of Bryn's stunned and horrified face. She was hurt and embarrassed, and there was nothing I could do to take it away. She believed what Reece had claimed, and I couldn't convince her otherwise.

Then she gave me the cold shoulder. Every time I called her, she sent me to voicemail. When I texted, she left me on read for days. When she finally got back with me, it was quick and full of excuses about why we couldn't hang out. She was busy with Harper or had picked up an extra shift.

A few times, I'd been tempted to stop by the bookstore to see if she was really there but wasn't sure I could handle it if she was lying to me. I also considered just dropping by when I knew she was home, but I didn't want to be pushy. I figured she'd come back around when she was ready. What I didn't realize was that she had no idea I'd broken up with Reece. She thought I was still with the person who'd said all those hateful things to her. She thought I valued our friendship so little that I'd allow someone to be cruel to her and then continue to date them.

I didn't know until last night that she was unaware of this change. Her eyes had gone wide as saucers, and her mouth fell open in shock when I announced to the table that Reece and I were no longer together. It all made sense in that moment. The dodged calls and unanswered texts, her stealthy avoidance maneuvers. Did she have so little faith in me to believe I wouldn't break up with Reece?

My presence there had unnerved her, so she smothered her emotions with rum. When she stumbled to the bathroom, I knew it was time to get her home. I hadn't expected the night to take the turn it did. I never dreamed she'd end up in my lap, her hot mouth devouring mine. I'd wanted so badly to give in. When her tongue slid against mine, it was all I could do not to take her right there in front of her house.

Her lips were soft and sweet. My hands molded perfectly to her curves as she pressed her hot center into my groin. I'd dreamed of having her body wrapped around me but hadn't known just how good it would feel. Somehow, I'd come to my senses and realized that what I was allowing to happen couldn't continue. She was intoxicated and obviously wasn't thinking clearly. There was no way I'd take advantage of her in that state no matter how badly I wanted her.

My wrench slipped and I cursed, my frustration causing me to lose focus on the task at hand. I lifted my shirt and swiped at my sweat-drenched brow. I promised Dad I'd finished this project this weekend, and time was running out. My mind was somewhere else, my thoughts completely consumed by Brynlee. I kept seeing her gorgeous legs in those short shorts and thinking about how that dark denim hugged her ass. When her thighs clamped down on my sides last night, I wanted nothing more than to strip her bare and lay her across the seat of my truck. I wanted her to wrap them around me as tight as she could as I thrust in and out of her, my lips exploring every corner of her mouth and inch of her exposed throat. But I couldn't. I wouldn't. She'd hate me if I did.

Checking my phone for the hundredth time, I was disappointed to find no texts from Bryn. There were plenty from Reece, but I left those unopened.

I'd sent Brynlee a message late this morning, trying to avoid waking her, but hadn't gotten a response. My mom complained that she hadn't seen her in a while and wanted to invite her to dinner. I extended the invitation but had yet to hear back. I hoped she would come. I needed to see her. This distance that had grown between us needed to be closed. Now that she knew the truth, perhaps we could start to bridge that gap.

I was packing up my tools, my job finally done, when my phone chimed from my pocket. Pulling it out, I was shocked to see Brynlee's name on the screen.

Brynlee: Sure, what time?
Me: 6:00
Brynlee: What do I need to bring?

I smiled to myself. Always the polite Southern belle, Brynlee was.

Me: Just yourself and your mini me.
Brynlee: Ok, we'll be there.

She punctuated her message with a smiley face, and the tension began to ease from my shoulders. I'd been worried about how things would be between us after that kiss. I hoped they would go back to normal, but at the same time, I didn't want them to go back to normal at all. That kiss we shared in my truck had been off the charts hot. If she remembered, maybe she'd want to do it again. And again. And again.

My body began to react to my ungentlemanly thoughts, and my jeans became a little more snug. I hurriedly tossed my tool bag into my truck and headed for home. I'd shower and wear my favorite cologne, the one Bryn got me for my birthday last year. I knew she loved the smell of it because she took a nice, deep inhale every time I wore it. It was all I could do not to bend down and kiss the top of her head whenever she did that. Maybe she'd do it tonight and I'd pull her in close. That is, if she still felt the way she did last night and wanted to pick up where we'd left off.

There was always the chance that she'd been too drunk to realize what she was doing. For all I knew, she could've just been missing Sean and didn't care whose lips were on hers. Pain sliced through me at that thought. I didn't want to be a faceless make-out session to her. I wanted our kiss to mean something. And if I knew Bryn, it had. She didn't just go around kissing anybody and was selective about who she spent time with, especially in a romantic capacity. She dated, but not often. I knew several of the guys she'd turned down. It always started the same way. They'd try to feel me out to see if she and I were an item, then ply me for information when they realized we were just friends. Then they'd come back and whine to me because she told them no. I was glad when she turned those guys down.

Would she turn me down? If I tried to kiss her, would she push me away? It killed me to stop her, but she *had* to know how badly I wanted her. She'd writhed all over the proof when she was in my lap. I hadn't turned down her advances, per se. I'd just hit pause on them.

Thirteen

BRYNLEE

WHAT THE HELL WAS I THINKING? I COULDN'T FACE Macon again so soon after I'd royally embarrassed myself. Obviously, he didn't hold it against me or he wouldn't have invited me to dinner at his parents' house, but I was still mortified. I would stick to my plan of pretending not to remember what I'd done. The memory had grown fuzzy but wouldn't go away completely despite my wishes. If I could just forget, maybe I wouldn't feel so awkward walking up to his parents' front door and lifting the knocker.

They lived in a beautiful home on one of the nicest streets in Willow Brook Falls. Macon's dad was a general contractor who got a lot of business from locals and folks outside the area, and his mom ran a cute little boutique in town. They weren't millionaires

—that I knew of—but they certainly weren't struggling.

Macon's mother came to the door a moment later and swung it open excitedly before pulling me into a hug. Sheila and Ben always treated me like family. From the first time I stepped foot inside their home while we were all still in high school and I was dating Sean, they made me feel welcome. Not like Sean's family. The few times I was at Sean's house, one or both of his parents were either high or drunk, and if they weren't intoxicated, they were fighting. That was why he spent so much time at my house or Macon's. He didn't have loving, supportive parents like we did. Naively, I thought he'd be different. He seemed to detest their behavior and the way they treated him so passionately, that I never dreamed he'd turn out to be a dead beat, absentee father.

Sheila ushered us inside and immediately crouched to Harper's level. "My, my look how big you've gotten," she crooned. Her voice was soothing and motherly, the type of voice grandmothers reserved for the grandchildren they adored. She reached out to her, and Harper stepped into her embrace without a moment's hesitation. My chest tightened as I watched Macon's mother pick my daughter up and cradle her close to her chest as she walked into the kitchen.

With a conspiratorial grin, she leaned in and whispered, "I baked cookies."

"Cookies!" Harper chirped excitedly.

"You can have some as long as you eat your dinner. Do you think you can do that for me?"

Harper nodded emphatically as they disappeared into the kitchen. I was about to follow them when Macon came trotting down the stairs.

"Hey," he greeted me with his signature crooked grin. My heart fluttered inside my chest, nearly stealing my breath. I had to remind myself to play it cool and pretend like the night before had never happened. "I thought I heard Mom baby talking to someone. Did she commandeer the kid already?"

I chuckled, and my body began to relax. "Yeah. They're in the kitchen, probably sneaking a cookie before dinner."

"I swear that woman is a different person with that child. She never would've let us do that as kids."

"That's how parents are. They act completely different with grandkids." As soon as the words were out of my mouth, I wanted to take them back, praying that he hadn't heard. His parents weren't her grandparents, no matter how much I wished they were. "I mean," I began with a stammer. "Not that she's her grandchild. It's just, um..." I was rambling, the panic setting in.

Macon's face softened, and he took a step toward me. "I know what you meant," he assured me. My relief was short-lived when his expression turned serious. "Hey, about last—"

He was mercifully cut off by Harper running into the living room, chocolate smeared across her mouth and soiling her hands. The damning evidence confirmed my suspicions that she'd already gotten into the cookie jar. I was so relieved she'd interrupted him, I didn't mind that she had sweets before dinner. Macon had been about to bring up the kiss, and I was thankful for the distraction.

"Hey, Half Pint." He crouched and scooped her into his arms.

"Watch out; she's covered in chocolate," I warned with a giggle.

"Eh, I don't mind," he replied and hugged her tightly. That damn ache returned to my chest. He was so good to my little girl. He was like an uncle, someone who could stand in as a father figure in the absence of her biological dad. It saddened me that was all he'd ever be. Macon had effectively drawn that line last night.

I'd never do that to you.

His words echoed in my mind, but I shook them away as Sheila came through with a paper towel, a sheepish look on her face. "I'm sorry, but she asked so nicely and looked so pitiful, I caved and let her have a cookie."

"It's alright," I assured her. And it was. I knew it wouldn't be long before my little girl suckered her into getting what she wanted.

"Dinner's almost ready," Sheila announced.

"I'll set the table," Macon offered, handing Harper over to Sheila, who wiped her hands and face.

"I'll help," I offered and followed Macon into the dining room. It was within earshot of the kitchen, so I was confident he wouldn't try to bring up the incident from last night again. I also had a plan for distracting him.

"So, what are you guys planning for Jonah's bachelor party?" Jonah and Haley were getting married soon. Both Macon and I were part of the wedding party, him as a groomsman and me as a bridesmaid. Macon was tasked with helping Jonah's brother—and best man—plan the bachelor party since he lived out of town.

"We haven't settled on anything yet," he replied, passing me half the plates to spread around the table. "But I was thinking of doing a poker night," he said, cradling the other half of the plates in his hand. We spread them out around the table, and I couldn't help but notice the way his forearms flexed when he set one gently on its place setting. Theirs was a formal dining room with a beautiful table made from cherry wood and expertly decorated with a floral centerpiece and silver candelabra. "Or maybe doing axe throwing," he added with a shrug. "The other guys haven't really given me any input. I think they're all expecting booze and strippers, but that's so cliché, and Haley would murder Jonah before they ever made it to the altar."

I let out a little snort of laughter and he chuckled, his smile growing wide. "You're right about that," I agreed. Haley definitely would not be happy with that choice of activities. "Why don't you do both? The axe throwing and poker night, I mean. Not the strippers and alcohol."

He thought about it for a moment before responding. "You think that would work?

"I think so. Start with axe throwing then round out the night with poker. Honestly that sounds like a blast."

"I guess it's settled then."

"I'm going to have to see if the girls will agree to the axe throwing because now I want to try it."

"I don't know. Doesn't really seem like Haley's thing." He was right. I didn't think the bride-to-be would enjoy something like that. She was more of a spa day type of girl. "But, if you really want to go, I could take you," he offered with a hopeful glint in his eye.

My pulse sped up just thinking of spending an evening with Macon. I could imagine him trying to help me with my form when I threw, his solid chest against my back and his arms bracketing mine. I'd fight the urge to lean into him, his hot breath on my neck sending shivers down my spine.

"That would be great," I replied, feeling my cheeks redden as though he could somehow see my thoughts.

We finished setting the table and returned to the kitchen. Sheila was helping Harper mash the potatoes, and my little girl looked like she was having the time of her life. Milk and potatoes flew in all directions as she clumsily slammed the masher down into the bowl. Sheila was positioned behind Harper who stood at the island in a kitchen chair, both hands held firm to the giant bowl as Harper went to town. A soft smile graced my lips as I watched. Macon's mom didn't care that she was making a huge mess or that Harper was wasting quite a bit of her side dish. All she cared about was that my daughter was having fun and learning a new skill. It warmed me to the soul.

Macon stepped up next to me and wrapped an arm around my shoulder. I froze, and my heart thundered in my chest at the unexpected contact. "See," he said, nodding toward his mom. "Completely different person," he announced, solidifying his earlier statement about his mom. "She never lets me help with dinner," he joked.

"That's because you're twenty-one and still have the same technique as a two-year-old," she replied without a moment's hesitation. He laughed, and I felt the vibration from the sound throughout my entire body. Macon's proximity was doing crazy things to me, and if I didn't put some distance between us, he was bound to notice how heavily I was breathing and that my heart was about to beat out of my chest. I stepped out of his embrace and walked toward his mom.

"Is there anything I can help you with?" I asked, hoping she'd give me a task. I needed a distraction.

"Can you slice the pork loin and add it to that platter for me?" She nodded toward the serving dish next to the stove.

"Sure!" I was glad to have a job, something that would take my mind off Macon. I couldn't look at him. I was too afraid he'd see the longing in my eyes. I was too afraid he'd finally notice how badly I wanted him and pull away. His friendship was too important to me to risk pushing him away by letting him know how desperately I wanted him.

When I finished cutting the meat and plated it, I lifted the dish from the counter and turned to take it to the table. I found Macon standing a few feet away. He reached his hands out to take the platter from me.

"I've got it," he said softly. His fingers brushed over mine, and we locked eyes. For a moment, I thought I saw something like yearning fill the golden sunbursts rimming his pupils, but I shook those fantasies away. I was surely imagining things. He didn't think of me the way I thought of him, and I would do well to remember that.

"Thanks," I muttered and slipped my hands from beneath his. His touch seared my skin, sending heat straight to my core. I didn't realize how much harder it was going to be to be near him after experiencing his fiery kisses and hard body pressed against mine. And the worst part was, I had to pretend like I didn't remember. I had to act like nothing had happened between us if I had any hopes of preserving our friendship and my pride.

That was going to be hard with him sitting right next to me at the dinner table, his arm brushing mine every time one of us reached for a serving spoon to add food to our plates. This was going to be the longest dinner ever.

Fourteen

MACON

HER SOFT SKIN GRAZED MINE AS SHE LIFTED A SCOOP OF mashed potatoes from the bowl and added them to her plate. A tingle ran up my arm, and I clenched my fork and knife harder to keep from openly reacting to her touch. I shifted, moving my arm away from her a bit when she reached for another scoop for Harper, hoping she wouldn't notice. The last thing I wanted was for her to think I didn't crave her touch like I needed my next breath, but this wasn't the time or place to broach that subject. We would talk later when my parents weren't around and Harper was occupied with a movie. We needed to clear the air about what had happened last night and why I pushed her away. The only problem was she acted like nothing had changed. She seemed unaffected by what had happened in my truck after drinks with our friends.

My stomach sank as realization hit me square in the gut. Maybe my fear was justified and she truly didn't remember. That was the only explanation for why she acted like nothing had changed. Maybe for her, it hadn't. Had she been too far gone last night to remember that we'd shared one of the hottest kisses of my life? Had the alcohol dulled her senses and made her forget she'd had her legs straddling my hips with my erection pressed into her hot center?

Fuck.

What would I do now? I'd wanted to talk to her about it, to see where her head was at. I needed to know where we stood. Most importantly, I had to know if she wanted to do it again. Because I sure as hell did.

Like always, she fell into comfortable conversation with my parents. She'd become a staple in our home over the years, so there was no awkwardness like there had been with the few girls I'd brought home to meet them. Even Reece had seemed a bit nervous and worried they wouldn't like her. Turns out, her fears weren't completely unfounded. My mother confessed to me after we broke up that she and my father never really cared for my ex, but didn't say anything because they wanted me to be happy. Looking back, I realized they never treated Reece with the same warmth and openness as they did Brynlee. They were always polite and welcoming, but there was definitely a difference in their demeanor around each of the women.

"Can you pass the potatoes?" my father asked.

Both Brynlee and I reached for the bowl and when our hands brushed, I could swear I heard her suck in a sharp breath.

"Sorry," she muttered and pulled her hand back.

"No worries," I replied with a half grin, but she never looked up at me. I rose slightly and reached over the table to pass my father the bowl. When I settled back into my seat, my leg brushed against Bryn's, and that zing of electricity traveled up my thigh and landed in my groin. I wanted her legs wrapped around me again so bad.

I left my thigh pressed lightly against hers to see if she would react. I yearned for any indication she felt the same, but she remained unfazed by the contact. She didn't pull away or press in closer. I considered rubbing against her to see what she would do, but I didn't want to be too obvious or make her uncomfortable. Finally I shifted in my seat, putting a little space between us. Dinner was almost over. I would know where we stood soon enough.

After stuffing ourselves full of cookies, Brynlee insisted on helping clean up. She always did, and she roped me into it too. My mom always protested, but I knew she appreciated the help. Before Bryn could rush out the door afterward, I asked her to stay and watch a movie. It wasn't unusual for us to hang out in the rec room and curl up on the couch with Harper to watch a kid friendly film, but it felt different this time. There was so much to say, and I wanted to do more with her than lounge on the cushions once Harper finally fell asleep, which she inevitably did every time.

She thought for a moment, looking as though she was trying to come up with an excuse not to stay, but my mom chimed in before she could respond.

"That's a great idea," Mom said, retrieving a damp paper towel to wipe more chocolate from Harper's hands and mouth. "We can keep an eye on this cutie pie if you guys want to watch something other than Disney movies," she added, reaching over and swiping the paper towel over Harper's nose playfully. Her face scrunched up, and she giggled as she swatted it away.

It was on the tip of my tongue to accept her offer when Brynlee spoke up. "Oh that's okay. I love Disney movies!"

"Are you sure? We don't mind at all. We love having her around."

"I really appreciate that, but she's probably going to crash soon anyway. It's almost her bedtime." She scooped up Harper who'd been playing with some pots and plastic cooking utensils while we cleaned, and settled her on her hip.

"Well, okay. Why don't you guys head on up, and I'll bring you some popcorn."

"Thanks, Mom. You're the best." I kissed the top of her head and grabbed Brynlee's free hand, leading her out of the kitchen and guiding her to the den. Harper was still wired from all the sugar, so she alternated bouncing around the oversized cushions on the sectional and playing with the toys I kept for her for the first fifteen minutes of the film.

"I'm so sorry," Brynlee announced as she tried to wrestle Harper down off the couch.

"Don't worry about it." I chuckled. "This old thing has held up to far worse than that little one jumping on it."

She visibly relaxed and gave up, sinking onto the cushion next to mine. The cushions were wide, and she was as far as she could get from me. I clasped my hands together and held on tight as I fought the urge to pull her closer. She leaned against the arm and curled her legs up beneath her like she had a hundred other times before, but this time, it felt like she was a world away. I couldn't get any closer to her without it being obvious.

"Are you warm enough?" I asked, hoping to have a reason to get up and grab a blanket so when I sat back down, I could spread it out over both our legs, bringing our bodies flush against each other. It was blazing hot outside, but it stayed cool in this room.

"Yeah, I'm good," she replied, her gaze never leaving the TV screen. A few minutes later, Mom came in with two bowls of popcorn: a big one for Brynlee and me to share and a small one for Harper. We thanked her, and she wished us goodnight since she and my father were turning in for the night. This was perfect. Soon we wouldn't have to worry about interruptions and could have the conversation we desperately needed to have.

Before the movie was even halfway over, Harper was passed out cold, snoring lightly. I got up and retrieved a blanket for her and brought one back to Brynlee. It had grown colder with the setting sun, so she accepted it with a grateful smile. I sat down, this time settling in closer to her.

I waited several minutes before broaching the subject I'd been dying to address with her. My palms dampened as nerves overtook me. This was it. This could be the moment everything changed between us. Rubbing my hands over my jean-clad knees, I took in a deep breath and turned to Bryn. I draped my arm over the back of the couch and tried to keep my posture relaxed even though I was wound tight as an eight day clock.

"Hey," I said softly to get her attention. She turned to me, shifting so that she faced me, her knee bumping against mine. A worried expression filled her eyes, and I realized my tone must've sounded more serious than I intended. I gave her a crooked grin, and her face slowly relaxed.

"About last night," I began, and her eyes widened.

"Macon, I'm so sorry," she exclaimed, her voice pleading. That was not what I expected, and I opened my mouth to tell her it was alright, but she cut me off. "I did not mean to get that drunk. I overestimated how much I could handle. I'm so embarrassed." She buried her face in her hands.

"Shh, it's okay. I just—"

"I know I must've been sloppy," she interrupted again, and I reached out a hand to comfort her. "I don't even remember leaving the bar," she admitted, and I froze.

She didn't remember.

"I'm just glad you got me home safely. Thank you

for that." Her wide eyes gazed up at me with gratitude. "And for the provisions you left on my nightstand. I really needed them this morning." No mention of the kiss. No indication that she remembered being in my lap with her breasts grazing my chest as she rubbed herself against my hard-on.

"Oh," I replied, deflating a bit. This was not how I saw this going. At. All. "You're welcome," I added hurriedly. That was the proper response. I wanted to tell her what had really happened last night, that we'd made out and it was explosive, and that I wanted to do it again, but she was already embarrassed, and I didn't want to make it any worse.

"You're the best friend a girl could ask for." She smiled and leaned into my side. Instinctively, I let my arm fall across her shoulders. Still bewildered by the turn of events, I slowly dropped my chin onto the crown of her head and pondered what this meant for us. We were still friends, but would we ever be more? I knew she was drunk last night, but still… There had to be more there. You didn't kiss someone the way she'd kissed me if there weren't any underlying feelings involved, intoxicated or not.

I pulled her in closer and she let me, melting into my embrace, hoping she wouldn't notice the thundering pulse beneath my skin. With her head nuzzled against my chest, there was no way she could miss it, but she never said a word. She let out a contented sigh and shifted, throwing her legs over my thighs like she had dozens of times before. But this time, it was different. I now knew what those legs felt like spread over my lap and braced against my hips.

I rested my hand on her shin. It was something I always did, but this time, I was hyper-aware of how close she was to my cock. It was growing harder by the second, and I prayed she didn't notice. Grabbing the edge of the blanket, I spread it over my lap, hoping to hide the evidence of my arousal. I wanted her more than I'd ever wanted anyone before, but I didn't want to risk scaring her off. My mind was so muddled that I couldn't think straight and didn't want to make any rash decisions. I'd have to figure out what to do with Brynlee Dawson when I could think more clearly.

Fifteen

BRYNLEE

IT WORKED. HE BOUGHT IT, HOOK, LINE, AND SINKER. When he opened his mouth to bring up the night before, I just knew he was going to say something to break my heart and let me down. I couldn't let that happen. If I had to hear him say the words, it would destroy me, so I did the only thing I could in that moment. I denied having any memory of drunkenly kissing him and trying to get him to make love to me in his truck. And it worked. Sure, he might have eyed me warily as though he debated whether or not I was telling the truth, but ultimately he believed the lie and dropped the subject.

Guilt twisted in my gut knowing I'd lied to him, but it was absolutely necessary. He could never know that I was falling for him if we had any hope of preserving our friendship.

Relief washed through me when he let me go, and I was able to return to my corner of the couch. I didn't want him to suspect anything was amiss, so I propped my legs up on his lap like I always did when we watched movies up here.

This old thing has held up to far worse than that little one jumping on it.

His declaration from earlier rang in my ears like a gunshot in the cozy space, and I fought the urge to recoil at the invasive thoughts pinging around in my head. Had he brought other girls up here and made love to them on this very couch? The space was private, strategically tucked away from the main living area. Plus, you could hear someone coming from a mile away. Had he screwed Reece up here on nights she spent in my spot?

I put a firm stop to that line of thought. It wasn't *my* spot. I had no claim to it. No claim to *him*, at least not the kind of claim I wanted.

We sat quietly through the rest of the movie, watching the animated film even though Harper had long since fallen asleep, the only light in the room coming from the jumbo-sized TV screen in front of us. I didn't mind. It was my kind of movie, and he'd chosen my favorite.

As the three little bears turned back into mischievous, red-headed little boys, I found myself growing antsy. I was ready to get out of here and away from Macon's woodsy scent and effortless sensuality. Pulling my feet from his lap was almost painful. Every now and then, he absentmindedly ran his knuckles up my arches, kneading some of the soreness out of them. The very *non* sexual contact made me ache elsewhere for his touch. I sat up, prepared to leave as soon as the movie was over.

When the credits began to roll, he clicked the TV off, plunging the room into darkness. My breath hitched, and my heart galloped in my chest.

"I should probably head home," I muttered and stood to my feet, colliding with something warm and hard: Macon's chest. I stumbled, the collision throwing me off balance. Strong hands gripped my forearms in the dark, and his intoxicating scent filled my nose.

"Whoa," he said, steadying me on my feet. "Sorry about that."

"S'okay," I spoke into his chest. He was so close that had I looked up, his mouth would've been mere inches from mine, so close I wasn't sure I could resist kissing him.

Don't do it, Bryn. He's just a friend.

Still, our breaths mingled, mine rushing in and out, the sensation of his skin on mine sending a spark of need through my entire body. His cheek was pressed to my temple, the stubble on his hard jaw grazing my forehead. And then his breath hitched, or at least I thought it did. It sounded as though he was just as affected by our closeness as I was. I longed to close the gap between our mouths and press my lips to his.

I couldn't trust myself, though. Hadn't I misinterpreted his actions last night, thinking he wanted more when, in reality, he'd just been taking care of a good friend who'd had too much to drink? I wouldn't make that mistake again. So even though it was going to pain me to pull out of his embrace, I took a step back, forcing myself to put some distance between us.

"I'd better get going," I said quickly, reaching down to pick up the discarded blanket. My eyes were starting to adjust to the dark, and I could see that he hadn't moved a muscle. He stood in the exact same spot he was in when our bodies collided only moments ago. When he finally moved, he took a step toward me, and I held my breath, waiting to see what his next move would be. He took the blanket from my hands and threw it haphazardly onto the couch.

"Thanks for inviting me over," I blurted out, afraid he would try to bring up the debacle from the night before again. He reached past me, and for a moment I thought he'd wrap his arm around my waist and pull me to him, but that was just wishful thinking. There was a click and then a soft yellow light from the lamp behind me filled the room.

He stepped past me, his expression unreadable, and scooped up my daughter. "I'll carry her out for you," he offered, and my belly did a somersault. He seemed so distant now, but as usual was taking care of us. He was always so thoughtful and helpful when it came to Harper that once again, I found myself wishing she was his.

THE NEXT WEEK PASSED BY IN A BLUR. MACON AND I fell back into our old routine. Mostly. We texted each day and spoke on the phone a few times. The bachelor party was coming up, and he wanted me to help him plan a few things for the poker night, so we met up one evening after I closed at the bookstore.

"Where are you hosting this little get-together? I hope for the sake of your parents, it's not going to be at your house," I said as we strolled down the snack food aisle at the local supermarket. My parents had Harper and were happy to keep her a little longer while I did my grocery shopping.

Macon chuckled and bumped his cart against mine playfully. "Of course not. Do you think I'm some kind of monster?" he asked in mock offense. "I would never subject my parents to that." He grabbed a few bags of chips from the shelf and dropped them into his cart. "Jonah's cousin has a house on the lake. He's one of the groomsmen," he clarified, tossing a jar of cheese dip in next to the chips. My nose curled up in distaste. Guys would literally eat anything, wouldn't they? "He said we could do it there. I just don't know how I'm going to get everything ready there when we're going to be axe throwing first."

"Can you go beforehand and set everything up?"

His brow knitted in concentration as he thought it over. "Some of it. The food and the keg are going to be tricky, though."

Of course they were getting a keg. I rolled my eyes. "Why is that?"

"I don't want to get the keg delivered too early, but

I'm afraid to schedule it later in case we don't get back in time. As for the food, I'll have to figure out how to keep some of it warm once it's cooked."

"Can you just put it in the crockpot?"

"Some things I can, but the wings need to be served fresh."

"I have an idea," I announced as we rounded the corner to the cereal aisle. "Why don't you leave me a key, and I'll go over while everyone is gone and get everything ready? Then you can have the keg delivered about thirty minutes before you expect to be back. Problem solved," I offered with a grin.

He stopped dead in his tracks and turned hopeful eyes on me. "You'd do that?"

"Yeah, it wouldn't be any problem. Then you could focus on having a good time."

"Are you sure? I don't want to take up your Saturday evening when you could be doing something else." His expression was difficult to read. It was a mixture of apprehension and hopefulness. I wouldn't let myself read too much into it, though. That tended to get me into trouble.

"What else would I be doing? Watching Harper sleep while I finish her uneaten Goldfish and browse serial killer documentaries?" He cocked an eyebrow at the last part but didn't address it.

"Well, when you put it like that," he said with the tiniest hint of a smirk tilting his lips. I reached over and elbowed him in the gut, and he let out an oomph. "I'm kidding," he attested, rubbing his solar plexus. "I just thought maybe you would end up having other plans, like a date or something."

Was he fishing? It felt like he was fishing. But that was crazy. He had no reason to probe for that kind of information. Except, if he was going to interrogate whoever I might be going out with like he did with Grady Vance. He ran that guy off before we even made it to dinner. Honestly, he did me a solid. Grady ended up in jail for selling his sick mother's pain medicine to an undercover cop. So really, I owed him.

"No, I don't have a date, and I don't plan on getting one either. So, yeah, as pathetic as it is, I am a twenty-one-year-old with no plans for Saturday night other than helping her best friend host the most epic poker night ever," I mused with the biggest, cheesiest grin I could muster.

"It's not pathetic," he assured me, pulling me in for a hug. His chin rested on top of my head, and I briefly let my eyes fall closed as I basked in his affection. "And you really are the most amazing friend ever. I just don't want you to feel like I'm taking advantage of you."

I wish you'd take advantage of me.

I kept those thoughts to myself and reluctantly pulled away. "I don't think that at all. I'm the one who offered. Besides, Jonah is my friend too, and I want his bachelor party to be awesome. I really don't mind helping."

"Alright, if you insist," he said with a smile that made my belly flip and skin tingle.

It was settled. I would help with the party. It was

the least I could do considering he'd fixed my car and my washing machine at no charge.

THE NIGHT OF THE BACHELOR PARTY, I SLIPPED INTO the lake house just before the sun went down and set to work. A couple crockpots filled with various dips sat warming on the counter. All the supplies that didn't require refrigeration were piled on top of the kitchen island. I'd grabbed a few things on the way that would add a little something extra to the party. Setting the bags full of decorations next to Macon's supplies, I grabbed the chicken wings from the fridge and began to prepare them. While they cooked, I decorated the main areas where there were card tables set up and ready to go.

When I finished, I looked around at the subtle hints of black and gold and mentally patted myself on the back. The space still had a masculine vibe with all the dark wood and leather, but now it looked like a celebration was about to take place. The doorbell rang, and I found the keg delivery guy on the front porch. I signed for it and had it brought to the kitchen and propped next to the island. Ensuring there were stacks of cups just above it, I began to get the rest of the food ready. Bowls were filled with chips, and sliders went into the oven. The wings were separated and coated in three different sauces and placed in foil pans. I wrote their flavors on the containers and covered everything so it would stay warm.

My phone chimed from my pocket, and I pulled it out to find a text from Macon.

Macon: We'll be back in about twenty minutes.
Me: Perfect. Everything is just about ready.
Macon: You're the best.

A small smile graced my lips as I read his last text. I tidied up and gave the space a onceover to make sure everything was ready. With only minutes to spare, I locked up, leaving the key where I'd found it, and snuck away before any of the guys saw me. I wished I could be there to see the looks on their faces but didn't want to intrude on their little male ritual. Me and the girls would have our day soon, and there were no boys allowed.

I giggled to myself at that thought. It was kind of ridiculous and made me think of every childhood movie where kids had their clubhouses with signs prohibiting anyone from the opposite sex to enter. It was so silly and got me thinking that if I ever got married, I might just decide to break tradition and have a coed party. That would really get everyone talking, maybe almost as much as me being a teenage single mom.

My mood instantly soured at the thought, and the resentment I thought I'd pushed far enough away came roaring back to life. Sean should've been there, not only for me but for Jonah on this special occasion. He was missing everything. He'd been Jonah's friend too. When he left, he left all of us behind, not just me.

I wondered how he lived with himself. Did he find new friends? Had he forgotten about all of us?

Another text came through, jarring me out of my thoughts. As I rolled to a stop at a red light, I checked my message and my bad mood evaporated.

Macon: You are an angel. I can't believe you did all this. Thank you!

The corners of my lips tipped up in an elated smile. I typed out my quick response and hit send.

Me: You're welcome.

The light turned green, and I headed home, all thoughts of Sean floating away like dandelion seeds in the wind.

Sixteen

MACON

I TUCKED MY PHONE INTO MY POCKET, A PLEASED GRIN lingering on my lips. Jonah approached, his hand outstretched. When I took it, he pulled me in for a friendly hug.

"Bro, this is awesome. How did you pull this off?"

"I had a little help," I admitted.

"Brynlee was here, wasn't she?"

"Damn, can't I get even a little credit? It was my idea; she just set up seventy-five percent of it."

He shook his head with a laugh. "For real, though. I couldn't have asked for a better bachelor party. Thank you," he added sincerely.

"Anytime."

"So when are you going to give in and ask Bryn out?" I froze at his question, fear rooting me into place. Did he know? Had he figured out that I was completely enamored with my best friend and wanted to be so much more with her?

"Wh-what," I stuttered, blinking away my surprise.

"Come on, man. You two are perfect for each other. Besides, I've seen the way you look at her, and I think maybe she likes you too."

What did I say to that?

If I admitted I had feelings for her, she might find out. Jonah would tell Haley, then Haley would tell Bryn. I didn't want her to find out like that.

If at all.

She deserved to hear it from me, but I wasn't sure she ever would. It was too much of a risk.

But damn if that kiss in my truck didn't have me all twisted up inside, wondering if she really did think of me like that.

I needed to say something. Jonah watched me with an expectant arch to his brow.

"I don't know. I think she's still hung up on Sean." He snorted and shook his head.

"Yeah, okay," he said mockingly, practically rolling his eyes. "Keep telling yourself that and you may end up missing out on something good."

Shit, maybe Jonah was right. Maybe I should just take a leap of faith and tell Bryn how I felt.

"You gonna tap that keg or what?" Cameron's booming voice pulled me from my thoughts, and I looked down at the silver barrel sitting next to me.

"Yeah, let's do it!" Tonight was all about having a good time and showing Jonah our support. I'd think about my own love life and Brynlee Dawson later.

Three hours later, Jonah had kicked most of our asses at poker, and the keg was surely almost empty. Some of the guys stepped out onto the porch to light a celebratory cigar. One of the groomsmen, a friend Jonah had met at college, tried to light one in the house and Jonah's cousin practically tackled him to the ground, claiming his wife would kill him if he let someone smoke inside the house. So half the party had moved to the large wraparound porch. After the remaining players finished up their last hand, the rest of us trickled outside into the balmy midnight air. I ensured everyone had a red plastic cup in their hand before raising a toast to Jonah.

"Cheers," we belted out in unison, smashing our cups together, some of us more exuberant than others. Plastic bent and collapsed as beer sloshed over the rims and onto our hands. No one seemed to mind, though. Every face was plastered with a lazy smile in different stages of drunkenness.

This night was a total hit. We'd been able to give Jonah one hell of a bachelor party, and there was one person I owed a debt of gratitude. And I couldn't wait to see her again to tell her how amazing this night had been.

THE NEXT MORNING WAS ROUGH. EVERYONE WAS hungover to some degree, but thankfully no one puked. That was one thing I couldn't handle. If someone even started to gag, it made my stomach churn. Cam and I were the first ones up, so we started on breakfast. The scent of frying bacon lured some of the guys from their slumber, but the coffee brought most of them back to life. By the time the eggs and pancakes were done, everyone had stumbled into the large, open space where the kitchen and main living area met.

When we finally all dispersed, it was well after noon. Once I was back home, I showered and dressed, planning to bring Bryn dinner at work as a thank you. When I walked into the bookstore, a bag of her favorite take-out in hand, my stomach sank. She was talking to a nicely dressed man who appeared to be a few years older than us. Something he said made her laugh, and she reached out and touched his arm. I had to fight back the urge to walk up and place myself between them and grunt possessively like a caveman.

I took a minute to calm myself and heaved a deep breath before approaching. Her gaze moved to me as she caught sight of me from the corner of her eye. Her growing smile matched mine. I didn't hesitate to pull her in for a hug, holding on a little longer than what could be considered friendly.

"Macon, what are you doing here?" she asked, her face filled with elated surprise.

"I brought you lunch," I announced, holding up the bag. "Or dinner, since it's kinda late in the day." I shot her my most charming smile, hoping the guy who'd been talking to her would take the hint.

He didn't budge, so I handed her the bag and turned to him. "Hi, I'm Macon," I said, offering my hand for a shake. It took everything I had not to do the macho, alpha thing and crush his hand in mine. I was tempted, but I decided I was better than that. I didn't need intimidation tactics.

Especially when Bryn wasn't even mine.

At that thought, I released his hand and took a step back, swallowing down my disappointment. His eyes darted back and forth between us as I casually draped my arm over Bryn's shoulders. They widened slightly. Bullseye.

"Oh, uh, I didn't realize you guys were—" he began but was interrupted.

Bryn stepped out from my embrace and held up her hand. "Oh, no, it's not like that. Macon is my best friend." I smiled through the stabbing in my gut. He looked to me for confirmation.

I shrugged and nodded. "It's true," I said, even though the words burned my throat. He eyed me skeptically for a moment, then finally began to relax.

If there'd been any doubt about how Bryn viewed me or felt about me, that cleared it up. I really was just a friend to her.

I finally noticed the man had a small stack of books gripped in his left hand and realized she wasn't just chatting up another guy—a potential date, no doubt—but was trying to do her job.

"I better let you get back to work," I announced, attempting to hide the fact that it tore me up inside to see her looking so interested in another man.

"Thank you so much for bringing me dinner. This is my favorite." She beamed up at me, holding the takeout bag closer. The other man eyed the bag, no doubt cataloging the name on the bag for later use.

Prick.

I pulled Bryn to my chest, hugging her close and placing a soft kiss on her hair. The familiar embrace was comforting, and I felt her relax and melt into me for a moment. When I pulled back, her sweet smile nearly undid me. God, she was beautiful. Not just physically, but in every way possible. She had the kindest soul and a wicked sense of humor. We could talk and laugh for hours and never get bored. She was perfect. I just wish she felt the same about me.

I had to get out of there before I did something stupid like confess my undying love for her right here in the middle of the bookstore or punch the guy who clearly didn't know when to take his leave. He lingered, pretending to read the inside sleeve of the hardback in his hands.

"I better get going." Book guy slowly looked up and closed the book. "It was nice to meet you..." I let the words hang in the air, hoping he'd take the bait and give me his name.

"Will," he offered with a tight smile, clearly aggravated with my intrusion.

"Ah, Will," I said, committing that name to memory. "I'll see you around." It wasn't so much as a threat, but a little warning. *Hurt Bryn and I'll find you.*

Seventeen

Brynlee

I watched Macon's retreating form as he neared the exit, my mind reeling. What had that been all about? He rarely visited the bookstore and had never brought me dinner before. Maybe it was a thank you for helping with the bachelor party. Jonah had texted me this morning to thank me and to tell me how amazing it had been. That had to be it. I shouldn't read too much into it.

But something about the exchange was eating at me. He'd gone all alpha male on Will as though he was trying to warn him off. Hadn't he always done that, though? He was always so protective over me and made sure anyone I dated knew better than to mistreat me. Maybe that was it. Maybe I saw it in a different light simply because my feelings had changed. Still, it felt different this time, almost like he was staking his claim.

Wishful thinking, Bryn.

Will prattled on about the last book in a series he was excited to read that was releasing soon. I'd zoned out temporarily but was now engaged in the conversation again, and I realized what had drawn me to him to begin with: his love of books. He was well read and enjoyed some of the same genres I did. He was easy to talk to and incredibly attractive. His blue eyes had small bursts of gold around the irises, and his dark hair was expertly styled. He was dressed nicely, casual, but professional, the complete opposite of Macon who'd shown up in ripped jeans, a plain T-shirt, boots and baseball cap. Will looked good, but Macon had that blue collar sex appeal that made you wonder what all he could do with those big, strong hands.

Heat creeped up my cheeks at that thought. Desperate to hide my reaction, I excused myself to put my food away and promised to come back. When I returned, Will was ready to check out, but he hesitated a moment and pulled his phone from his pocket.

"I hope this isn't too forward, but I'd love to take you out sometime."

I chewed on the inside of my lip, conflicted. From what I could tell, he checked off all the boxes, but I couldn't get Macon out of my head. Maybe this was what I needed to get over him. This man was nice, funny, well read, and probably had a good job considering he planned to purchase three hardbacks. Those suckers weren't cheap. It was time to take a chance. I wouldn't know what could potentially be waiting for me if I never put myself out there.

"Okay," I replied shyly, a small fluttering starting in my belly.

A huge grin split his face, and he unlocked his phone. "Could I have your number?" he asked in such a gentlemanly way, it reassured me I made the right decision. It was time to forget about this silly crush I had on Macon and move on with my life.

That thought was short lived when I sat down for my break a half hour later. As I bit into my club sandwich, I nearly moaned at how good it was. He'd even got me extra pickle spears. They were my favorite. I polished off my meal before discovering the blondie— my favorite dessert from the restaurant—in the bottom of the bag. I sent Macon a quick text thanking him for the food again.

Me: Thank you for the food, especially the blondie. How did you know this was exactly what I needed? Macon: I know you better than anyone, Bryn.

My breath caught, and my heart leapt into my throat. That sentence felt oddly intimate and left me feeling exposed.

Macon: I'm always here for you, whatever you need.

Why did he have to say things like that? I was

trying to move past my feelings for him, but he was making it nearly impossible.

Me: I know. I'm here for you too.

Three little dots appeared as Macon typed his response, and I held my breath, unsure how he'd respond. They disappeared, and I frowned. Seconds later they reappeared again. I was so focused on my phone and what he would say that the building could've been burning down around me and I wouldn't have known.

When they went away again, I groaned in frustration. *Just say it*, I wanted to scream.

A full minute later his response finally came.

Macon: Call me when you get out of work. I want to tell you all about the party.

My frown deepened, disappointment shuddering through my body. That was what took him so long to say?

What had I been expecting, though? For him to confess his undying love for me? That was ridiculous, and I knew that. I just couldn't seem to squash that hope.

Me: Okay.

A couple hours later, I locked up after the final customer left and headed to my car. I started it up and called Macon, placing it on speakerphone so I could drive. He picked up on the second ring.

"Hey you." His deep voice rumbled, sending butterflies flitting through my stomach.

"Hey," I said, my voice sounding more breathy than I had intended.

We talked the whole ride to my parents' house. I sat in their driveway for several minutes so he could finish telling me about the party. Warmth filled my veins as he proclaimed it the best bachelor party in history. I knew that couldn't possibly be true, but it made me giddy knowing he felt that way.

Before hanging up, we made plans to get together and hang out. Nervous energy hummed through me at the thought of being mostly alone with Macon. Of course, whatever we did would include Harper. He always included her, and that made me long for things that could never be.

Eighteen

MACON

OUR DAY AT THE LAKE WENT MUCH LIKE THE LAST TIME we were there, only there was no Reece pouting under the canopy this time. Looking back, it was clear that was what had been happening. I thought she was just being cautious about sun exposure, but now I realized she felt put out by the fact I was playing with a toddler. I was instantly grateful I'd seen her true colors before it was too late. At one point, I thought I could see myself settling down with her. What a nightmare that would've been.

The second difference was that I knew when we left here today, Harper would go to her grandparents' house and Brynlee would go home and get dolled up for her date with Will. And I'd go home with nothing but my thoughts to keep me company. What if she and Will really hit it off and she decided to continue seeing him?

I wanted to hit something. That asshole got to take Bryn out on a real date tonight. She'd gone on dates before, but this time, things were different. Now I knew just how good her lips felt on mine. I knew what her moans sounded like and how well her body molded to mine as she ground herself against my erection. Will could be the one who got to experience her like that tonight. That thought hit me like a punch in the gut, and I fought the urge to double over in pain.

I couldn't stand the thought of someone else touching her or kissing her. What if it led to more, and she ended up falling for him? I'd have to sit back and watch their relationship blossom. And I didn't know if I was strong enough to do that.

A soft hand met the bare skin of my back, and I jumped. Turning, I found Bryn watching me, concern etched over her pretty face. She wasn't wearing any makeup and her hair was pulled into a messy bun, but she was the most beautiful woman I'd ever laid eyes on.

"Hey, are you alright? You seem really tense."

I let my shoulders relax and gave her an easy smile. "I'm fine," I assured her. "I'm just a little worried you're going to hate me after this." Before she could register what was happening, I threw her over my shoulder and walked into the water.

"Wait, Macon, what are you doing?" she asked, panic rising in her voice.

"It's so hot out here," I replied casually. "You need to cool off."

"Don't you dare," she warned. "Let me down! Harper needs me." I glanced back at the shore where Harper lay sleeping under the canopy, Brynlee's mom perched next to her reading a book, an amused grin on her face. She obviously saw what I was doing and heard Brynlee's pleas.

"Nice try." I smirked and shook my head as I waded further into the water.

"Macon James Lewis, you better no—" Her threat was cut short when I dunked us both under the surface. She gripped onto my shoulders, her fingernails digging into my skin. I couldn't help but wonder if she'd do the same as I hovered above her, thrusting in and out of her body.

Those thoughts were short-lived.

We burst out of the water at the same time, and I knew by the look on her face, I was in big trouble. I turned to swim away, but she was fast and lithe. In a flash, she was on my back.

"You jerk! Now I'm gonna have to wash my hair again." She tried to put me in a headlock, but loosened her grip when I dunked us both beneath the water again. She came up sputtering and cussing, and I knew I was in for it. She came at me again, but I was expecting it this time. I reached out and grabbed her, and spun her around, pinning her against my chest.

"I'm sorry. I just couldn't help myself." I chuckled as she squirmed against me. The laughter fell from my lips as my body came alive against hers.

Shit. She was definitely going to feel that if she kept her back pressed against my front. I released her, hoping she hadn't noticed the stirring in my trunks. Unfortunately it gave her just enough space for a punch to the gut. I let out an exaggerated oomph when her puny fist connected with my abdomen. Luckily, she aimed high enough not to accidentally encounter the erection that had grown to full strength at the sight of her breasts, the tips peaked from the cool water surrounding us, bouncing in her bikini top.

I held up my hands in surrender hoping she wouldn't attack again. If she got that close to me this time, I wasn't sure I could help myself. She'd definitely know what her sexy legs and perky breasts did to me then.

"Truce?" I offered, hoping she'd accept. Her eyes narrowed as though she didn't trust me. That was fair after what I'd just done to her. But that was how we were. We horsed around and teased and fought like siblings.

I swallowed thickly, stuffing down disappointment at that thought. No wonder that was how she viewed me. If I treated her like a sister, then she'd never see me as a lover. I had to make a mental note to stop doing stupid shit like that, because I wanted her. I couldn't get what Jonah said the other night out of my head.

You two are perfect for each other.

I've seen the way you look at her, and I think maybe she likes you too.

Could he be right? I was so conflicted, unsure of how she felt about me. She kept saying we were just friends, but that kiss in my truck said otherwise. Whether she remembered it or not, she'd wanted me. I felt her need and experienced her passion firsthand. That had to mean something.

"Alright," she agreed, snapping me out of my thoughts. "But if you mess with me again, I'll make you pay," she warned.

"I won't. I promise." She looked like she didn't believe me, but I was sincere. That was the last time I would play a brotherly prank on her.

Nineteen

BRYNLEE

I stared down at the text Will sent me earlier and debated on how to respond. He wanted to go out on another date. We'd gone out a couple times, and although we had fun and he'd proven to be a proficient kisser, there was something missing. There were no butterflies or sparks like there were when Macon was near. My heart didn't race when he brushed against me, and he certainly didn't set my skin ablaze when his lips touched mine. I needed to let him go but was afraid any potential he had was overshadowed by my unrequited feelings for Macon.

I sighed and stuffed my phone into my clutch, leaving his text unanswered.

"Everything okay?" Shayla asked as she poked an earring through her lobe. It was the day of Haley and Jonah's wedding, and we were in one of the back rooms where the bridal party had congregated to finish getting ready.

"Yeah, I'm good," I offered with a smile. I knew she was worried about me since the last wedding I'd been a part of was my own, and that had ended disastrously. Memories flooded me when I walked into the church and saw the decorations. I swallowed hard, trying to push down the ache welling up in my chest. This was Haley's day, and I wouldn't let my heartbreak from the past overshadow her joy.

I slipped into my dress and added simple jewelry that matched the other bridesmaids. We joined the rest of the wedding party just outside the sanctuary and took our places in line. When the procession began, I looped arms with Macon, and he gave me an encouraging smile. My skin tingled everywhere it made contact with his body. It made the slow walk down the aisle a sweet torment.

An hour and a half later, the ceremony was completed, and the photographer had taken at least five hundred pictures to commemorate Haley and Jonah's special day.

"You ready to have some real fun?" Macon asked as we headed toward the parking lot. I'd ridden with Shayla to the church, but she was hitching a ride to the reception with someone else, so I accepted Macon's offer to ride with him.

"Yes," I answered excitedly as I tossed my bag into his truck and slid into the seat beside it. "I'm happy for Jonah and Haley, but I sure am glad that's over." He nodded in understanding. "Do you mind taking me home after the reception? I have those books your mom ordered and was going to send them home with you." Sheila asked me to grab her book order when I was at work Thursday, but I hadn't had time to take them to her yet.

"Of course. Whatever you need." His eyes flashed briefly to mine, and I knew I was reading way too much into it, but it felt like he meant more by that statement.

Dinner was served shortly after arriving at the venue, and I was thankful we didn't have to wait long to eat. I was starving. The bagel and coffee I'd had for breakfast were long gone. Macon was seated on the opposite end of our long table along with the other groomsmen, and I hated it. We couldn't even talk while we ate.

Once the cake was cut and both the best man and maid of honor gave their speeches, it was time for the first dance. The DJ put on a slow, romantic song, and the newlyweds stepped onto the dance floor. I slipped out as soft music floated from the speakers, ensuring the doors closed behind me as I found my mom's number and clicked on the icon to start a video chat. She answered right away, her face, so much like mine, filling the screen.

"Hey, sweetie. Are you having a good time?" she asked, and I nodded.

"I am, but I miss my girl. Is she around?"

"Hold on just a moment. I think Blake just finished polishing her nails."

A moment later, Harper's face popped up and she

smiled. "Mommy," she trilled excitedly, her eyes going wide. "You wook so pwetty." She looked at me like I was her favorite Disney princess come to life, and my heart melted.

"Thank you, baby," I crooned, my smile growing exponentially.

"She's right. You look amazing." I turned at the sound of Macon's voice. He'd slipped into the corridor and was slowly stalking toward me, his appreciative gaze burning into me. My cheeks warmed at his praise as I drank him in. He'd removed his suit jacket and had his shirtsleeves rolled up to his elbows, exposing his muscular forearms. I swallowed thickly as I tried to ignore the sensual masculinity rolling off him in waves. He stepped right up to me and invaded my space. For a moment, as he looked down into my eyes, I thought he might kiss me. I'd almost convinced myself of it when he turned his attention to my phone and a wide grin spread over his lips as he greeted my daughter.

"Hey, Half Pint."

"Hi, Macon!" she practically squealed. Once she saw him, I was no longer of any consequence to her. The corners of my mouth turned down into a frown, and Macon smirked at my pout. She prattled on for several minutes, Macon nodding and interjecting a few "uh huhs" and "wows" at the right moments, despite not understanding half of what she said. Once we finally wished her goodnight and ended the call, muted sounds from inside the reception were the only thing piercing the silence between us.

She's right. You look amazing.

Macon's compliment echoed in my head as his warm eyes found mine. Tension radiated between us. There was something in that look that resembled longing. My breath caught when he opened his mouth to speak.

"Bryn," he began, but before he could say anything else, the door flew open and Cam stepped out into the hall. Music from the reception poured out into the corridor and filled the small space between us. It was like a shield had gone up between us, an invisible force field meant to keep him just out of reach when it seemed he was finally ready to come closer.

"There you guys are!" Cam announced as though he'd been looking for us a while. "Haley wants everybody back in there for bouquet and garter toss." He held the door open and motioned for us to follow with a nod of his head. I let out a soft sigh and walked toward him, afraid to look at Macon, lest I discover I'd imagined the heat in his gaze when he'd looked upon me.

As we entered the dimly lit room, all the single ladies began to gather in the center. Shayla caught sight of me and motioned me over. I joined her and Delilah on the fringes, hoping Haley aimed for the opposite side when she slung her flowers over her shoulder.

I was in no hurry to get married, especially since I was single and the only man I'd even consider spending my life with was watching me with a teasing grin from the crowd gathered around us. It was the grin of a friend, not someone who wished to be more. I guess I really had imagined the look of desire flashing in his eyes a moment ago.

Haley's bouquet went sailing and was quickly plucked from the air by one of her cousins. My shoulders sagged in relief as I joined Macon in the crowd.

"You're turn, big guy." I smirked, patting him on the back as I motioned to the gathering group of men. He pushed off the wall and sauntered over to join them, positioning himself nearly dead center. It was almost like he *wanted* to catch the garter.

Fighting off catcalls from the guys, Jonah waved his dismissal at the rowdy men in the group and knelt in front of his new bride. He slowly shimmied the tiny garment off her leg, his eyes never leaving hers as a wicked grin tugged at the corners of her lips. When he finally stood, he balled the garter in his fist and tossed it over his shoulder. A familiar, muscular arm reached up and grabbed it over the other grappling hands.

Macon pulled the scrap of fabric to his chest, grinning triumphantly. His gaze landed on me momentarily, and he held my stare. Our connection was broken when Cam slapped him on the back, and the rest of the guys shouted and cheered around him.

We spent the rest of the night dancing and laughing with our friends. Neither Macon nor I brought up the look that passed between us after the garter toss, and I convinced myself it had been nothing. Perhaps I'd read his expression wrong, and he was remembering the devastation from my wedding three years ago. Maybe it wasn't longing I'd seen flashing in his eyes but sympathy.

"ARE YOU READY TO GO?" MACON SAID, LEANING DOWN to speak into my ear as the clock ticked closer to midnight. I'd sat down to remove my high heels and rub my aching feet, but even that sensation faded to the background as goosebumps pebbled my flesh. Macon's breath stirred the loose strands of my hair at the nape of my neck, and his deep voice stirred something low in my belly.

I nodded my response, not trusting my own voice, and slipped on my shoes. He pulled my chair out as I stood and grabbed my clutch from the table. It was all I had with me since the rest of my things were already in Macon's truck.

We bid our friends goodbye, and I gave both Haley and Jonah congratulatory hugs.

"I'm so happy for you two," I proclaimed, gripping Haley's hands.

"Thank you," she replied with a soft smile and gave my hands a gentle squeeze.

We walked out into the balmy night air and headed for his truck. The engine roared to life when he turned the key in the ignition, a low rumble taking its place as he pulled out of the parking lot. I tried not to think about the last time he'd driven me home, but I couldn't keep the memories from resurfacing. I quietly winced and turned my face away from him as warmth flooded my cheeks, the sting of his rejection still fresh in my mind. Squeezing my eyes shut, I slowly inhaled a deep, calming breath and pushed those thoughts aside. We spent the rest of the drive back to my house chatting casually about the evening with no indication of what he was about to say when Cam interrupted us earlier.

When we pulled into my driveaway, I grabbed my bag and hopped out of the truck. Macon followed me inside, and I instructed him to make himself at home while I changed. The box containing his mom's books was in my bedroom, so I promised to bring them back out with me, but I had to get out of this dress before I did anything else. I took down my hair as I strode down the hallway to my room, shaking it out and rubbing my tender scalp as I slipped the last bobby pin from my updo. Kicking off my shoes, I reached for the zipper on my dress. I'd only pulled it down an inch or so before it got stuck. Tugging on it, I grunted in frustration. The bastard wouldn't budge. There was only one way I was getting this dress off.

I poked my head out of my bedroom door. "Umm, Macon," I called into the hallway. "Can I get a little help in here?"

"Coming," came Macon's reply. I slipped back into my room, waiting for him to arrive. He appeared in my bedroom door, and my heart rate kicked up a notch. He looked all rugged and handsome with his shirtsleeves rolled up, a five o'clock shadow darkening his sharp jaw. My breath hitched as he approached, his easy, relaxed stride a contradiction to the sudden fluttering in my belly. His large, muscular body moved with a surprising litheness that made me wonder how it moved in *other* ways.

"What do you need?" His head tilted to the side, and he watched me inquisitively.

"My zipper is stuck," I admitted, turning my back to him. "Can you finish unzipping me? I need to get out of this dress," I lamented. It was snug and pushed my breasts up to the sky. I was ready to be done with it.

He was quiet for a moment and when I looked up, I caught our reflection in the full-length mirror in the corner. It was off to the side, so I could see most of his profile with a clear view of his face. He swallowed thickly as he stared at my back, and I watched as his expression morphed. His brows knitted in concentration as though he was trying to hold something back.

I averted my gaze, feeling as though I was invading his privacy by watching him without him knowing, but when he spoke, I couldn't help but look into his reflection again.

"Uh, sure," he said, clearing his throat. "I can do that." His gaze dropped, and I could've sworn he checked out my ass as he took a step closer to me. He reached out and pushed my hair over my shoulder so he could see the zipper in question, his fingers brushing gently over my skin. The soft contact sent shivers down my spine, and I fought the urge to let my eyes fall closed to savor the feeling because I couldn't stand the thought of not being able to see him as he practically undressed me.

He gripped the metal puller and tugged it gently. It didn't move. He tried again, pulling a little harder this time, and it finally gave way. Slowly he dragged it down, opening my bare back to him. His breaths were coming faster, the rise and fall of his muscular chest visible beneath his white dress shirt. His eyes skimmed over me, a look of desire I'd never seen flashing over his features. I wasn't imagining it this time. He looked like a man who'd been deprived of water staring into a well. He was ready to dive in, but something was holding him back.

Perhaps I'd been wrong this whole time. Maybe, just maybe, Macon wanted me as more than a friend too. The way his eyes skimmed over my bare skin when he thought I wasn't looking made me second guess everything I thought I knew about our relationship and how he thought about me. Had he actually been longing for me the way I longed for him, but was too afraid of ruining what we had to make his move? If the look in his eyes was any indication, the answer was a resounding yes.

It was now or never. I needed to take this chance. And loving Macon Lewis was worth the risk.

"I remember," I murmured softly as the zipper reached the bottom. He froze, his hands still on my dress. His gaze lifted, and he caught sight of me in the mirror. It felt as though he could see straight into my soul. It was time to lay myself bare and admit what I'd been afraid to tell him for so long. "That night in your truck," I elaborated, and recognition flashed in his eyes. He knew exactly what I was talking about. "I remember all of it."

I turned to face him, my arms held over my chest to keep my dress from falling. He took a step back, giving me space I didn't want. I suddenly felt cold in the absence of his warm skin on mine.

"I didn't want to take advantage of you. It caught me off guard. I'm sorry." He scrubbed his hand over his face, looking distressed.

"*I'm* not."

Surprise registered on his face. "You're not?"

"I'd wanted to do that for a long time." At my confession he took a step closer. "I never wanted to jeopardize our friendship, but I don't want to be just friends anymore. I want to be m—"

Before I could finish that sentence his hands were on my face, cupping my cheeks as his mouth slammed against mine. It took my brain a moment to register what was happening, but then I was kissing him back. My lips parted as his tongue swept inside, and I groaned. Dropping his arms, he wrapped them around my waist, and I released my dress, no longer caring about keeping anything covered. Macon was kissing me, and that was all that mattered.

My hands snaked over the hard planes of his chest and encircled his neck. His palm flattened over my lower back, and I arched into him, reveling in the feel of his solid torso pressed against me. He began to harden against my belly, and my blood heated.

He pulled back and pinched his eyes closed. "Bryn," he groaned, and my pulse thundered even harder against my ribs. His eyes fell to my exposed breasts where the fabric had fallen away somewhere in the midst of our kiss. "Are you sure about this? There's no going back after we cross that line."

"We've already crossed it." I stepped back and let my dress slide further down my torso. Gripping it in my hands, I pushed the fabric over my hips and let it pool on the floor, stepping out of it to stand in nothing but my undergarments. He gulped at the sight of me in nothing but my lace thong. The dress had built-in cups that eliminated the need for a bra, so all I had needed were panties.

Then his mouth was on me again. He started at my lips and worked his way down my neck until he found one tender peak and pulled it into his mouth. I cried out, and my fingers speared into his hair. I held him against me as he swirled and flicked his tongue over one nipple, leaving it sensitive and wet before moving to the other side.

My body was practically vibrating by the time his lips found mine again. He lifted me gently in the air, and I wrapped my legs around his back as he brought me to the bed and laid me down. He hovered above me, his hips settling between mine. His kisses slowed and became more tender, more reverent.

"We don't have to do anything you're not ready for. Just tell me if you want me to stop."

"Don't stop," I breathed. "I want everything."

He made a low sound in the back of his throat, and my thighs involuntarily tightened at his sides. Large, deft hands slid down my ribs and over the curve of my waist and gripped my panties. He worked his way down, his mouth trailing kisses over my breasts and abdomen as he rid the last thread of clothing off my body.

I expected him to undress and rejoin me on top of the sheets. That was all I'd ever known, but Macon wasn't Sean, and he had other plans. His hands gripped my calves, pushing my legs apart as his lips skimmed up the inside of my leg. I gasped as he neared my center, realizing what he was about to do. He grinned up at me wickedly when he noticed me watching and took one long swipe over my sensitive flesh with his tongue. My head fell back, and my eyes closed at the unfamiliar sensation. It had been a long time and had never amounted to much when it happened, my previous partner too impatient for his own orgasm to care about mine.

"Look at me," he commanded, and my eyes shot open. "I want you to watch."

My core tightened as I grew slick with need, Macon's demands stirring something inside me that had lain dormant too long. Was this what I'd been missing out on all this time? Those thoughts evaporated as his hot tongue flicked over my clit. My hips bucked, and he chuckled, clearly amused by my enthusiasm. I didn't care as long as he didn't stop.

My skin was on fire, my heart pounding like a drum inside my chest. Seeing Macon's dark head between my thighs, devouring me like his last meal had my body wound so tight, I would shatter into a million pieces once my release came.

My legs shook, and the pressure built as he slipped first one finger and then another inside me and curled them forward. Every nerve ending in my body was on high alert waiting for the explosion that was sure to come. My back bowed, and Macon's name left my lips on a shout when I came.

Sated from the earth-shattering, life-changing orgasm he just gave me, I felt limp and boneless as Macon crawled up the bed and hovered above me. His mouth descended to mine, and I kissed him, tasting myself on his tongue.

"Fuck, that was hot," he proclaimed, pressing his forehead to mine. I agreed but couldn't manage to form the words. "I wish we'd done that sooner."

"Mm-hmm," I replied lazily. My body was more relaxed than it had ever been in my life. I was contemplating sleep when Macon shifted, and his hardened length brushed against me. I was suddenly wide awake and craved more.

He was still fully clothed. That was the first thing we needed to change. I reached for the buttons on his shirt, popping them out of the buttonholes.

"I need more," I demanded. Macon chuckled and sat up, giving me room to work. Once his shirt was open, I moved to his pants, flicking open the button and unzipping him.

"Let me grab the lights," he said as he stood to push his pants down.

"I want to see you first," I blurted out. I hadn't meant to admit that out loud, but it was true. He'd had me sprawled wide open, able to take in every inch of me. I yearned to see him that way too.

He smirked, pleased with my request. "Okay," he said, stepping out of his dress pants. Hooking his fingers inside his boxers, he slowly, torturously, brought them over his hips, freeing his erection. My eyes went wide, and I swallowed thickly. I had felt it before. I knew it was big. I just hadn't realized it was *that* big. It had been a long time since I'd had sex, but I'd had a baby. Surely, I could handle it, right?

He turned and walked to where the light switch was on the opposite wall. I crawled across the bed to my nightstand and flicked on the lamp seconds before the lights went out, not wanting it to be completely dark. I wanted to see his face when we made love for the first time.

He bent and picked up his pants, pulled his wallet from the back pocket, and retrieved a small square of foil. I was suddenly aware of the fact that I'd been so lost in him, I hadn't even considered protection, but I was thankful he had. Not only was this our first time together, and I knew he'd been with other women, but I also wasn't ready to give Harper a sibling.

All that faded away as I watched him roll on the condom. I was mesmerized by the motion and the way he gripped himself. For some reason, the act was so sensual. Maybe it was because I hadn't had many partners, but it made me yearn for him even more. He glanced up and caught me watching. The corners of his mouth lifted, and I blushed.

"Come here," he growled, and I leaned up from my

kneeling position on the bed. We reached for each other at the same time, and his hands cupped my face. He kissed me, lips and tongues crashing and tangling as his hard cock bobbed against my belly. For a moment I wished he hadn't covered it because I wanted to taste him.

Maybe next time.

That thought made me giddy. After this, there'd be no more pretending. No more acting like he didn't make my pulse race and butterflies to take flight in my belly.

"Lie back," he instructed, releasing me. I followed his command, willingly letting my legs fall open to welcome him in. He came over me, planted one hand next to my head and the other pressed into the mattress next to my ribs. "Are you ready?"

"Yes." The sound came out breathy, and I feared he hadn't heard. He didn't move for several seconds as his eyes roamed over my face as though trying to capture every detail. Finally, he positioned himself at my entrance, and I felt him parting me. He let out a low curse as he slowly slid into my body.

"Brynlee," he groaned, and my heart squeezed in my chest. He rarely used my full name, but I loved the sound of it on his lips. It sounded so special, like it meant something more to him.

When he was fully seated inside me, he paused, giving me a moment to adjust to him. It was a nice gesture, but I wanted—no *needed*—him to move. I rolled my hips, encouraging him to thrust, and he granted my wish.

He kissed me reverently as he gently moved in and out of me. It felt good, better than anything I'd felt before, but it wasn't enough.

"More," I demanded, and he locked eyes with me. I wanted to see him lose control, to show me what he really wanted. He leaned back slightly, changing the angle of his entry, and lifted one leg. His arm curled around the back of my knee, and that delicious pressure began to build again. With each thrust, he brought me closer and closer.

Shudders ran through my body, and I cried out, my climax pulsing in waves. He let me ride it out, pumping in and out of me until tipping over the edge himself. He collapsed against me, his damp forehead coming to rest on my shoulder.

"Wow," he muttered against my skin. "That was…"

"Intense," I finished for him.

"Yeah," he agreed breathlessly before rolling off me. Excusing himself, he headed to the bathroom to dispose of the condom. When he came back, I was in the exact same position in which he'd left me. I wasn't sure I'd ever be able to move again after that. He let out a little chuff of laughter when I told him as much.

Lifting the blanket, he helped me maneuver beneath it and pulled me against him. Slipping his arm under my shoulders, he cradled me close to his chest. We were completely naked, not one single scrap of fabric between us. I never dreamed we'd get to this. I'd hoped for it but never let myself believe it could happen.

Twenty

MACON

"I HAVE A CONFESSION TO MAKE," I ANNOUNCED AS Bryn and I laid naked in her bed. The sex had been mind-blowing, even better than I could've imagined, but the connection we had was almost magical. I'd never felt closer to anybody before.

"What's that?" she asked, propping her chin on my chest. She looked so cute doing it, I nearly forgot what I was going to say.

"I had the biggest crush on you in high school."

"What?! Really?" she exclaimed.

"Really."

"Why didn't you ever say anything?" she questioned, pushing herself up on her arms.

"I was working up the nerve to ask you out, but Sean beat me to it."

"He knew and asked me out before you could?"

"It wasn't like that. I never told him. If he had any inkling that I liked you, he kept it to himself."

"He's been gone for three years. What took you so long to tell me this?"

"I kept thinking he'd come back, you know. That he'd finally get his act together and beg for your forgiveness. By the time I realized that wasn't going to happen, we'd already become such good friends that I didn't want to risk losing what we had by asking you out in case you didn't feel the same."

"I have a confession too."

"Oh?"

"I always thought you were cute. But you were so quiet and studious. I never would've guessed you liked me. Sean made no secret that he was into me. If you had asked me out first, I would've said yes."

My heart hammered against my chest at her admission, and I found myself struggling to catch my breath. If I'd just had the balls to ask her out back then, all her pain could've been avoided. We could've been celebrating many happy years together right now instead of just finding out we'd always had feelings for each other.

I shifted so I could hover above her, and she flattened herself on the mattress, her eyes widening slightly.

"Do you mean that?" I had to know for sure. At this point, it wouldn't change anything. We'd already crossed that line, but sixteen-year-old Macon had to know that she would've chosen me over Sean if given the opportunity.

Her legs fell open, and my hips settled between hers as her lips turned up in a sweet, yet sensual grin.

"Yes," she breathed, and I dropped my forehead to hers, pinching my eyes closed to savor the moment.

She wriggled beneath me, and I lifted away, staring into her eyes. They dropped to my mouth, silently asking for a kiss. I granted her unspoken request, swallowing her moan as I flexed my hips, pressing my growing arousal against her.

A moment of coherent clarity broke through the haze of lust, and I lifted off her welcoming body. "I don't have any more condoms."

A blush bloomed across her cheeks, and she looked away. "I have some," she confessed almost in a whisper, but then her brows furrowed. "I'm just not sure they're going to fit you." It was on the tip of my tongue to ask who exactly they did fit, but ultimately it was none of my business. Instead, I took in her worried expression and almost laughed.

"Only one way to find out." I quirked a brow suggestively, and she grinned. That look and close proximity of her naked body was making me hard all over again. "Where are they?" She pointed to the bedside table, and I opened the drawer.

"All the way in the back," she instructed. "Might have to wipe off the dust before you open the box." It was meant to be a joke, but I was secretly thrilled she hadn't needed them.

Locating the box, I tore it open and took what I needed, returning to Brynlee's warm and inviting body in a flash. She wrapped her legs around me as I peppered soft kisses over her neck and jaw before finding her pink, swollen lips. I pushed into her just as her mouth opened and our tongues met. She sucked in a gasp, and I took the opportunity to deepen the kiss.

Her soft moans spurred me on. I wanted to make her forget there was ever anyone before me. I wanted her to feel how cherished she was. There was no more holding back with her. No more pretending. After this, things would never be the same, and I couldn't be happier. She was now more than my best friend. She was my everything.

Her body tightened and spasmed around me, drawing me closer to my release. I leaned back slightly, gripping her thigh with one hand while bracing myself with the other. Three long, hard thrusts and she was crying out, her tightening core tipping me over the edge. Sweat trickled over my brow and down my back as I came with a shout. Our groans and cries mixed and mingled until I collapsed against her, our sweat-slickened bodies sliding over each other.

The room fell silent in the absence of our moans of pleasure as we both caught our breath. I brushed a damp tendril of hair from her face and softly pressed my lips to hers.

"That was incredible."

"Yeah," she replied simply. "I'm gonna need a shower after that."

"Same," I agreed.

Her shower was thankfully big enough for both of

us. We took our time getting cleaned up. I gently washed her back, and she scrubbed shampoo into my scalp with her magical fingers. By the time we were both clean, I was ready to get dirty again. My cock grew hard at the sight of her wet, soapy breasts, and her eyes darkened as she took in how my body reacted to her. We explored each other with hands and lips and mouths, and by the time we were finished, we both fell into bed, exhausted and sated. Within seconds, I drifted off to sleep, dreaming of a future I always thought was out of reach.

Twenty-one

BRYNLEE

My cheeks ached from smiling so much. I'd finally admitted my feelings for Macon, and to my surprise, he confessed he felt the same.

"What are you so happy about?" my sister, Blake, grumbled from the doorway. I was standing in my parents' kitchen, nursing a cup of coffee.

My baby sister was a typical teenager. She slept until noon, then still woke up with a bad attitude. Her hair hung slightly off center in a loose, lopsided bun with the remnants of yesterday's makeup smudged beneath her eyes. Last night was her high school cheerleading squad's annual fundraiser and as a returning senior, she was one of four girls in charge of helping to organize the event. So, while I was standing next to one of my best friends as she said her vows, Blake had a fake smile plastered on her face

139

while she sold overpriced baked goods at the craft fair that was held in our local high school gymnasium.

Before I could respond, Harper came running in with her arms stretched wide. "Bwake," she crooned, slamming into my sister's legs.

Blake bent and scooped Harper up, settling her on one hip.

"Hey ya, little Harpy," Blake chirped her usual greeting and tickled her neck. Harper giggled and squirmed, and my smile grew at the sight. My sister and daughter were two peas in a pod and absolutely adored each other.

"How'd the fundraiser go?" I asked, hoping she wouldn't notice I had just avoided her question. I wasn't ready to tell anyone about me and Macon just yet, and we agreed to keep it on the low for now. We hadn't discussed labels, but we both wanted to give ourselves time to get used to this new aspect of our relationship before announcing anything to our families and friends. I would be lying if I said that didn't give me a little thrill. It felt kind of taboo and totally hot to be seeing him in secret.

Blake rolled her eyes and hefted Harper higher on her hip. "It was lame." Typical teenager response. "But I guess we raised enough money to get new uniforms and warm-up suits."

"That's good," I offered encouragingly before taking a sip of my coffee. It wasn't nearly sweet enough, so I added another heaping spoonful of sugar to it.

"Yeah, I guess." She shrugged, looking unimpressed. "I still think we would've made more money with the silent auction. Then we wouldn't have to pay so much out of pocket to travel for competitions." The silent auction had been Blake's idea, but the craft fair/bake sale was somewhat of a tradition. They'd held one every year for the past decade. It was familiar and a surefire way to raise money, but Blake was probably right. The silent auction she proposed had sounded like a very lucrative venture.

"There you guys are," Mom announced, coming into the room. "I was trying to get this little stinker changed, and she ran away." She reached for Harper, but my little girl pulled away, clinging tightly to my sister. Blake totally played into it by turning away and putting more distance between the two.

"Ugh," Mom huffed when Harper peeked at her from behind Blake's neck. "You little traitor," she accused teasingly.

"Do you want Auntie Blake to help you get dressed?" my sister asked in a sweet, placating tone, and Harper nodded. "Okay, let's go." They swept out of the kitchen and presumably upstairs to what was now Harper's room. Decorated with all the pinks, purples, and sky blues a little girl could want, my once drab, boring room was now my daughter's own little paradise. I'd never been allowed to paint my walls with anything but neutral colors, but for Harper, the sky was the limit.

"How was the wedding?" my mother asked, pulling me from my thoughts.

"It was good," I answered, trying to hide my smile

behind my coffee mug as I took a sip. One brow lifted as she watched me closely. I knew my eyes gave me away, but I hoped she'd let this one go. I wasn't so lucky.

"How good we talkin'?"

"The ceremony was beautiful, and Haley looked absolutely stunning. Then the reception was—"

"Spill," she demanded, motioning for me to give her more. "I know something happened. You're practically glowing."

Shit, she knows.

"Mom," I whined, pleading for her not to probe any further. She just gave me that look, the one that said she'd find out one way or another and it was best for me to just tell her now. She perfected the look when I was in junior high and had been caught in a lie my friends and I concocted to go to a high school party. It was the classic one where everyone told their parents they were sleeping over at someone else's house but were really getting wasted in a field. It didn't take long for our moms to figure out what we were up to since they'd all done the same thing back in the day.

Damn gen X-ers.

I finally gave in under the weight of her stare. "It's still new, and I don't want to jinx it. Just let me keep it for myself for a little while."

Her lips curved up in a devious smile. "Well, you look happy. And if you're happy, then I'm happy for you."

Relieved, I let myself relax against the counter. "Thank you."

"I just hope you and Macon used protection."

"Of course we—"

Wait. What? How the hell had she known it was Macon?

The mug nearly slipped from my hand as I stood there slack-jawed, my chin nearly on the floor. "How did you know?"

She smirked as she lifted the steaming mug to her lips. "A mother knows these things." I eyed her skeptically. "Plus, I got a call from Donna Wilson saying she saw him leaving your house this morning wearing the same clothes he had on at the wedding," she admitted ruefully.

I winced and worry churned in my gut. I wasn't ready for the whole town to know about us, and that was what would happen now.

"Don't worry," Mom soothed, recognizing the panic in my eyes. "I told her not to read too much into it and that he probably fell asleep there after dropping you off. Besides," she added in that faux sweet, Southern voice, "she wouldn't want anybody to know that the secret ingredient to that famous cake of hers is a box of Duncan Hines." She winked at me over the rim of her coffee cup, and I shook my head. My mother never ceased to amaze me.

"Thanks," I replied gratefully, knowing she'd just saved me from being the talk of the town. Again. But it wouldn't last forever. Eventually people would find out. Macon and I just needed to figure out what we were doing before that happened.

I DIDN'T GET TO SEE MACON OR EVEN TALK TO HIM much over the next several days. He was busy helping his dad with a big project in another town, and I was working extra hours at the bookstore. The lack of communication had me on edge. Doubt and insecurity plagued me, the worry that we'd never be able to make this work tying my stomach in knots. I wanted us to work. I didn't think I could go back to just being friends after what we shared the other night. He was it for me.

I was arranging hardbacks on the display table featuring new releases when a static charge filled the air around me. I felt him before I heard him.

"Hey, Bryn."

I turned to find Macon standing behind me. He kept a respectable distance, but there was a fire in his eyes I recognized from Saturday night and again on Sunday morning. We'd lazily made love in my bed as sunlight peeked through the blinds, bathing us in little beams of soft morning light. My cheeks flushed at the memory. He'd been even more glorious in the light of day, his hard muscles sculpted from years of sports and manual labor, his jaw covered in day-old scruff.

"Hey," I breathed, finally finding my voice. There was a seriousness to his features that I rarely saw, but it started to relax now that I'd spoken. It was as though he'd been worried I wouldn't want him showing up here. That wasn't the case. I was thrilled that he was here. It was my first time seeing him since everything went down five nights ago.

"I was in town and thought I'd stop by. Brought you a latte," he announced, holding out the sweet, iced offering. My growing smile matched his as I reached for the drink. My fingers slid over the cool plastic gathering condensation before meeting his warm skin. Desire flashed briefly in his eyes at the contact, and I stilled, taking in the moment. It was the first time I'd touched him in days, and it had been far too long. I wanted to touch more of him, to slide my hands up his arms, over his broad shoulder, and around his neck so I could pull him close to me. If I hadn't been on the clock, I would've done just that.

"Thank you." Our eyes locked and held as he released the cup, and I pulled it to my chest. His gaze dropped briefly to the v cut of my top where just a tiny bit of cleavage showed. He swallowed hard before lifting his gaze to mine.

"I've missed you." His voice was so low that no one around us could hear, but it sounded like a chorus of angels singing in my ears. I'd missed him desperately and wanted nothing more than to jump into his arms and kiss him silly.

"I missed you too."

"Let's have dinner tomorrow night." I glanced around to make sure nobody was listening in on our conversation. We hadn't made anything official yet, so I was nervous someone would overhear.

"I have the late shift tomorrow. It will be well after nine before I get home from picking up Harper." My little girl would most likely be asleep by the time I got to my parents' house to get her after work and would stay that way the whole ride home.

His smile fell a bit, but he didn't give up.

"Saturday then?" I thought his proposal over for a moment, trying to decide if it would work. I would get out of work early enough, but we'd have to take Harper with us or see if Mom wouldn't mind keeping her just a little longer. I hated to do that to my parents, though. They barely got any time to themselves because they had my daughter so often.

"If you want, I could pick something up and bring it over so you don't have to worry about having Harper out too late," he added hopefully. He'd already thought ahead and considered my daughter a part of the equation. My heart swelled at the prospect knowing she was included in his plans.

"That sounds perfect," I agreed.

"Alright. I'll see you Saturday then." With that, he leaned in and pressed a soft kiss to my cheek, lingering a moment before pulling away. From the outside, it might have looked like a friendly kiss, but it certainly hadn't felt like one. It was a kiss full of promise. A kiss that guaranteed there was more where that came from.

Twenty-two

MACON

I HAD A DATE WITH BRYNLEE. SURE, IT WAS JUST DINNER at her house and Harper would be there, but as far as I was concerned, it was our first official date as a couple.

I thought about her all day, wondering what it would be like now that I wasn't fighting my attraction and feelings for her. Would we be able to relax and hang out like we always had only with kissing involved now, or would it be nerve wracking and awkward at first like it was anytime you started dating someone new.

My phone buzzed, and I pulled it out to find a message from Brynlee.

Brynlee: Thanks again for the latte. I'm convinced

**that was the only thing that got me through my
busy morning.
Me: Anytime.**

I punctuated the message with a big smiling emoji and hit send. I wanted to bring her coffee every morning if it meant getting to see her look at me that way on a daily basis.

**Brynlee: What time should I expect you on
Saturday?**

Her question sent a thrill through me and caused my pulse to quicken. She was thinking about our upcoming date too, and damn if that didn't make me infinitely happy.

**Me: What time will you be home?
Brynlee: Around seven.
Me: Expect to see me then.**

She sent back three red hearts, and my grin widened. I had something special planned for her. It would be the best first date she ever had.

"Quit goofing off and get back to work," Daryl intoned, dropping a box of screws at my feet. He loved to bust my balls since I was the boss' son, but he was actually a pretty cool guy. After a stint in prison for a drug charge, he cleaned up his life, but nobody would hire him. He jumped through all the hoops the courts required of him, but the damage to his reputation had been done. My dad was the only person willing to give him a chance, and now he was the best roofing guy he'd ever employed. He was even getting side jobs when Dad didn't need him for a project.

I tucked my phone away and tried to suppress the grin I knew was splitting my face. The job site was no place for sharing my excitement about a girl I was seeing. I learned that the hard way. The guys ribbed you relentlessly. Besides, I wasn't ready to share my newly updated relationship status with anyone yet. Everything happened so fast with Bryn that we hadn't even discussed what we were, but I wanted to rectify that. I planned to ask her to be my girlfriend, officially. Then I'd shout it from the rooftops.

"Did they deliver that lumber yet?" I asked, eager to change the subject.

He smirked like he knew what I was doing but didn't call me on it. "It's out front," he replied, pointing a thumb over his shoulder. "Jonesy and Porter are unloading it now."

"Good." Wiping the perspiration from my brow, I straightened my tool belt and went back to work.

I fought the urge to stop by the bookstore the next day, not wanting to appear clingy, but damn I missed her. Now that I knew just how good we were together, I was hooked. She was the drug I didn't know I needed and now that I'd had a dose, I never wanted to stop.

That struggle bled into Saturday, the day we'd be having dinner. Knowing how close I was to holding her and kissing her again should've been a relief, but all it did was add to the anticipation. By the time I picked up the food from the local Italian restaurant, I was ready to burst out of my skin. I shouldn't have been nervous. This was Brynlee, my best friend of the past three years. We knew everything there was to know about each other.

Or did we?

Somehow, we'd both hidden our true feelings from each other for a long time, not knowing the other reciprocated those desires. Had we inadvertently hidden other parts of ourselves? I, for one, was looking forward to finding out. I wanted to know everything there was to know about her.

I parked in her driveway just after six thirty and hopped out of my truck, take-out bags in hand. The key she'd given me long ago felt cool and hard against my palm, the metal warming as I gripped it tightly in my fist. I hoped she wouldn't mind that I was using it. It was the only way I could pull off this surprise. She'd never given any stipulations to the use of this spare key, but I always thought of it as something to be used in an emergency. Now that we'd been intimate, did that change the meaning of this small, flat silver object?

My nervousness grew tenfold wondering if she'd be upset that I'd let myself into her house. Before I could let my reservations cause me to pack up and run, Brynlee sent a text to tell me she would be home soon. Scrambling around the small kitchen, I pulled everything together, putting the final touches on my surprise seconds before the door opened.

Twenty-three

BRYNLEE

MACON'S TRUCK WAS PARKED IN MY DRIVEWAY WHEN I pulled in, and my pulse accelerated. I hadn't expected him to beat me here. Panicked, I glanced in the rearview mirror to check my reflection. Despite the long, hectic shift, I didn't look too disheveled. I smoothed down my hair, ensuring that all my fly-aways were tucked away and applied some lip gloss. That was the best I could do with what I had.

Unbuckling Harper, I scooped her up and went to the front door. Macon wasn't in his truck, so I assumed he'd let himself in. The door was unlocked, confirming my suspicions. I couldn't have guessed what waited for me on the other side.

At the sound of the door closing, Macon turned, a dinner plate in each hand. He looked up and gave me a heart-stopping smile before placing them both on the table. Candlelight flickered through the room, and the heavenly scent of rich sauce and fresh baked bread filled my nose. Nestled in the center of my tiny table was a beautiful bouquet of roses. Between the two large plates filled with pasta was a smaller pink plate with a kid's sized portion of our chicken fettuccine and some applesauce.

My mouth fell open as I took in the sight before me. He'd done this for me and had made sure Harper was included. Tears stung the backs of my eyes as emotion welled in my throat. It was the most thoughtful, romantic thing anyone had ever done for me.

"Hi." Macon's deep voice came from across the table, and I lifted my stunned gaze to his. His smile was hopeful but pensive, as though he was worried I'd be disappointed. He had absolutely nothing to worry about. I was elated.

"Hi," I returned his greeting.

"I hope you're hungry." I'd been ravenous, but now it felt like my belly was full of tiny butterflies, hundreds of little wings fluttering to the beat of my racing heart.

"Starving," I responded, despite the feeling. It was the right response. His grin widened, and he came around the table to stand in front of me.

"I hope you don't mind me letting myself in. I wanted to surprise you."

I let out a little relieved laugh. "It worked," I assured him. "And you're welcome to let yourself in anytime. I don't mind." I hadn't meant for that statement to come out sounding so salacious, but as soon as the words left my mouth, Macon's eyes darkened. My breath caught as he took a step closer to me. My head tilted back as I held his heated gaze.

"I'm glad to hear that." I felt the deep rumble in his voice from my chest all the way down between my legs, and I pressed my thighs together to quell the ache. He leaned in but before he could get close enough for a kiss, Harper began to squirm and demanded to be put down. I granted her request, and she went straight to her highchair. Helping her into it, I secured her tray in place and gave her the plate Macon had prepared along with her juice.

Once I had Harper taken care of, I turned to find Macon holding out a chair for me. I took the offered seat, wishing he'd finish what he started a moment ago. Just one kiss. That was all I wanted, to feel his lips on mine. It had been nearly a week since the last time we kissed, and I needed more. I craved it with every molecule in my body.

He took the seat across from me and picked up his fork. I followed suit and tried to calm my nerves. The food smelled and looked amazing.

"Did you get this from that place on Main Street?" I asked, spearing a morsel of chicken onto my fork before swirling it into the creamy pasta.

"Yeah," he replied with a knowing grin. He knew how much I loved the place and had even ordered my favorite dish. My heart swelled in my chest. He'd put so much thought and effort into this date.

I wanted to crawl across the table, straddle his lap,

and show him my appreciation. That wasn't an option with my daughter in the room, so I settled for thanking him.

"This is really amazing. Thank you," I offered with a soft smile.

"You're welcome." His lips turned up in a grin, and the fluttering returned. I'd wanted this beautiful man for so long, and he was finally mine. I just hoped I could keep him.

After dinner, I put on a movie for Harper and went back to the kitchen to clean up. Macon had already stored the leftovers in the fridge and rinsed our plates.

"Come here," he demanded once the dishes were in the wash and only one candle remained lit. I eagerly stepped into his embrace as he leaned against the counter. Much to my chagrin, he didn't kiss me right away. He simply tucked my head beneath his chin and held me for a long moment.

"I missed you this week," he confessed. "I thought about stopping by so many times." I leaned back so I could look at him.

"Why didn't you?"

He studied me for a moment, gauging his response. "I didn't want to freak you out. Everything happened so fast, and even though I was ready to dive in headfirst, I didn't want to push you."

He could never push me. It wasn't possible. I wanted everything with him. Instead of saying that, I leaned up on my tiptoes and pressed my lips to his. He responded instantly, wrapping his arms around my waist and pulling me to him. The hard planes of his chest met my breasts and I shuddered, a soft moan escaping my lips. I opened to him, letting his tongue probe inside my mouth as my hands curled around the back of his neck. I was panting, ready to rub myself against his erection growing against my belly when he pulled away.

"I want you so bad," he growled. "What time does she go to bed?" He nodded toward the living room where the couch was barely visible from our spot at the kitchen counter, his voice low enough not to be heard over the animated film.

"Between eight and nine," I replied, my tone filled with a desperate need I felt all the way down to my toes.

"I'm gonna make out with you so hard," he proclaimed, one side of his mouth lifting. I chuckled as warmth spread through my veins. It was a relief for us to still be able to joke like we always had. Now, I got to kiss him after he made me laugh. It was the perfect arrangement.

We joined Harper in the living room, and she was so enthralled by the movie, she hardly noticed our presence. Soon her eyelids started to get heavy and finally fluttered closed. Once I was sure she was fully asleep, I moved her to her room and laid her gently in her bed. I snuck away to my room to quickly freshen up and changed into more comfortable clothes.

After brushing my teeth and adding a tiny spritz of perfume, I returned to the living room to find that Macon had put a different movie on. I sank down next to him on the couch, and he instantly wrapped an arm around my shoulders. The movement was so familiar and comfortable that for a moment, I merely sank into his embrace, snuggling into his side. Then his woodsy scent invaded my senses, and his arm tightened around me. My pulse hummed in my veins as awareness prickled my skin. He shifted in his seat next to me, turning his body toward mine. I looked up at him and took in his profile. His strong, chiseled jaw was covered in dark stubble and his thick, dark brows pulled together in concentration.

His features morphed when he noticed me looking at him, and he turned fully to face me. Those dreamy whiskey eyes zeroed in on my mouth, and I instinctively licked my lips. He brought his hand to my face, sliding his palm over my cheek before spearing his fingers in the hair at the nape of my neck and pulled me to him. His lips crashed against mine, his tongue sweeping past the barrier and tangling with mine. I moaned into his kiss, and his fingers tightened in my hair.

My head spun, and my chest tightened. Would I ever stop feeling this way when Macon touched me? Would his kisses ever stop making my lips tingle and set my skin ablaze with anticipation?

He released my hair and slid his hand down to graze my neck. His palm curled around my throat, and his thumb ran over my pulse point. I was certain he could feel my heart pounding, the blood pumping through my body faster and faster. He continued to explore, dropping his hand lower to cup my breast through my tank. He sucked in a sharp breath when he felt nothing but the thin cotton fabric between us. I'd ditched the bra when I changed earlier, but it was dark in here and he hadn't noticed. *Until now.*

My body hummed, moisture pooling between my thighs. Every brush of his skin against mine increased my arousal. By the time he made it all the way down, I would be soaked and ready for him.

His fingers danced across my belly, lower and lower until they found the elastic waistband of my shorts. My eyes were already closed, but I pinched them shut even tighter as he dipped a finger inside. He pulled the material away from my body and brought his hand lower.

Cupping me, he groaned against my mouth. "You're already so wet."

"Yeah," I agreed, nearly panting.

He rubbed one finger over the tender bud and circled it. I leaned up on my knees, wanting more. If I gave him more room, maybe he'd give me what I needed sooner. He chuckled at my enthusiasm and slid his fingers down further, dipping one inside only to bring it out and repeat the circular motion. I fought the urge to growl in frustration.

He did it over and over again, thrusting and curling his fingers inside of me longer each time. By the time I was ready to explode, he had me on my back, legs spread wide, my shorts and panties discarded somewhere on the floor. When he sucked my clit into his mouth, stars exploded behind my eyelids and my back arched off the cushion. His fingers dug into my thigh, holding me in place as I rode out the waves of my orgasm.

He worked his way back up my body, his slick lips fluttering kisses over my abdomen and chest until he hovered above me.

"Macon," I whispered, and his eyes fell closed.

"I fucking love that sound," he declared before kissing me. After a long moment, he pulled back and gazed down at me. "I need to be inside you."

My thighs clenched at his admission. I needed the same thing. "Not out here," I warned, unwilling to take this any further out in the open. We needed to be behind a closed door in case Harper got up in the night. It wasn't common but still happened on occasion.

"Your room?"

I nodded, and we both sat up. Gathering my discarded clothes, I rushed to my room, Macon hot on my heels. He gently shut and locked the door behind us, and immediately his lips were back on mine. He backed me up toward the bed, but before he could lay me down, I turned the tables. I flipped around and pushed against his shoulders. He complied and sank onto the edge of the bed, a surprised look on his face. There was something I'd been dying to do to him. I'd thought about it so many times after seeing his glorious, naked body last weekend. I just hoped I did it right. It had been a long time, and I'd never been into it like I was right now.

Slowly, I lowered to my knees in front of him, and his widened gaze became hooded and full of lust. I removed my tank and reached for his belt. He leaned back, resting his weight on his hands and watched as I worked.

Flicking open the button, I dragged his zipper down, anticipation lighting every nerve ending on fire. He lifted his hips in a coordinated effort as I tugged the denim down his thighs, his cotton boxer briefs coming with it. Freed from its confines, his rock-hard length bobbed. I licked my lips as I reached for him, ready to take my first taste.

Twenty-four

MACON

I WATCHED, ENTRANCED AS BRYNLEE'S PINK TONGUE darted out to swipe across her lips the moment before her head descended. Her mouth met my tip, and I sucked in a sharp breath, the sensation almost too much to bear. *Almost.* My head began to fall back and my eyes drifted closed, but something across the room caught my attention, and they popped back open. I had a perfect view of the mirror in the corner and therefore Brynlee's naked form kneeling in front of me.

"Fuck," I hissed through my teeth. It was one thing to have her lips wrapped around my cock, but it was something else entirely to be able to see everything I was dying to touch.

She moaned around my length, and I nearly exploded right then and there, the vibration sending shockwaves of pleasure straight through me. I'd be lying if I said I never imagined this, but it was always just a fantasy, something that was firmly out of reach.

All thoughts left my brain as she swirled her tongue over the head and took me to the back of her throat. Her grip tightened around the base as she stroked me in the same rhythm she used to bring me to the edge with her mouth.

"Bryn," I warned, unable to utter anything else. "I'm gonna..."

I erupted in hot, pulsing waves before I could say another word. She pulled back at the last possible second as I spilled everything I had onto my stomach. Spent, I let myself fall back and land on her mattress. Brynlee quickly retrieved a towel and wiped me clean as I caught my breath.

I laid there boneless, my pants around my ankles as she discarded the towel and returned to the bed. She let out a little giggle at the sight she found on her return.

"You want some help pulling your pants back up?" she asked with a mischievous snicker as she plopped down next to me.

"Hell no," I replied, kicking them off the rest of the way. "I'm not done with you yet." I lifted off the bed and rolled over, pinning her beneath me, and kissed her soft lips. In no time, we were both ready for the next round.

I AWOKE GROGGY AND CONFUSED, WONDERING WHY THE room was so bright. Rolling over, I threw the blanket over my head to shield my eyes. Something tugged at my foot and I shot up, scooting toward the headboard.

"Macon!" Harper squealed from the foot of the bed, and I swallowed down the scream rising in my throat. Her blonde hair stuck straight up, creating a pale halo in the bright morning light. I thought I'd died and tiny angels were here to carry me off into the afterlife.

Brynlee came awake with a gasp, sitting straight up in the bed. She looked at Harper then turned and startled when she saw me.

Shit, we fell asleep last night after making love.

The fog began to clear, and last night came back to me in a rush of vivid images flashing in my mind. My head between Brynlee's legs, her kneeling in front of me, and finally sinking into her as she called my name and dug her nails into my skin. I felt my body stir to life and attempted to suppress those memories. The last thing I needed to do after being caught in bed with my girlfriend by her toddler was get a boner.

"Harper, honey, how did you get in here?"

Harper turned and pointed to the door. "I open it," she proclaimed proudly.

Brynlee dropped her head into her hands and scrubbed her face, mortification and frustration reddening her cheeks in equal measure. I reached over and rubbed my hand soothingly over her back. She flinched, pulling away slightly. I fought back the hurt her reaction caused and told myself she was just tense because her little girl had just walked in on us sleeping in the same bed. She wasn't ashamed of what we'd done last night.

Was she?

"I hungry," she announced, her "r" sounding more like a "w" and rubbed her tummy.

"Okay, baby, I'll make you some breakfast," Brynlee promised.

Harper scooted up the bed and reached a hand out to me. "Macon, you tum wif me," she commanded.

"Um... I..." I tried to come up with an excuse not to get out of the bed. I didn't have on a stitch of clothing and couldn't let her see that.

"Macon has to use the potty. He'll be out in a minute." *Nice save.*

"I pee on potty," Harper chirped, jumping from the bed and bouncing out the door.

"Shit," Brynlee hissed, shaking her head.

"It's okay. She won't remember this."

"It's not just that," she lamented but didn't elaborate. Slipping out of the bed, she hastily pulled her shirt on and stepped into her shorts. I quickly put my underwear and pants on, not bothering to zip them up. I needed to catch her before she walked out the door. I crossed to her, gently gripping her by the arms as she watched her open doorway nervously.

"What is it then?" I was starting to worry. I didn't know what this reaction meant for us. She acted guilty and remorseful, and I couldn't stand the thought that being with me was what made her feel that way.

"It's just…" she began, letting out a frustrated huff. "I never wanted to be that kind of single mom." I eyed her, confused. "You know, the type who parades guys in and out of her child's life and lets men sleep over on the first date. I didn't want to ever do that with someone unless I knew it was serious."

I reared back as though she'd slapped me. It was as though she thought of me as some random hookup, not the person who'd been her best friend for years.

"Is that really how you think of me?" She froze and looked at me wide eyed, regret washing over her face.

"No, of course not! I'm just not ready for sleepovers and all this next level stuff. We just started this, and I don't even know what I am to you," she rambled on, pacing the room.

"Well, I was going to ask you to be my girlfriend last night, but we got a little distracted." That stopped her in her tracks. She faced me then, a hopeful gleam shining in those seafoam irises.

"You were?" she asked, nervously fiddling with the hem of her tank. The stretchy material pulled tight over her chest and torso, and it took all the will power in my body not to let my gaze fall to her breasts.

"Yeah," I replied, closing the distance between us. I grabbed her hand and laced my fingers with hers so she'd stop pulling at her top. "It was all part of my grand scheme. What did you think the candlelit dinner and flowers were for?" I gave her a teasing lopsided grin, and a soft chuckle fell from her lips.

"I assumed it was so you could get laid," she joked.

"Nah. That's not enough." My tone turned serious, and her eyes darted back and forth between mine. "I want more from you." I cupped her face gently and pressed my forehead to hers. "I want everything. I want us to be official. And I sure as fuck want to be exclusive." The thought of her seeing other guys had me tied in knots. I didn't think she would do that, but it didn't stop me from worrying.

"I want that too."

Our breaths mingled as I held her close. She was mine, and I was hers. I always had been, even when we were with other people. She owned me completely.

After breakfast I headed home to shower and change, promising to come back so we could spend the day together. Brynlee wanted to go to the lake so I dressed in my swimming trunks and a tank and packed a bag with extra clothes.

"Where are you headed?" my mom asked as I came down the stairs.

"To the lake," I answered.

"You didn't come home last night and now you're leaving again." She eyed me suspiciously. There was no accusation in her voice—I was a grown man after all—but there was a hint of curiosity in her statement.

"I should've called or texted. Sorry if I worried you guys." My parents didn't try to control me, but since I lived in their house, it was common courtesy to let them know if I wouldn't be coming home.

"Who is she?" Mom asked, taking me by surprise. I

hesitated a moment, trying to decide how to answer. I finally settled on playing dumb.

"What do you mean?"

She shot me a smirk. "You came in whistling this morning. *Whistling*, Macon. And just now, you had the biggest smile on your face like you were looking forward to seeing someone. Now spill," she demanded.

"Mom," I groaned like a petulant teenager. She simply crossed her arms and waited. "Look, it's really new, and I don't want to jinx anything."

"So new, you thought it was a good idea to spend the night with her?"

"It's not like that. I've known her for a while."

Her eyes widened and she uncrossed her arms, sucking in a gasp. "Wait a minute." The wheels were spinning in her mind, and she was putting two and two together.

"Gotta go, Mom. Love you." I wasn't about to confirm or deny her suspicions, so I placed a swift kiss to the side of her head and rushed out the door before she could ask any more questions.

Our day at the lake was more fun than I could've imagined. I didn't have to worry about entertaining another adult or splitting my attention between my date and my favorite kid on the planet, unlike the time I came with Reece earlier this summer. Now, I had the woman of my dreams by my side and could spend as much time building sandcastles as I wanted.

The sharp sting of guilt speared my chest. Maybe I hadn't hidden my feelings for Brynlee as well as I thought, and Reece had known the whole time. Had she felt like second best every time we were around Bryn? I'd certainly never meant to make her feel that way. It didn't negate how horribly she'd treated Brynlee, nor was it an excuse for her to be so cruel, but it made me wonder if I wasn't partially to blame. I regretted hurting her in any way, but she hadn't been the one for me. It just took me about six months too long to realize it.

It had always been Bryn. I simply couldn't let myself believe that she felt the same. How long had we both been secretly pining after each other, thinking friendship was the only option on the table?

"Hey, why so glum? Are you not having fun?" Bryn's worried expression came into view as she stepped up to where I was perched in the sand next to Harper. My eyes fell to her bikini-clad torso, and I swallowed hard. If I didn't want to embarrass myself, I needed to stop looking at her firm breasts, soft curves, and toned legs. I stood and refocused on her face, my lips curving into a smile.

"I'm having a great time," I assured her and pulled her to me, placing a kiss on top of her head. "I'm just bummed the weekend is almost over and we both have to go back to our busy schedules next week." We were trying to meet a nearly impossible deadline at work, so I'd be putting in extra hours this week, and Brynlee had a shift at the bookstore nearly every day. I wasn't sure we'd have much time to talk let alone see each other. And I wasn't sure I could stand to be away from her that long now that she was finally mine.

Twenty-five

BRYNLEE

I'D HAD THE WEEK FROM HELL, AND IT WAS ONLY Wednesday. It was my only day off this week, and I was spending it at the doctor. On top of having to call the cops over a shoplifter Monday and a visit from the fire department after someone smoking in the bathroom set off the alarms yesterday, Harper was now running a fever and tugging at her ear. My mom called me yesterday while I was trying to talk to the firefighters about the incident, but I hadn't heard my phone over all the commotion. By the time I called her back, she'd already given Harper something to bring down the fever.

Wracked with guilt, I damn near worried myself sick on the way home. Did she have an ear infection because I let her go under while we swam at the lake?

Did she have some kind of deadly bacteria that would go to her brain if left untreated?

Her kind, gentle pediatrician eased some of my fears after examining her. She gave us a prescription for ear drops and an oral medication to take care of the infection and assured me she'd be better in a couple of days. With the sudden attack of mom guilt subsiding, I sent Macon a text to let him know what was going on and to cancel our dinner plans for this evening. We'd had plans for him to come over and make homemade pizzas with us, but I was sure he wouldn't want to hang out with a sick, cranky kid.

I was wrong.

Harper had just swallowed the last of her evening dose of medicine when there was a knock on the door. I peered out the window before opening it and saw Macon's truck parked in my driveway. The corners of his mouth turned up when he saw me standing in the doorway, disheveled hair in a messy bun and scroungy clothes hanging from my tired body.

"What are you doing here?" I asked, silently cursing myself for not being more put together. But I'd been taking care of a sick kid all day. I was lucky to have brushed my teeth and had a shower.

"I know you canceled our plans," he replied sheepishly, uncertainty filling his eyes, "but I didn't want you to have to do this alone. So I brought the pizza to you and stopped to grab some supplies for the Half Pint." He held a square cardboard box in one hand and a bag from the pharmacy in the other.

I was so touched—and relieved—that I practically tackled him. My arms came around his waist, and my cheek met his solid chest. "Thank you," I whispered into his shirt.

"Anytime," he offered, and I could hear the smile in his voice.

"Come in," I instructed and stepped aside to let him pass. He went straight to the kitchen and placed his wares on the counter, pulling several items out of the bag: a jug of Pedialyte, some children's strength fever reducers, a temporal thermometer, and a couple of Harper's favorite snacks. I was already prepared to cry at his thoughtfulness, but then he pulled the remaining two items from the bag. I almost wept when he handed me the bottle of wine and king-sized chocolate bar.

On top of everything else, I'd had a visit from aunt flow this morning and was in desperate need of the solace his simple gifts provided. Plus the hormones were making me extra emotional.

"How did you know?" I looked up at him with unshed tears threatening to spill over. A laugh bubbled up my throat at his confused expression.

"I just know what you like," he said with a shrug. When I filled him in on the situation, he nodded in understanding.

"Ah, fate was on my side today. I'm glad I chose wisely then," he added teasingly. I playfully slapped his stomach, and he let out a little grunt. He was no stranger to my feminine troubles and had brought me special treats before when he knew I was struggling with cramps and headaches. It was yet another reason I knew how incredibly lucky I was to have him.

He poured me a glass of wine while I added slices of cheesy pizza to plates. I tried to get Harper to eat some, but she only took a few bites before asking for a popsicle. Since she still wasn't feeling well, I agreed, letting her nibble on it while Macon and I finished our dinner.

"Do you want half?" I asked, breaking off a generous piece of my candy bar and offering it to Macon.

"Sure," he replied, gripping my hand and leaning in to take a bite. His eyes met mine, and I sucked in a breath.

"You can't do things like that to me right now!" I blurted out. My cheeks instantly warmed, and one corner of his mouth lifted in amusement.

"Sorry," he offered without an ounce of regret in his tone. He knew just how to push my buttons. It wasn't fair, not in the least.

Seeking comfort, Harper climbed into my lap and laid her head on my chest. I stroked her hair until she drifted off to sleep, then held her for a long time. Her skin was cool to the touch, her hairline slightly damp when I finally placed her in her bed. Macon stuck around for all of it.

We spent the next hour cuddling on the couch, watching the latest episode of a medieval fantasy series. My eyes grew heavy, and I let out a very unflattering yawn at the height of the action.

"I should let you get to bed. I know you must be exhausted."

"S'okay." I blinked up at him, fighting the fatigue. I wanted to spend time with him, and this was the only chance we'd get all week.

"Alright. I'll stay a little longer," he promised and before long, I was dreaming of Macon in a long, white-blond wig wielding a sword and growling as a form of communication.

I awoke in my bed in the wee hours of the morning to the sound of Harper crying. The spot next to me was surprisingly empty. Macon must have carried me to bed before leaving last night. I slipped out from under the covers and went to Harper's room. She reached for me pitifully, and I scooped her up, cradling her to my chest. She felt a little warm and was pulling on her ear again, so I gave her another dose of medicine and placed her in bed with me. I held her close, speaking soothingly into her hair until she fell asleep again.

She was starting to feel better when I dropped her off to my mom just before noon the next day. I had to work the late shift, so she would likely be asleep when I picked her up later. I gave Mom her bag and some instructions I'd jotted down so she'd know when her medicine was due and how much to give her. Before I could escape, Mom launched into the interrogation I knew was coming.

"How are things going with Macon?"

"Good," I answered, unable to suppress a smile. I

told her about how he'd surprised us by stopping by with pizza and supplies for Harper the night before.

A dreamy look crossed my mother's face, and she pressed both hands to her chest. "I knew that sweet boy was one of a kind. Better keep ahold of that one," she instructed with a wink.

That was what I planned to do, but there was something inside of me that worried I wouldn't be able to. Some deep-rooted fear that my joy would only be temporary.

SUMMER WAS RAPIDLY COMING TO A CLOSE, AND Macon and I had only officially been a couple for a few weeks. He would head back to school soon, only visiting on the weekends, and I'd go back to being a full-time student at the local community college and only working a handful of hours here and there. Luckily I'd padded my savings account quite nicely over the last few months. The checks still came in from Sean. Some months they were a godsend, especially when Harper grew out of her clothes and shoes and I had to buy her a whole new wardrobe or when I needed to buy books for class. Others, it was a painful reminder of his absence.

The financial support was nice, but it wasn't a replacement for him being in his daughter's life. I appreciated the help, but it would've been nice if he'd actually wanted to be involved with his child.

I pushed all thoughts of Sean McEntire out of my

mind so I could focus on Macon's last day at home. He would only be a couple hours away and would probably come home frequently, but it unnerved me that he would be so far out of reach on a daily basis. I'd gotten used to him being around. We might have been busy, but he was never too far away. He could stop by the bookstore or we could hang out in his parents' den on the evenings I didn't have to work. But now, I wouldn't have those options.

"You alright?" Macon asked after sliding into the driver's seat of his truck. We were headed to dinner with our friends. It would be our first time hanging out with them as a couple.

"I'm fine." I gave him a soft smile for assurance.

"Uh oh. You're not fine. No woman who has ever said 'I'm fine' has actually been fine." His joke eased the tension from my shoulders, and I let out a small chuckle.

"I'm going to miss you when you go back to school. I don't want you to forget about me," I joked, but his expression turned serious.

"I've never once forgotten about you, Brynlee Dawson. Not even for one day." His eyes dropped to my mouth as he brought his hand to my face. "That certainly isn't going to change now." He urged me toward him, and our lips met. I opened to him and he deepened the kiss, tangling his tongue with mine.

My stomach tightened, and my breath hitched. I wanted to make love to him again, but we were already running late. I'd had to fix my makeup and re-curl my hair after he'd come in wearing a baseball cap and jeans that hugged his perfectly sculpted backside like a glove. I hadn't been able to resist, and neither had he. I was on my back with his hips settled between my legs in no time.

"We better get going," I breathed, reluctantly pulling away.

"Do we have to?" he asked, running a hand up my thigh.

I chuckled and swatted his hand away. "Yes," I commanded. "Everyone wants to see you before you head out tomorrow. We don't know when we're all going to be able to get together again."

"Oh, alright," he said with a faux pout and shifted into drive. When we arrived at the restaurant, I got out and met him by the tailgate. Without hesitation, he grabbed my hand and laced his fingers with mine. My heart rate sped up not only at his touch, but at the realization that our friends might not have known yet that we were together. We hadn't made any kind of formal announcement, but people around town had probably seen us, and news like that spread fast in small towns like ours. However, it wasn't unusual for us to hang out, so unless someone saw us kiss, they wouldn't necessarily know anything had changed.

He peered down at me when we got to the entrance. "Ready?" he asked. I nodded and took in a deep, calming breath. He held the door open for me, and we stepped inside. It didn't take long to find our party and as we approached, Haley looked up and caught sight of us. She started to smile, but then her mouth fell open in surprise. She elbowed Jonah who was sitting next to her talking to Cameron, and he looked our way. His eyebrows shot to his hairline when his gaze landed on our combined hands. Everyone else turned to look at us, and cheers erupted from the entire table when they noticed our entwined fingers.

"It's about damn time," Jonah shouted over the commotion.

"Oh my God, you guys!" Shayla gushed, jumping out of her chair and throwing her arms around me. She moved to Macon next, giving him an enthusiastic squeeze. "Why didn't you tell me?"

Macon and I exchanged glances, and I shrugged. "It hasn't been very long, but I figured someone would've blown our cover by now." She rolled her eyes and grabbed my free hand to pull me toward the table. Macon and I took our seats, and he rested his hand on my thigh.

He leaned in, placing his mouth next to my ear. "You don't know how many times I've wanted to do this when we've been at dinner together," he whispered, his hot breath sending shivers down my spine as he squeezed. I fought the urge to moan and let my eyes fall closed at his touch.

"You realize we all saw this coming, right?" Haley asked, waving a hand between us, and shared a knowing look with her new husband.

"What? No!" Shayla exclaimed. "We did *not* all see this coming. I had no idea." She exchanged glances with Delilah who just shrugged as if to say she hadn't expected it either. Shayla then looked at us like we owed her an explanation. "Tell me everything!"

"Well…" I began, looking to Macon for support, and he nodded for me to proceed. "We both have had feelings for each other for a while but were too afraid to admit it lest it ruin our friendship."

When I didn't say anything else, Shayla scowled at us. "That's it?" She held up her hands as though she needed more of an explanation. "I know there has to be more to the story," she demanded.

"I may have drunkenly kissed him after our last get-together here and tried to seduce him." Jonah snorted his laughter, and Haley snickered from across the table. I proceeded to recount how he'd turned me down, and Macon butted in to explain that it was because I was drunk. Everyone nodded in under-standing. Then I admitted to lying about remem-bering until the night of Jonah and Haley's wedding when we finally came together.

"You two have been seeing each other for an entire month and didn't tell me?" Shayla looked aghast and a little hurt.

"I'm sorry. It's still new, and we're still figuring things out. This was a big change for us."

"I guess that makes sense," she conceded. "Either way, I'm happy for you guys. You both deserve to be happy."

"Thanks."

The rest of the evening was spent laughing and enjoying our friends' company. It was nearly closing time when we finally headed back to my house. My mom had offered to keep Harper since she knew it was Macon's last night at home, and I gratefully accepted.

The house was dark and quiet when we stepped inside. I'd barely deposited our leftovers in the fridge when Macon grabbed me from behind.

Twenty-six

MACON

MY HANDS GRIPPED BRYN'S HIPS AS I PULLED HER toward me. Her back slammed into my chest, and I savored the feel of her soft curves against my hardening cock. She let out a little gasp, surprised at the sudden contact, but moaned when she felt me hot and hard against her ass.

I slid one hand to the front and flattened it over her stomach, pressing her harder against me. "I need you," I confessed, my voice laced with desperation.

She reached back and slid her hand around the back of my neck, pulling my mouth to her as she looked back over her shoulder. My fingers dipped into the waistband of her shorts and slid lower until I found her wet and ready. I cursed under my breath, basking in how quickly she became wet for me.

Circling my fingers, I found the spot sure to make her come on my hand, but the tight denim restricted my movements. With a groan of frustration, I pulled my hand out of her shorts and flicked open the button. I had them unzipped and yanked down her legs in no time.

Kneeling in front of her, I removed her panties and threw one leg over my shoulder. With a yelp of surprise, she fell back against the counter. Soon a moan replaced the sound as my tongue slowly circled her clit. I flicked and sucked the tender bud into my mouth as she writhed against me. Her eagerness fueled my desire. I couldn't wait to be buried deep inside her, but I wouldn't deny her the building orgasm that was sure to explode any second.

She came hard, grinding down on my face, and I lapped up everything she gave me. I couldn't wait one second longer to be inside her, so I lifted her onto the counter. No time to waste taking her to her bed. I pulled a condom from my wallet, rolled it over my erection, and nudged her entrance with the head.

"Look at me," I demanded. Her eyes lifted from where she watched me settling between her legs. I slid in slowly, inch by agonizing inch until I was fully inside her. I captured her lips in a scorching kiss before pulling back to slam into her. Her cries of plea-sure filled the room along with the sound of our slick bodies slapping against each other.

I gripped her hips, holding her into place as I plunged in and out of her tight, slick heat. Both of us were still wearing our shirts, and I regretted not taking the time to remove her top so I could see all of her; her lush, pink tipped breasts bouncing with each thrust, and the muscles of her stomach clenching with her impending release. At least I could see her face and watch her brows dip and mouth form an "o" as her orgasm ripped through her.

Her muscles spasmed around me and a moment later, I spilled everything I had into her. I dropped my head to her shoulder, panting as sweat beaded my skin.

"Wow, that was hot," Brynlee mused. I looked up to find her cheeks flushed and hair mussed, a look of feminine satisfaction curling her lips.

"Yeah, it was," I agreed, removing the condom and discarding it before pulling up my pants.

"I can say with confidence I've never been fucked in my kitchen before." Bryn was no angel and cussed on a daily basis, but I'd never heard her say anything like that before, and for some reason, it sounded so salacious and forbidden coming from her mouth.

"Careful," I warned, helping her down from her perch. "Keep talking like that and I'll find something to occupy that pretty little mouth." Her eyes widened as she sucked in a sharp breath, and I feared I'd gone too far. Then her eyes darkened and dropped to my mouth as her teeth captured her bottom lip. Shit, she liked that idea.

My body roared back to life at her heated gaze. I slid my hand over her cheek and tangled my fingers in her hair to pull her in for a punishing kiss. If that was what she wanted, I was happy to give it to her.

ROLLING BACK INTO CAMPUS WAS A NECESSARY EVIL. I was a senior this year and would be graduating in the spring. There was a light at the end of the tunnel, but damn if I didn't suddenly want to stay in my hometown just to be closer to my former best friend turned girlfriend.

Once I was settled in, I hit the shower and dropped onto my bed with my phone in hand.

Me: I already miss you.

I hit send on the text to Brynlee and waited for her reply. Most guys probably wouldn't send a message like that to the girl they had just started dating, but this was Bryn. She knew me better than anybody. I wasn't going to play games or avoid saying the things I wanted to tell her for fear of coming on too strong.

Her reply came a few minutes later and solidified my decision to send her that message. It was a cute picture of her in a pale yellow tank top with her hair pulled into a high ponytail and her lips puckered in an adorable pout.

Brynlee: I miss you too.

We would have to find the time to video chat until I could come home. The cute pic was nice, but it wasn't enough to keep me going. I'd need more than that to make it through a week of classes without being able to touch her. She sent me several winking and kissing emojis when I told her as much and promised to oblige.

The next morning, my alarm went off way too early. I considered snoozing it but wanted to hit the gym before my morning class started. Everything was going smoothly for my first day back until I walked into my afternoon class.

"Fuck," I gritted out under my breath. I'd forgotten about signing up for classes back when Reece and I were hot and heavy. We'd both signed up for this one knowing it meant we'd get to see each other frequently.

I turned to walk out and head to the admissions office to see about getting my schedule changed when she spotted me.

"Macon, wait!" I ignored her, but she caught up to me just outside the classroom. "Macon, please." She grabbed my arm, and I was forced to stop. I turned to her, an uninterested expression settling on my face.

"What do you want, Reece?" If she thought this was her chance at winning me back, she was sorely mistaken.

"I just wanted to apologize. I know I've already said this, but I'm really sorry about what happened at your parents' party. What I said to your friend was terrible, and there was no excuse for it." *My friend?* She couldn't even say her name. "I was feeling really vulnerable and insecure, and I took it out on her." She stared down at her hands, dejected, and I couldn't help but wonder if this was all an act or if she'd really seen the error of her ways.

"Apology accepted." I turned to leave again, but she wasn't ready to let me go.

"Can we start over?" she asked, eyes bright with hope. "As friends?"

"Look, Reece, I don't think that's a good idea." She opened her mouth to argue, but I cut her off. "You were right about one thing." She snapped her mouth shut, surprise washing over her features. "There was no excuse for how you treated Bryn, but some of your suspicions held merit." Her mouth fell open in shock, and hurt filled her eyes. "I never lied to you about dating Bryn or sleeping with her because at that point, I hadn't, but I've had feelings for her for a long time. And now I know she feels the same way." Reece winced and averted her gaze, nostrils flaring with humiliation.

"I'm not telling you this to hurt you, but I don't think it's a good idea to be friends with my ex who treated my current girlfriend like shit." Her gaze snapped back to mine, fury flashing in those bottom-less, ocean blue eyes.

"How long did you wait to start fucking *her* after you broke up with *me?*" she spat.

"Not that it's any of your business, but she didn't

talk to me for weeks after that. She thought you and I were still together." She scoffed and rolled her eyes.

"So I was right the whole time," she stated matter-of-factly. "I really wasn't a priority to you. You were too busy pining after your friend's sloppy seconds."

Her dismissive tone and condescension set my teeth on edge. There was so much I wanted to say, but I wouldn't engage. It was what she wanted, and I wasn't about to give her the satisfaction.

I nodded and walked away, preparing to change my whole schedule if necessary just so I could avoid having to see her again.

That night, I called Bryn and told her about my run-in with Reece. She was quiet for a moment, and I worried she'd be mad.

"I'm glad you were able to change your schedule, but I hope you did it because you wanted to and not just for me." My shoulders sagged in relief. I should've known better, really. It wasn't like Bryn to get jealous or mad about petty crap. But then again, I'd never been her boyfriend before. That probably changed the way she felt about me being around other women, especially ones I'd slept with before.

"Believe me, I wanted to." Reece wasn't someone I really wanted to spend time with. Even before we broke up, she wasn't exactly into the same things I was and was much more uptight than what I was used to. There was really only one thing that had kept our relationship going, and it hadn't been conversation.

The rest of the week went much smoother, and by Friday afternoon, I was ready to jump in my truck and head home. I would've gone straight to Bryn's if she hadn't been at work, but since she wouldn't be home for a while, I headed back to my parents' house. After a quick nap and shower, I ate dinner with my folks and spent a little time with them before heading out. There was somewhere I needed to be.

Twenty-seven

BRYNLEE

WHEN I PULLED INTO MY DRIVEWAY AT A QUARTER after eight, Macon's truck was parked in its usual spot. My heart pounded in my chest, and my palms grew damp. It had only been a week since he'd gone back to school, but I was still nervous to see him again. He leaned against the passenger side door, both hands buried in his pockets and feet crossed at the ankles. He was the epitome of cool and collected while I was on the verge of hyperventilating.

I threw the car in park and jumped out, leaving a sleepy Harper behind. A huge smile split Macon's face as he pushed off the truck and started toward me. I slammed into him, my arms going around his neck. His lips found mine, and his arms tightened around my waist.

After a moment, he loosened his grip, and I pulled

back slightly, staring up into his warm, honey eyes. "Welcome home," I said softly, and a small smile tugged at his lips.

"Thanks. It's good to be back."

Macon unlocked the door and held it open as I carried Harper inside. She rubbed at her bleary eyes when she caught sight of him but was too tired to keep them open. Once she was tucked snug in her bed, I rejoined Macon in the kitchen. My skin began to hum the closer he got as we stood talking in the dim glow of the light over the stove. We'd hardly spoken all week due to our busy schedules. It was nice to finally catch up.

But it wasn't the only thing we needed from each other at that moment.

As if reading my mind, Macon brought his mouth to mine, simultaneously wrapping me in his strong arms. His kiss was hard and intense, a demand I was more than willing to answer. His tongue slipped inside, tasting and teasing as it tangled with mine.

Lifting me off the floor, he urged my legs to wrap around his waist. My fingers tangled in his hair, and my lips found his throat as he carried me to my bed. We spent the next hour getting reacquainted.

And so it went, for the next couple months. Macon came home almost every weekend, and we spent as much time as possible together. When I wasn't working, we went to the home games to watch Blake cheer and root for our old high school team. Sometimes my mom watched Harper so we could go to the movies or have dinner by ourselves, but mostly my daughter was with us no matter where we were or what we did, and Macon didn't seem to mind a bit. He always made sure our plans included kid-friendly activities if he knew she would be with us.

When Halloween rolled around, Macon joined us in dressing up for Trick-or-Treat. He insisted our little Dorothy needed a not-so-cowardly lion to make our themed costumes complete. My entire family participated with my mom as Glinda, my sister as the Wicked Witch of the West, and my father as the tin man. With a painted nose and straw sticking out of my hat, I completed the ensemble as the scarecrow. Miraculously, I'd managed to find a costume with a skirt that was long enough to cover my ass and stockings that came up to meet the hem. Most of the other costumes I'd found were more for drunken college parties, not going around asking for candy with your kid.

Insecurity crept into my mind at the thought of Macon attending parties like those. He didn't go to them often, but I couldn't help but wonder how many of those college girls wearing barely there costumes he'd encountered recently. Had he flirted and flashed that perfect, pearly white smile at them. Had he been tempted to take one of them home for the night? I shook those thoughts away, knowing all they would do was cause me anxiety. We had built-in trust that came from years of friendship. I had to rely on that.

I added the finishing touches to my costume and turned to face Macon who was zipping up the front of his lion suit and burst into laughter. He gave me a crooked grin and brought the hood up over his head. It was made to look like a lion's mane with two ears popping out of the top. He looked ridiculous but adorable.

"There's something missing," I observed, tapping my chin with my forefinger.

He looked down at himself, smoothing his hands over his torso. Not seeing anything amiss, he glanced at me and shrugged.

"Your whiskers," I clarified with a sly grin. He arched one brow like I was teasing him, but I was dead serious. "Sit." I motioned to the chair in front of my vanity.

"This is ridiculous. I don't need whiskers."

"Oh, yes you do."

He stared at me, and I looked right back at him, crossing my arms over my chest.

"Fine," he huffed and plopped down onto the chair. I sifted through my makeup and located the black eyeliner I needed to make perfectly pointed whiskers. Pushing his hood off his head to keep the faux mane out of my way, I leaned in to make dots on his cheeks.

"Come closer so you don't have to lean over so far." Macon placed his hands on my hips and pulled me toward him, his knee pressing in between mine. I had no choice but to spread my legs and straddle his thigh. I'd only made two lines, each shooting out from one of the dots when he cupped the back of my thigh and lifted it, swinging it over his other leg. I was fully straddling his lap, and he was face to face with my chest.

"Sit," he commanded in a low tone that had my pulse racing and belly tightening. I obeyed, resting my weight on his thighs.

Attempting to finish the job at hand, I swiped the felt tip over his skin, making a hairlike stroke. I was painfully aware of how close we were, and if I scooted just a couple inches closer, I'd feel him against my quickly dampening core. His large hands came down on my thighs, inadvertently lifting my dress. I nearly ruined one side of his face with an ill placed black stripe when one hand moved higher, curving around the front of my thigh.

I fought back a groan as his fingers toyed with the edge of my panties. There was only one line left to draw, but my brain was beginning to short circuit and my hand shook. Slipping his fingers beneath the cotton, he ran one knuckle over my slick center. I sucked in a gasp at the delicious contact.

"Can you keep working or do you want me to stop?" he asked, voice laced with deviousness. He stroked me a few more times just for emphasis.

"Don't stop," I breathed, zeroing in on his cheek with laser focus.

I managed to make the last line and replace the cap on the pen before my hips began to undulate on their own. He yanked on my panties, and I felt the material pull until I heard a ripping sound, and suddenly there was no more tugging. His finger plunged inside me, and I cried out. His mouth came down on mine to swallow the sound. Harper was just down the hall playing in her room, and the last thing I wanted was for her to hear us and come to investigate.

His fingers moved in and out of me furiously as his thumb found the tender bundle of nerves just above my entrance. My orgasm built as my legs squeezed his sides. Soon my body shuddered, my release coming on fast and hard.

Tiny footsteps sounded down the hall, and I heard Harper call my name. I jumped out of Macon's lap, landing on wobbly legs, and smoothed my skirt down. My shredded panties lay limp against my skin. What little was left of them at least.

I lifted my gaze to meet Macon's heated one. His look told me he wasn't done with me yet. I let my eyes fall to his lap where his arousal showed even through the loose-fitting costume. He brought his fingers—the two that had been inside me—to his lips and stuck them in his mouth, licking them clean. I nearly whimpered, the action oddly arousing. If I didn't get out of here, I was going to combust from the fire burning in his eyes.

I caught Harper just before she reached the door to my en suite and scooped her into my arms. She giggled and brought her tiny hand to my face, gently pressing her fingers into my scarecrow makeup.

"You ready to get dressed, Dorothy?" I asked, and she nodded enthusiastically. Together, we pulled her dress on over her head, and I slipped her little red shoes onto her feet.

My family was dressed and ready when we arrived. We only had a few minutes to spare to get pictures before trick-or-treaters began to arrive. My sister and her best friend, Maren, passed out candy while the rest of us escorted Harper around the neighborhood.

We were almost back to my parents' house when my phone buzzed in my pocket. I pulled it out when we got to the end of the driveway and saw a text from an unfamiliar number. When I opened the message, it felt like someone had punched me in the gut. All the air left my lungs in a rush, and I fought back the scream building up in my throat.

"What's wrong," Macon asked, coming into my field of vision. I couldn't speak, could hardly breathe, when I looked into his face. I felt betrayed. Glancing around, I ensured my mom had Harper before pushing past him and rushing into the house. I needed to be alone. I needed a moment to think and to come to grips with what I just saw.

Jogging up the stairs, I went straight to the bathroom and leaned over the sink, my chest heaving. Seconds later there was a knock on the door.

"Bryn, are you okay?" Macon asked from the other side. Anger rose in my chest like a raging inferno, scalding my insides.

I walked to the door and ripped it open, fuming as I took in his concerned expression. "Would you care to explain this?" I turned my phone screen to face him, and he leaned in to get a closer look at the damning photo.

"What the hell?" he murmured, brows pinched together. They lifted in surprise when he realized just what he was looking at. "Where did you get this?"

"Someone sent it to me." My chin wobbled as I pulled my phone back to my chest.

"Bryn," he said, pleading and taking a step toward me. I backed up, the thought of his touch causing me physical pain.

"Are you seeing her behind my back?"

"No," he proclaimed vehemently. "I would never do that to you. I don't want anything to do with her."

I let out a humorless laugh. "This picture would suggest otherwise."

"I didn't realize someone had taken a photo of us."

"That doesn't make it any better!" I cried.

"That's not what I meant. This is someone trying to hurt you, to make you think there's more going on between me and Reece. I promise you there isn't." He looked so sincere. I wanted to believe him, but the evidence…

"Can I see the number it came from? I have a feeling I already know, but I need confirmation."

I opened the text again and tried to avoid looking at the photo in question. It was of Reece with her lips planted firmly on Macon's cheek. She was dressed in a sexy devil costume complete with red horns, short skirt, and pointed tail with red pumps on her feet. Pretty damn fitting if you asked me. Macon held a red plastic cup with a wide smile on his face, the same one he wore when he was laughing. Reece's arm was looped around his neck, and though he wasn't looking at her, he had to have known she was there, hanging all over him. My stomach churned as I handed the phone back to him so he could see the number.

"Son of a bitch," he barked before passing it back to me. Scrubbing his fingers through his hair, he looked at me from beneath his lashes. "You have to see what she's trying to do here. She sent that to you on purpose to cause problems between us. She's angry at me for rejecting her."

"She's kissing you!" I screeched, holding up the proof. "And you let her. I don't care why she sent the damn picture. Her lips are on your skin."

"I didn't *let* her do anything," he growled, anger pinching his features. "She surprised me. I didn't even know she was there. Can't you see I was looking at one of the guys when she did that. I pushed her away as soon as I realized what she was doing."

"Then why didn't you tell me about it? If you're so innocent, why did you keep it from me?"

"I'm sorry. I should've told you. It was stupid of me to keep it from you. I didn't want to upset you or make you worry."

My heart was torn. One half wanted to believe him. It knew he would never betray me and that he'd waited too long to have me as his own to throw it all away for Reece, but the other half was reinforcing her armor. She was trying to keep me from getting hurt again. My trust had been shattered into a million pieces before and was finally being put back together. If he broke it, it would never be whole again.

The conflicted look in my eyes must've given me away. He took a step closer, and then another, until he was so close I could feel the heat from his skin. His hand came up to my face and slid over my damp cheek, swiping away a tear with his thumb.

"I would never do anything to jeopardize what we have. You're it for me. I don't want anyone else, especially not someone who would treat you the way she did." I swallowed past the lump in my throat. "And I'm sorry I kept this from you. It was a mistake. I should've trusted you enough to know you'd understand. I hadn't known what she was up to, but that's no excuse." He pressed his forehead to mine, and I could feel the anguish rolling off him in waves.

When I remained silent, he stepped back, his dejected look crushing me. "I guess I'll just..." He let his words fall away and turned to leave. I didn't want him to go, but it hurt to have him so close. All I could see was that horrible woman's lips on my boyfriend's cheek. It was clear from everything he had told me that she was jealous. She'd always hated me, but now she had a reason. I had what she wanted.

"Wait," I called just before he disappeared into the hallway. He halted, heaving a deep breath before turning to face me again, pain flashing in his eyes. "Don't go," I said softly, pleadingly. He came back in slowly, approaching me like one would a wounded deer. "I think we need to put an end to this once and for all."

Twenty-eight

MACON

PAIN SLICED THROUGH MY CHEST, AND I NEARLY doubled over. What was she saying? We'd finally found happiness with each other. At least that was what I thought. Now she wanted to end this?

"She needs to know that we aren't that easily broken and that we won't let her come between us." I breathed a sigh of relief at her declaration. For a moment, I thought she meant to end *us*.

"How do you suggest we do that?"

"We're going to have to call her, but I don't want to do this here." She waved a hand around us. "We'll do it once we have Harper home and settled in for bed."

"Okay," I agreed and grabbed her hand, pressing my lips to the back of her fingers. She gave me a sad smile and reached past me to open the door. Blake stood on the other side, hand held up like she was about to knock. Her eyes darted back and forth between us, and her nose curled up in disgust.

"Ew. Can't you guys wait until you get home to do that?"

"That's not—" I began, denying her suspicions, but Brynlee yanked me through the door before I could finish that thought.

Brynlee's mom insisted on keeping Harper for the night, so we were all alone on the drive home. We spent that time planning on how we would approach Reece. I wanted to call her from my phone to see if she would admit to setting me up. It had been long enough since she'd sent that text that she probably thought I was alone. She also had to know that confronting her about it was the only reason I would call her.

"Hello, Macon," she purred. "Ready to come crawling back to me now?"

"Why did you do it?" My voice was low and menacing, a clear indication I was in no mood to mess around.

"Do what?" she asked with faux innocence. If we were face to face I was sure she'd be batting her eyelashes.

"Send Bryn that picture?"

"I just wanted her to see what an unfaithful bastard you are and to know what it feels like to have someone else stealing all your man's attention."

"You didn't have my attention. You snuck up and kissed me so you could have someone take a picture."

"Ugh, whatever. It was just a means to an end. I'm

assuming you're calling me because she broke up with you. Believe me, I did you a favor. That girl was boring as hell. I'm sure she's no different in the bedroom. At least you know that with me, it will never be boring. I am rather adventurous."

Bryn's nostrils flared as she gritted her teeth. She'd been quiet up until now, but it was time to make her presence known.

"Just stop, Reece. I know you're still mad about the breakup and think that I wronged you somehow, but you need to leave us both alone," Brynlee commanded with a calm but assertive tone. She was met with silence for several long seconds.

"I see you didn't heed my warning after all. That picture just goes to show your *boyfriend*," she said with a sneer, "can't be trusted while away at college. He's out partying and hanging out with other girls for crying out loud. What did you think was going to happen?"

Pain and uncertainty flashed in her eyes, but it was gone as quickly as it came. "I certainly never expected his ex-girlfriend to stalk him, kiss him without consent, and then harass me. I suggest you leave us both alone. Otherwise, we'll be obligated to get the law involved, and I don't think your parents would appreciate you running their good name through the mud like that."

Stunned, my mouth fell open. I'd never seen Bryn stand up to anyone like that before. I was damn proud of her for it too. The fact that it was partially in my defense was oddly kind of a turn-on. A lioness defending her king. God, I wanted her so bad right now.

Before Reece could even respond, I hit the end call button and tossed the phone aside. Framing her face with both hands, I brought my lips down on hers. They softened, opening up to me as I ran my tongue along the seam of her mouth.

"You're fucking amazing," I praised, lifting her into the air. She giggled, the drama from moments ago quickly forgotten. Hopefully, this put Reece in our rearview mirror for good. The last thing she wanted was to get in trouble with her parents and risk losing her inheritance.

Brynlee moaned as I laid her on her bed and settled between her legs, flexing my hips so my hardened length rubbed against her. She'd been so sexy earlier when she was in my lap trying to paint whiskers on my face. I'd been dying to get her alone like this when that picture damn near ruined our evening. I was so thankful that she saw through the bullshit and recognized it for what it was: a petty attempt to damage and potentially ruin our relationship.

I gazed down at the beautiful woman beneath me with gratitude and adoration. She smiled softly, affection shining in her eyes. She was everything to me, and I'd spend every day for the rest of my life showing her that if she'd let me.

That night, instead of our usual insatiable and

frantic love making, I took my time with her. It was slow and steady, a passionate joining of two souls. Every sigh and gentle brush of our skin, our hearts knitted together, creating a bond no man could ever break.

Twenty-nine

BRYNLEE

As the days grew colder and Macon and I both got closer to finishing school, I couldn't help but wonder what the future held for us. Would we be living together this time next year? Would we spend Christmas morning opening presents in a home we made together? Would I have finally built up the courage to tell him I was in love with him?

Maybe I was getting ahead of myself. We hadn't technically been together that long, but hadn't our time as friends counted for something? I could see myself settling down with Macon one day. I just hoped he felt the same.

The week of Thanksgiving found us in a flurry of activity. We were on break from school, but I still had to work. I was only able to see Macon a couple times before he and his parents left to visit family out of state. He would be gone for three long days.

Blake and I helped Mom bake all the cakes and pies the night before and began the process of decorating the numerous trees my mother insisted on putting up for the holidays. It was almost midnight by the time we finished. Harper had long since fallen asleep, so I decided to stay the night.

The next morning, I awoke to the smell of bacon and freshly brewed coffee. Glancing at the clock, I saw that it was after ten and hustled downstairs. Harper was surely awake by now and would be with my dad in the den watching cartoons.

"Mornin', sleepy head." Blake smirked, sweeping past me on her way to her room. I poked my head into the den and found Harper just where I'd expected: nestled in the crook of my father's arm with the TV playing her favorite show.

My mom was in the kitchen, straightening up before she had to start on dinner preparations. I opened the dishwasher and started filling it, silently joining her. She grabbed a dish cloth and began wiping down the counters.

"How are things with you and Macon?" she asked.

My lips curved in a small smile. "They're good." They were *really* good. We got along brilliantly, and aside from the issue with Reece at Halloween, we hadn't fought or hit any snags in our relationship. Not to mention the sex was phenomenal. I couldn't exactly tell my mother that, though.

"That's good. I'm happy you found somebody who

appreciates you and treats you right. Plus, he seems to adore Harper. I know how important that is to you."

She was right. It was the most important thing I could look for in a partner. Harper was my number one priority. I would always put her first, no matter how I felt about a man. If he couldn't understand that, then he didn't need to be in my life.

"He's amazing, Mom. I wish I'd taken a chance sooner and told him how I felt."

"I think it all happened at just the right time," she assured me with an encouraging smile.

It was after dinner when everyone had added a slice of pie to their plate that they were too stuffed to eat when a knock came at the front door. I stood, plate in hand as I swallowed my first bite of pumpkin pie piled high with whipped cream on top. "I got it," I announced to my mom as she began to rise. She'd worked so hard all day. I wanted to let her relax and kick her feet up. Swallowing the bite, I swiped a napkin over my mouth before pulling the door open. Looking back, I wished I had looked to see who it was before opening the door. I stood there frozen as he greeted me, and the china slipped from my hand, shattering on the floor.

"Hey, Bryn," Sean McEntire said from my parents' front porch.

Thirty

BRYNLEE

My head swam and I swayed on my feet, the sound of porcelain breaking on the hardwood floor echoing inside my skull. Sean sprang into action, catching me before I could hit the floor.

"What the hell?" my father roared as he came into the foyer.

A moment later, someone—probably my mother—gasped behind me.

"What's *he* doing here?" Blake's irritated voice sounded much farther away than it should have.

"Are you okay?" Sean asked, looking down at me with those startling blue eyes, his brows pinched in concern.

"I think so," I replied as he righted me, and I found my footing once again. My mother came up to me and wrapped a steadying arm around my waist. My pulse thundered in my veins and drowned out every other sound in the room.

"What are you doing here?" I asked, echoing my sister.

"I uh," he began, bringing his hand to the back of his neck nervously, "came to meet my daughter."

"Like hell," my father bellowed, taking a step toward him. Mom released me to grab his arm before he could do something rash.

"Dad," Blake cried, reaching for him at the same time.

"You have every right to be angry with me. All of you," he announced, swallowing hard. His eyes found mine, imploring me to listen. "Especially you, Bryn." My hands shook, and I folded them across my stomach so he couldn't see. A rush of unwanted emotions flooded me as those clear blue depths penetrated straight to the heart that had locked him out long ago. He was finally here. He came back to us and wanted to see his daughter, something for which I'd prayed for a long time. But I'd lost all hope and given up that dream. All that was left in its wake was simmering anger.

"A lot has changed over the last three years. I've had to grow up and own up to my mistakes. And leaving you was the biggest one." Tears pricked the backs of my eyes, and I didn't know if they were from anger, hurt, relief, or a mix of all three, but I refused to cry. He didn't deserve my tears or my time.

"You need to go," I warned.

"Please, Bryn. I just want a chance to make this right. I want to get to know my child."

"You could never make this right!" I spat, pointing an angry finger at his chest.

"I'm sorry," he said, dropping his head pitifully. Was I supposed to feel bad for him? He left me on the day of our wedding, pregnant and scared. I wasn't the bad guy here. He was.

"Mommy," Harper's little voice called out to me a second before she appeared in the hallway. She ran to me, and I scooped her up, cradling her close to my chest.

"Is that... Is that her?" he asked, eyes glimmering in wonderment. I nodded, and she turned to the sound of his voice.

"Who dat?" she asked, pointing to him.

"I'm your—"

"Sean," I answered in a rush before he could tell her he was her father. "His name is Sean."

"Oh," was all she said, her disinterest evident. She squirmed and asked to be put down, so I placed her on her feet. She took off, my sister trailing close behind her. A mixture of pain and hope flashed in Sean's eyes as he watched their retreating forms.

"I think perhaps you two should take some time to talk," my mom announced, giving my hand a gentle squeeze. My gaze shot to hers, and I saw my fear reflected there. She was right. He was here, and we needed to talk. I wasn't prepared for it. After the first couple years, I'd given up on believing he'd ever come back. Why now?

Both my parents stepped away and disappeared into the dining room, my father grumbling lowly to my mom. Sean and I stared at each other across the room. It might as well have been the Grand Canyon considering how far apart we'd grown.

"I suppose we could use the living room," I offered. It was on the opposite side of the house from where the rest of my family was so we'd have a bit of privacy. Leading the way, I hoped he couldn't see that I was shaking. It had been so long, and there was so much to say, but I didn't know where to start.

I sank down onto the chair where my father sat the day he had his man to man talk with Sean more than three years ago. Looking back, I wished he'd never done that. Now I realized how pressured Sean must've felt. He never really wanted to marry me but had been guilted into it. Maybe if things had gone differently, he wouldn't have run away and Harper would've had her father all this time.

Sean stepped up to the adjacent couch, and I noticed there was something strange about his movements. He had a slight limp and moved with the stiffness of someone three times his age. He lowered himself slowly onto the edge of the cushion, one leg sticking out as though he couldn't fully bend his knee.

"Why are you here? Why now?"

"Like I said earlier, I wanted to meet my daughter. I've been gone too long."

"You think?" I snapped without hesitation, and he winced.

"It was always my intention to come back. Once I

got my head on straight, I was going to come home and make things right."

"What happened?"

"I joined the Army."

Stunned, my eyes grew wide. That wasn't what I'd expected, but it explained the money.

"When I left, I had no idea where I was going. I ended up on my uncle John's doorstep in Fort Bragg." I'd never met John, but I'd heard about him. He was an officer in the Army. I wasn't sure exactly what kind of officer he was, but he'd left an impression on Sean. Unlike Sean's dad, John had made something of himself and Sean always admired him for that.

"Is that how you got hurt?" I asked, motioning to his leg. He'd been absentmindedly rubbing it as though it ached. He pulled his hand back and rested his elbows on his knees.

"Noticed that, huh?" He gave me a crooked, half-hearted grin.

"Yeah."

"That's part of why I'm here. I…" He paused, drawing in a breath and searching for the right words. "Witnessed some things recently that made me realize what I've been missing out on. My life was passing me by, and I had a child I'd never met. The things that should've been top priority had been waiting on the back burner, and I needed to change that. I didn't want to die with so many regrets."

The pain in his voice tugged at my heart, and I nearly cracked. Had he watched his brothers in arms die? Was that what he'd witnessed that caused this epiphany? When I asked about it, he confirmed my suspicions.

"I was thrown several feet from the blast. My leg was mangled and my face and arms were cut, though I couldn't tell how deep." Looking more closely, I could now see that he had a fresh scar slicing through one eyebrow and another on the side of his face just in front of his ear. His long sleeves covered any that might have been on his arms. "All I could do was look up at the sky and imagine your face in the clouds. When I was finally able to crawl to safety and wait to be rescued, I promised myself there'd be no more waiting, that I was going to man up and face my past."

He straightened his spine, his jaw set with determination. It was sharper and more defined than it had been. Come to think of it, so was the rest of him. He wore long sleeves, but I could still make out the bulge of his biceps beneath the material. His chest and shoulders were much broader, and the short haircut and clean shaven look suited him. Another woman—one whose heart he hadn't trampled on already—would probably be swooning over him. I, however, knew better. I was no stranger to the pain that came with loving Sean McEntire, and I wasn't going to fall for it again.

Thirty-one

MACON

SEAN'S BACK.

I stared at the text for a long time, long enough that my mom asked if I was okay. My eyes snapped up to meet hers. Worry creased her brow, and the corners of her lips turned down.

"Oh, um…. Yeah I'm fine," I replied, shaking off the shock from receiving Bryn's message.

What the actual fuck? Why was he back? Of all times to return, he had to wait until Brynlee and I were finally together. Things were going so well between us. Was he going to swoop in and fuck it all up? I always suspected she still had some feelings for him. Now I had to wonder if they were stronger than what she felt for me.

My stomach clenched with worry, and my dinner threatened to make a reappearance as I pushed away from the table. I needed some fresh air and some time to clear my head.

Slipping my jacket on, I headed outside to take a walk through the orchard my grandparents owned. The sun sank lower in the sky, adding to the chill in the air. My breath came out in a white puff against the cold evening air. Shoving my hands into my pockets, I trailed the lines of bare trees as fallen leaves crunched beneath my feet. If Sean was back in town, he would probably try to win Brynlee back. Even if that wasn't his intention now—Bryn stated in her message he returned to meet his daughter—I had no doubt he would see how amazing she was and want another chance to make things work.

If that was the case, there was only one thing for me to do. I had to fight for her. I had to prove to her I was the better man and show her how much I loved her.

I halted in my tracks, realization slamming into me at what I'd just admitted to myself. I was in love with Brynlee. She had become the most important person in my life, and I'd be damned if I was going to sit by and give Sean a chance to weasel his way back into her heart. No fucking way. She was mine.

We weren't set to leave until the next day, but I was itching to get home. I hated being this far away from Brynlee. She was probably struggling with Sean's return, and I wanted to be there to comfort her. This was the man who'd made me give her a note on their wedding day saying he wouldn't be there. That betrayal cut deep, and Brynlee's wounds hadn't yet healed completely. We were working on it, though. I was the one mending her broken heart and had been since the day he'd left.

I didn't waste any time when we arrived home the next day. Hopping out of my parents' car, I went straight to my truck and slid behind the wheel. I sent Brynlee a text to let her know I was home and was headed her way. Knots formed in my stomach and settled there like a lead weight as I tore down the road toward her house. My phone dinged with an incoming text, and I glanced down at it when I came to the stop sign at the end of my road.

Brynlee: I'm not home. Harper and I are at my parents' house.
Me: I'll be there in 5.

Stuffing my phone into my pocket, I immediately changed course. My mind ran wild with possibilities on how Sean's return could change things between us as I headed to the Dawson residence. She was going to need time to adjust to him being home; that much I was sure of. But what if that meant she needed to put the brakes on our relationship? On top of working and going to school, she would have to navigate co-parenting with him if he planned to stay.

Worst of all, what if they decided to get back together? They'd spent years as a couple, whereas she and I had only been dating a few months. Hell, they'd almost gotten married once. Could they rekindle that old flame and choose to see if they still had a connection?

My head was spinning by the time I pulled into the driveway and parked my truck. I hopped out on unsteady legs and went to their door, knocking twice. Bracing my arms on the frame, I waited for her to answer, my heart pounding in my chest. A fine sheen of sweat coated my brow as worry gnawed at my insides.

When she opened the door, I blurted out the first thing that came to mind. "You're not getting back together with him, are you?"

She recoiled slightly, the shock of that question lifting her brows before creasing them with concern. "Of course not. Why would you ask me that?"

I scrubbed a frustrated hand over my face, my day-old stubble scratching my palm. "I'm sorry. I've been going crazy over the news of him being home."

She stepped closer to me and lifted her hands to my chest. Her palms flattened against the hard planes, and I prayed she didn't notice how fast my pulse was racing.

"I don't want him," she proclaimed, her eyes pleading. "I want you. Him coming home isn't going to change that."

My chest heaved with every ragged breath I drew. Her touch ignited my desire even as relief washed over me. I pulled her to me, wrapping my arms around her and resting my chin on her head.

"Well, this was unexpected."

I nearly jumped at the sound of his voice. It was

almost as though he was a ghost come back to haunt me, a specter sent to remind me of the past and toy with my future.

I slowly released Brynlee as he stepped forward. She gripped my hand and nestled into my side. He forced a smile, but his eyes betrayed him. He was not happy about what he'd just witnessed. I wasn't sure how much he'd heard, but it was obvious he was aware of how things had changed between Bryn and me in the last three and half years.

"Welcome home." I nodded and reached for his hand. He took it, holding my gaze as we shook.

A mixture of emotions swirled inside my chest; relief that he was home safe, nostalgia from having my childhood best friend back in town. But the bigger emotion, the feeling that overshadowed them all was worry. I feared his return would derail everything I'd built with Brynlee these last few months.

"It's good to finally be back." His grip was firm, just on the brink of threatening, but just when I thought he was going to let go, he surprised me by pulling me into a brotherly hug.

My shoulders relaxed, and I returned his hug as we patted each other's backs like male friends did after a long absence. He'd changed so much since I last saw him. His lean jaw was more cut, and he was much bulkier than before. I had no doubt he'd gotten taller too, but I still had an inch or two on him.

When he stepped back, I noticed for the first time he was wearing a gray T-shirt with the word "Army" stamped across it in black letters. Before I could stop myself, I asked, "That where you been?" and pointed to his chest.

He looked down at himself and took a moment to process what I was asking before answering. "Yeah."

Nodding in understanding, the realization that he'd gone off to serve our country hit me square in the chest. I couldn't help but respect his decision. It was better than him going off and becoming just like his parents.

I couldn't believe that in all the time he'd been gone, he hadn't bothered to let any of us know where he was or that he'd joined the military. What if something had happened to him and nobody knew? He could've been killed in action, and none of us would've even known he was in danger. Anger burned through me at his selfish and inconsiderate behavior. He could've died and none of the people who cared about him would've had a chance to say goodbye or talk to him one last time.

"Would've been nice if you had told somebody," I chastised, the words falling from my mouth before I could think better of them. He winced, regret flashing in his eyes. "None of us have known where the hell you were for years. Would it have killed you to pick up the phone or written a damn letter?" Brynlee pressed a soothing hand to the middle of my back, and her touch grounded me.

"I'm sorry. It was never my intention to leave everyone out in the cold. I was in a really bad place when I left. I had a lot of growing up to do and needed to find myself, as cheesy as that sounds." I scoffed, not buying his lame excuses. His jaw ticked, and his eyes narrowed on me. "There's a lot you don't know, and quite frankly I don't need your judgment. I'm here now, and my main focus is getting to know Harper. I thought you, of all people, would be glad to see me back. You were like a brother to me." His expression filled with sadness, and I bit back my retort. He was right. I should be glad he came home. I *was* glad. Wasn't I?

Thirty-two

BRYNLEE

A HEAVY TENSION SETTLED AROUND US, THE AIR SO thick with masculine energy, it was nearly suffocating. I wished Macon hadn't come until Sean was gone. I tried to warn him, but he never responded to my last text message. Had he ignored my warning on purpose so he could stake his claim on me, show Sean who I belonged to now? He seemed so worried that I was going to take Sean back when he first showed up. Had he so little faith in me to believe I'd ever go back to the man who turned his back on me when I needed him most? None of this set right with me.

Sean walked away, leaving Macon and me alone in the foyer. I turned to him and tried to tamp down my frustration, but it bubbled up despite my efforts.

"Why did you come?"

His head jerked toward me, and surprise flitted in

his eyes as they connected with mine. "I... I'm sorry. I wanted to see you. I thought you'd feel the same." Confusion and hurt warred in his whiskey gaze.

"I do. I just thought it would be best if you waited until he was gone." Sean had sat quietly, taking in every word when I told him that Macon and I were seeing each other. He voiced his surprise but nothing else. He didn't have to. The tight set of his jaw told me everything I needed to know. He wasn't happy about this new development and would need some time to get used to the idea of his ex being with his best friend. Despite all the pain he'd caused me in the past, I didn't want to rub his face in it.

For a moment, I thought I detected suspicion in Macon's expression, but it was gone as quickly as it came. "I didn't realize he was here."

"But I texted you. I tried to let you know."

He pulled his phone from his pocket and unlocked the screen. A few seconds passed as he tapped and scrolled, then cursed on his breath. "I didn't see this until now," he explained, shaking his head. He looked at me then, his brow pinched. "Did you not want him to know about us?"

"That's not it at all." I reached for him and settled my hands on his arms as they hung at his sides. "I've already told him. He didn't say much, but I could tell he wasn't happy about it. Even though it's been over between us for a long time and he's the one who left, I just thought it would be best if we let him get used to the idea, before having to see us together."

His arms snaked around my waist, and he pulled

me closer as he let out a long breath. "Fuck, I'm sorry. This is just…"

"A lot," I finished for him, knowing there were no other words to describe what was going on. I let him hold me for a minute before pulling away. "Let's take a walk." I needed to get out of this house and away from prying eyes and ears.

"Okay."

Grabbing my coat from the hook by the door, I peeked in on my family. Sean was on the living room floor, playing a game with Harper while my mom sat in her chair, quietly observing. My dad fiddled with one of Harper's toys, trying to get the bottom panel off so he could change the batteries. He'd come to terms with Sean's return and could now be in the same room with him without scowling the entire time.

Seeing that Harper was in good hands, I met Macon by the door. We stepped out into the chilly fall evening, the gold and orange sky slowly darkening as the sun moved lower in the horizon. The air was just a bit chilly, but the wind made it feel much colder. My hair whipped and swirled around my face, so I pulled it all to one side and tucked it behind my ear. We were silent for several minutes, both of us absorbing everything that had happened the last couple days.

"How are you doing?" he asked finally.

"I'm okay. Still a little in shock, but okay." He nodded like he understood. "The last thing I expected was for him to show up at my door yesterday."

"How long will he be here?"

"I'm not sure. He's waiting to see if they are going to medically discharge him." He turned to me, his head tilting to the side, his gaze inquiring. "He was injured on active duty and nearly lost his leg from the sound of it."

"Damn," he said, barely loud enough to be heard over the wind.

"I guess his brush with death reminded him of his own mortality, and he realized what he was missing back home." I shrugged like it meant nothing to me, but deep down, it made my heart ache to know how scared and full of regret he'd been.

We continued walking, both of us quiet as we looped around the neighborhood. If we stayed on this path, we'd be back at my parents' house right at dusk. It came early this time of year, the days growing shorter and nights getting colder. It made me want to curl up beneath the covers and snuggle up next to Macon's warm body, his strong arms cradling me to his chest.

"Did he tell you why he left in the first place? Aside from the obvious?" The obvious being the fact he didn't want to get married or face any of his responsibilities. That much was clear in the letter Macon handed me on my wedding day.

"He did," I answered, chewing on the side of my lip. Macon looked at me expectantly, but I couldn't divulge what Sean had told me in private. It was his story to tell. I relayed as much to Macon.

"I will tell you this," I began as we rounded the corner, my parents' house coming into view. "Nothing excuses his actions, but at least now I know why he left the way he did," I explained, thinking back on the conversation I'd had with Sean earlier.

"I WAS USING," HE CONFESSED, HIS EYES FOCUSED ON HIS folded hands. He sat with his elbows resting on his knees, head slightly hung as though he felt ashamed. It took me a moment to understand what he meant, and when it finally clicked, my eyes widened in shock. I knew he drank on occasion back then. Most of our friends did, but I had no idea he was into drugs. I'd always gotten the impression he hated them because of what they did to his parents.

"It started our senior year. I just dabbled at first, only getting high on the weekends, sometimes not even that often. But when you told me you were pregnant..." His voice trailed off as he pinched his eyes shut. "I just couldn't take the pressure. It was all too much. I started using more and more until it was happening daily. I knew if I didn't do something, I'd turn out just like them." Them meaning his mom and dad.

"There was only one way to get clean and get my life back on track, and I knew who could help me."

"John," I whispered. Sean's uncle had been his only hope, at least in his mind.

"He took me in, helped me detox, and set me up with a recruiter. And I never looked back."

I sat in stunned silence, blinking as though I could clear the scene playing out in front of me. He looked so damaged with his mouth twisted in regret, scars lining one side of his face and his shattered leg that wouldn't bend in the confines of his brace.

"By the time I was better and bringing in a paycheck, it was too late to come back. I figured by then you hated my guts, and the only thing I could do to make up for abandoning you was send money for our child. I couldn't face you. I couldn't face your family. I didn't really want anything to do with mine since they were a big part of the reason I was in that mess. So I stayed away. Figured you were all better off without me."

"Sean." Sadness filled my voice, and he shook his head, refusing to accept my pity.

"I brought this all on myself. I know I can't make up for leaving you. I can't make up for leaving Harper." His voice cracked when he said our daughter's name. "But I hope you'll give me a second chance. I want to get to know her and be there for her. For both of you."

That was when I told him about me and Macon. I didn't want him to get any ideas about us getting back together. Getting to know his daughter and spending time with her? Sure. Walking back into my life and picking up right where we'd left off? Not a chance. Before delivering that blow, I made sure he knew that he would have a place in Harper's life as long as he was good to her and didn't abandon her again. He knew if he left her again, that was it. There was no third chance.

"I won't. I promise," he swore, pressing a closed fist to his chest. As an added layer of assurance, he gave me all his contact info—as well as his Uncle John's—so I would always be able to find him.

"You should talk to him," I said when we reached

the end of the sidewalk that led up to the porch. They'd been friends. Maybe they still were. It was hard to say where they stood after everything that had happened, but I didn't want to be what came between them.

Thirty-three

BRYNLEE

SEAN WAS ALREADY GONE WHEN WE RETURNED FROM our walk. I let out an audible sigh, relieved by his absence. I wasn't sure if having him and Macon in the same room together was such a good idea. They both needed time to adjust to our new circumstances— Macon to Sean being back and Sean to Macon and me being a couple.

Before Macon showed up, Sean and I had agreed to a visitation schedule so he could spend some time with Harper. We met at my parents' house for a few hours Saturday before I went to work and then again on Sunday. Macon stayed away while Sean was around, claiming he didn't want to intrude or inter-fere, but that left little time for us. When we finally fell onto my bed after dinner Sunday evening, he took his time, making love to me slowly.

He slid his hand up my thigh and over my stomach before cupping my breast and bringing his mouth down on my rosy, peaked nipple. I moaned as he sucked it into his mouth, biting down gently before swiping his tongue across it. My inner muscles clenched, squeezing him tighter as he rolled my hips, giving me exactly what I needed. My orgasm crashed over me, my legs shaking as I threw my head back and called out Macon's name.

"Are you gonna be home for Harper's birthday party?" I asked as Macon slipped on his shoes.

"It's Saturday, right?"

"Two o'clock," I confirmed.

"I wouldn't miss it for the world." He grinned up at me, and a soft smile tugged at my lips as he stood and bent down to kiss me.

It was going to be a long week without him here, especially with Sean hanging around. I'd have to see him almost every day. I wasn't prepared for it. I was even less prepared for the man he'd become over the last three years. He was different: calmer, quieter, more introspective. And he treated me better now than he had when we were together. He was attentive and caring and even ... considerate. It was a strange shift, one I hadn't anticipated.

When it came to fatherhood, he was hesitant at first, uncertainty plaguing his every action. But he was catching on, according to my mom. She kept me updated, giving me a report of sorts after each of his visits while I was at work or school, and I was surprised at what she told me. By the time I picked

Harper up after my shift Monday evening, he'd learned all her likes and dislikes along with her favorite foods, movies, and toys.

She yawned and rubbed her eyes sleepily as he carried her to my car. When I opened the door, he placed her into her seat and, to my surprise, buckled her in. My eyes narrowed with suspicion. *How did he know how to do that?* My mind raced with possibilities. Had he dated someone who had a child while he was gone? Did *he* have another child somewhere? Was there a kid out there who'd gotten all his attention while my daughter didn't get so much as a letter or phone call? I'd worked myself up to the point of snapping by the time he shut the door and faced me.

"Where did you learn how to do that?"

Shock and confusion filled his face at my terse tone. "Learn to do what?"

"Strap her into her car seat." It wasn't rocket science, but it was something most twenty-one-year-old men wouldn't know how to do right off the bat unless they'd done it before.

"Oh that?" he asked, nodding toward a now sleeping Harper. "YouTube," he offered with a shrug.

"You've never done it before?"

"No," he replied. "But I figured it was something I needed to know how to do, so I watched some videos."

"Oh," I said, my shoulders relaxing as my suspicion faded. We said our goodbyes, and he promised to see me tomorrow. I had class in the morning but was off the rest of the day, so he'd only get a short visit with Harper unless he showed up super early.

Which he did. And he came bearing coffee.

For me.

I nearly collided with him as I stepped onto the front porch of my parents' house after dropping off Harper. He handed me a steaming cup, and the scent of French vanilla wafted to my nose. Stunned, I stared down at the cup as though it held all life's answers. I finally lifted my gaze and met his eyes, swallowing hard at the soft smile playing on his lips. Perhaps this was his way of thanking me. In a sense, I'd extended the olive branch by allowing him into Harper's life without making him jump through hoops. This much needed dose of caffeine before my eight a.m. class was a small kindness, but one I appreciated.

"Thank you," I offered, bringing the cup to my lips for a sip. "I needed this. I had to stay up late to finish writing a paper."

His smile fell, and he glanced away briefly before his gaze returned to mine, guilt shimmering in his blue eyes. "You've worked so hard to give our daughter a good life. You're an amazing mother. I wish I could've been better."

Before I could formulate a response, he ducked into the house and out of sight.

He was gone when I returned to pick up Harper and hadn't yet arrived when I dropped her off the next day. But when I returned to get her after work, he was there. He sat crouched next to her kid-sized princess table with a tiny cup in his hand and a tiara on his head. Covering my mouth with my hand, I stifled a laugh as he and Harper clinked their glasses together and pretended to sip tea.

He glanced up and caught me watching, his eyes dancing with amusement.

"Would you like to join us?" he asked, motioning to the empty spot next to him. Harper noticed me and shot from her chair, squealing her excitement as she barreled into my legs.

"Mommy! Me and Sean dust had a tea pawty," she mused, framing my face with her tiny hands.

"You did?" She nodded her head emphatically. "That sounds like so much fun." She squirmed to get down, and I placed her back on her feet.

"It is! Tum sit wif us," she urged, tugging on my hand.

I let her guide me to the table and sank down onto my knees as she fixed a place setting for me. Sean smirked, amused that I'd been roped into her game just like he'd been. Little did he know, I'd done this dozens of times before.

The next day was my day off, and I didn't have class, so I got Harper all to myself. I hadn't realized how tense the last several days had been until I had a moment to catch my breath. Our world had been turned on its head with Sean's return, and I'd been antsy since the moment I opened my parents' front door on Thanksgiving and saw him standing there.

We spent the day decorating our tree, baking cookies, and watching Christmas movies. As I was packing up the cookies, Harper grabbed a couple and set them aside, declaring that they were for Sean. My chest constricted at her sweet gesture as warring emotions churned in my gut. I was relieved she'd connected with him, but there was an underlying current of indignation swelling in my veins, rising like the flood waters following a rain storm. He'd been in her life less than a week. He didn't deserve her thoughtfulness. He didn't deserve the fruits of my labor. I made the damn cookies with no help from him, just like I hadn't had any help raising our daughter.

I leaned against the counter, bracing my weight on my palms as I closed my eyes and inhaled a calming breath. Guilt washed over me as I released a long exhale. I shouldn't think like that, but damn if it didn't make my blood boil every time I thought of him leaving me at the church that day with nothing but a scrap of paper offering his goodbyes, then simply waltzing back into my life when he felt like it. His timing couldn't have been worse. I was finally over him and falling for someone else. I was happy for the first time in more than three years.

Gritting my teeth against the onslaught of annoyance, I grabbed a container and held it out to Harper. "Here you go, baby. You can put Sean's cookies in here." I mustered a smile as she excitedly placed the baked goods into the container and secured the lid.

I dropped them off along with Harper the next day, thankfully avoiding Sean since he hadn't shown up yet. It was a good thing because I was too tired to deal with him. I'd stayed up far too late last night talking to Macon on the phone, but it was the only time we'd been able to talk all week. We'd both been incredibly busy and had only been able to text here and there since he'd gone back to school. I hated him being gone and couldn't wait for him to be home for winter break.

My phone buzzed, and I pulled it out of my pocket as I walked into my first class. It was a text from Sean.

Thank you for the cookies. I can't believe you remembered they're my favorite.

My brow knitted in confusion. I hadn't known they were his favorite. *Had I?*

The peanut butter cookies with the chocolate candy pressed into the center were a staple in our house around the holidays. My mom made them every year and now, so did I. Harper loved them. She would eat them until they made her sick if I let her. Maybe that was where she got it from, but I didn't remember him ever telling me they were his favorite.

Then an image of the Christmas before he left came flooding back into my brain: Sean standing in our kitchen, a plate full of those cookies in his hands with a huge grin splitting his face. My mom had made a whole batch just for him, and he'd nearly cried. Back then I thought it was just because his mom wasn't like mine. She didn't bake him cookies or make him feel special in any way. Looking back, I guess that was a big part of it, but also, she'd paid attention and had given him his favorite treat.

I didn't know how to respond to him, so I simply replied, "You're welcome," and stuffed my phone back into my pocket. I hoped he didn't read too much into it, but I also didn't want to hurt his feelings by telling him it was all Harper's idea, and I hadn't wanted to share with him simply out of spite. It was petty and immature, and I certainly wasn't proud of myself for thinking that way.

Several hours later, I was at work stocking shelves with a new release that had been selling like hotcakes when my phone buzzed again. Expecting it to be Macon or my mom with a picture of Harper—she usually sent me at least one a day while she babysat—I nearly dropped the phone out of shock when I saw the text from Sean.

Would you like me to bring you lunch? I can pick up anything you want.

Stunned, I stared at my phone in disbelief. Sean McEntire was full of surprises these days. The old Sean never would've offered to do something like that for me. Then again, he hadn't had a car or extra money back then. If his circumstances had been different, would *he* have been different? I shook those thoughts away and tapped out my response.

Thanks for the offer, but I already ate.

It wasn't exactly a lie. I'd grabbed a quick bite after class, but it had been a while. Still, there was no way

I'd let Sean bring me lunch. It was too personal. It was something a boyfriend did or even a close friend. Sean was neither of those things to me anymore.

Maybe I was reading too much into it, and he was just trying to thank me for the cookies. Either way, I wasn't comfortable with it and hoped he wouldn't ask again. I didn't really know this version of Sean. He was almost like a stranger to me.

After a long day at school and work, I was exhausted when I finally returned to pick up Harper. I cursed when I saw Sean's vehicle in their driveway. He should've left two hours ago. Annoyance flared inside me that he hadn't stuck to our visitation schedule.

He glanced up when I walked into the family room and stood when he saw it was me. "Hey, Bryn," he offered as he approached.

"What are you still doing here?" I asked, keeping my voice calm and steady, despite my irritation. Harper heard my voice and came running. I scooped her up and held her tight, planting a gentle kiss on her cheek.

"I had to duck out to get some testing done at the hospital earlier and was gone for a few hours," he explained, absentmindedly rubbing his leg. "It wasn't supposed to be until next week, but they had a cancellation and asked if I could come in. Your mom said it would be okay if I left and came back to make up the time I lost," he offered, his voice tinged with nervousness.

Worry replaced vexation as I took in the concern

that flitted across his face. It was gone in an instant. I hoped there wasn't something wrong. Had it just been routine testing or something more?

"It's fine," I assured him and shifted Harper to the opposite hip. She was getting heavy, and my back ached from lifting and carrying her as well as hefting boxes of books at work.

"Do you want me to take her?" Sean offered, reaching a hand out to Harper. I accepted gratefully, and she went to him without hesitation. That was a good sign. He carried her to my car and once she was all secure, he stood and pulled me into a hug. All the breath left my lungs in a whoosh, and I stood there dumbly, my arms hanging limp at my sides.

He released me and stepped back, something I couldn't name shining in his eyes. The cold night air was still as he watched me silently for several heartbeats.

"Thanks again for the cookies," he said finally, "and for being understanding about my appointment."

I simply nodded, unsure how to respond. I hurriedly got into my car and drove off, the awkward encounter leaving me unsettled and confused.

Thirty-four

MACON

THIS WEEK SEEMED TO MOVE INFINITELY SLOWER THAN normal. I couldn't wait to get back home. I never got a chance to talk to Sean, but I knew it was coming. We would have to have a conversation at some point. According to Brynlee, he hadn't seemed too pleased at the news of us being together, and that could only mean one thing: he wanted her back. Otherwise, he had no reason for not wanting to see both of us happy.

As soon as my last class ended on Friday afternoon, I was in my truck, heading toward home. Brynlee had a shift that evening, so it was late by the time I got to see her.

"How has your week been?" I asked as she lay naked in the crook of my arm. She nuzzled closer to me beneath the fluffy duvet.

"It's been alright. The arrangement I have with Sean is working out for now. We're kind of testing the waters before we pursue anything official." Her goal had been not to involve the courts unnecessarily—or prematurely since who knew if Sean would stick around—since these situations could get sticky. It was much easier if they could agree on how to handle things on their own.

"Good." *I hope it stays that way.* I didn't want to say that part out loud since I knew it would add to her anxiety over the whole situation.

"He's eventually going to want to take her somewhere or keep her overnight, and I'm just not ready for that."

"Where is he staying?"

"In a hotel for now. Apparently he was going to stay with his parents, but when he went there, it was really bad." A shudder ran through her. How much worse could it have gotten? Their trailer was a dump with trash strewn about and the smell of stale beer mixing with old piss permeating the air. And that was back when we were all still in high school. I didn't want to see or smell what was worse than that.

The next day, I arrived for the party early to help Brynlee decorate and set everything up along with her mom and sister. Harper ran around the fellowship hall connected to the church the Dawsons attended, kicking and smacking at the balloons as Blake blew them up. At the sound of the toilet flushing, I turned to see the door to the small bathroom swing open, and Sean stepped out. My shoulders went rigid, and my mouth clamped shut at the sight of him. He noticed me and gave me a curt nod before walking toward me. I was reminded of his injury as he weaved in and out of the tables. His limp was noticeable but didn't seem to slow him down.

"Hey, man," he greeted, reaching out to shake my hand.

"Hey," I offered in return. *What are you doing here?* I wanted to ask but kept my mouth shut. I shouldn't have been surprised to see him. It was his daughter's birthday party after all. *But he'd never bothered to show up before.*

"Did you come to help decorate?" he asked, releasing my hand.

"Yeah. You?"

"Nah, I'm here to wrangle the munchkin so her mom can work," he announced, a huge grin splitting his face when he finally spotted Harper. My chest tightened. Now that he was in her life, where would that leave me? I had always been Uncle Macon to her. I was the only father figure, besides Brynlee's dad, that she'd ever known.

She looked up to see us both standing there and covered her mouth as an exaggerated gasp left it. She ran toward us, and I was certain she would throw herself into Sean's legs.

"Uncle Macon," she squealed, surprising us both. I scooped her up and placed her on my hip, and faced Sean. His jaw ticked with irritation, and I'd be lying if I said that didn't soothe some of the ache. Harper still chose me for now. She knew she could rely on me.

She knew I would always be there to keep her safe. Sean was little more than a stranger to her.

"Hey, Half Pint. Are you excited for your party?" She nodded, her two blonde pigtails bobbing with the motion. She wore a white top with a unicorn printed on the chest and a frilly rainbow-colored tutu.

"I bet you can't wait to open presents." She clapped her hands excitedly.

"Hey, Harper, you wanna come with me and play with your dolls?" Sean asked, holding out his hands. He expected her to reach for him, but she didn't. Instead she curled further into me and nuzzled into my neck.

"I stay wif Macon," she proclaimed, her voice pouty. Disappointment flitted across his face, but he quickly covered it with a tight smile. He looked to me, and something I couldn't name flashed in his eyes. Anger? Resentment? Jealousy? Whatever it was, I had a feeling it would become a problem.

I walked over to Brynlee who was spreading a pink plastic tablecloth over a table and tapped her on the shoulder. Turning, she smiled when she saw who was behind her. She kissed Harper on the cheek then stood on her tiptoes to press a chaste kiss to my mouth. As we spoke, I felt Sean's stare on my back, the heat of it penetrating my thermal and warming my skin. When I looked up, he was tying off balloons as Blake filled them from the helium tank and handed them to him. His gaze flickered from her and back to me, his tension palpable from across the room. For the first time, he was seeing what he'd left behind, what he could've had. A beautiful, kind, warm-hearted woman by his side and a sweet, energetic little girl who could light up any room. He was finally seeing what he'd been missing out on, and it was too late to get it back.

What he'd given up was now mine. The woman he'd tossed aside when things got too real and too hard. The child he'd abandoned when he couldn't face the consequences of his actions. He didn't deserve them, and I was determined never to let him hurt them again.

The party went off without a hitch, and Harper came away with some incredible toys including a pink Barbie Jeep from Brynlee's parents. When the last of the partygoers were gone, I passed Harper to Bryn and gave her a quick peck then hoisted the heavy toy into my arms so I could carry it to my truck. I'd just placed it in the bed when I heard Sean's voice from behind me.

"What the hell, man?"

I turned to find him storming toward me, his fists balled at his sides. He looked furious, but I hadn't done a damn thing to him. However, I had my suspicions about what had him riled up.

"What's the problem?" I asked, lifting the tailgate, releasing it when I heard it click into place.

"I'll tell you what the problem is," he fumed, shoving a finger in my face. "You're in there trying to play daddy to my little girl and acting like she and Bryn are your family. They're not," he demanded, his nostrils flaring. His blue eyes burned like the hottest fires, rage roiling beneath his skin. "And you and Bryn? Really? She was my girl, man. How could you go after her?" He'd clearly been holding in all his fury over Bryn and me being together since learning we were a couple. Now, after seeing it play out in front of him, all that anger boiled to the surface.

"You've been gone for three fucking years, Sean! What did you expect? Did you think she wouldn't have moved on by now?"

"Not with you!" he shouted, pointing at my chest. "You're my best friend." His accusing tone inflamed my already heated temper. He acted as though I'd stolen her from him, like I'd taken her right out from under his nose.

"Not anymore," I informed him. "I'm *her* best friend. And I plan on being her best friend for the rest of my life."

He huffed out a humorless laugh. "Not if I have anything to say about it."

"You don't," I asserted and turned to walk away.

"I was her first love, and I'm the father of her child." His words stopped me in my tracks. They were facts. Facts I already knew, but now they felt like a threat. "Don't underestimate the power of my position in her life. It might be precarious at the moment, but we share a child. It's not like she can cut me out of her life completely, and if she tries, I'll get a lawyer. I have all the receipts where I've sent her money, and I know those checks were cashed. I've provided financial support, and that counts for something in the eyes of the courts."

A chill ran up my spine. I had no doubt Brynlee would allow him to remain in his daughter's life. She would never try to keep her from him, but if she didn't take him back, would he try to take her to court for custody? He'd been absent Harper's whole life. Surely no judge would allow that. He'd had zero contact with Bryn or their daughter and had no right to make demands.

He was bluffing. He had to be. I didn't know what the laws were when it came to situations like this, but if he decided to make Brynlee's life difficult, he had the power to do *that*, at the very least.

I whipped back around and walked right up to him, getting in his space. He cowered for a second, fear flashing in his eyes. He was scared. Good.

"Brynlee is a good woman. Far too good for you," I sneered, and his jaw tightened. "She would never try to keep you away from your daughter. She's not like that. And if you think a family court judge would ever rule in your favor, then you're insane. Sending a little money every now and then doesn't make you a good father. You abandoned Bryn when she needed you the most. I was there to pick up the pieces when she fell apart, and I've been there ever since."

My chest rose and fell rapidly, anger burning through my lungs with every word I spoke. His ire grew, and I knew I was getting under his skin. I shouldn't have said what came out of my mouth next, but knowing the effect it had on him almost made it worth it.

"Hell, I've been more of a father to your daughter than you have."

Bullseye.

My words hit their target. Rage burned in his eyes, and his face flamed with fury. The veins in his neck protruded, and I only had a second to take in his reaction before his fist landed on my jaw.

Pain shot through my face, and I stumbled back a bit, surprised at the force behind the blow. He was much stronger than he was three years ago.

"You son of a bitch!" He raged, spit flying from his mouth. "That's my little girl! I know I haven't always been here for her, but I am now. And I'm not going anywhere!"

"You mean you've *never* been here for her. There's a difference." I was poking the bear, but I didn't care. It was the truth, and it seemed he needed to be reminded of it. I wiped my busted lip with the back of my hand and spit blood onto the asphalt. I'd have one hell of a bruise from his hit.

"That's the one and only shot you get," I warned. "The only reason you're not on the ground right now is because I refuse to get in a fight at a kid's birthday party." I looked up just to make sure no one had come out of the building. I didn't want Brynlee or Harper to see what was happening. "But trust me, if you hit me again, you'll be the one wiping blood off your face."

Thirty-five

BRYNLEE

MACON HISSED WHEN MY FINGERS PRESSED INTO HIS purpling skin. I'd come outside just as Sean peeled out of the parking lot. Macon stood watching him leave, his face tight with anger. When I asked him what that was all about, he relayed the events that transpired just moments before and Sean's behavior over the last week started to make sense.

He'd been unusually attentive and thoughtful, even going so far as picking up coffee for me and offering to bring me lunch at work. The night he hugged me after his visit with Harper, he'd held on to me longer than could be considered friendly. I tried not to read too much into it despite being able to sense his regret and longing through the embrace.

He finally realized what he'd lost three years ago, and I suspected he wanted it back. But that would never happen. The damage was done. He broke my heart, and in his absence, someone else mended it back together.

Despite the regret and anger he clearly felt, there was no excuse for Sean's actions. He couldn't just go around punching people when he didn't like what they had to say. Sean would definitely be hearing from me soon. This behavior couldn't continue if he was to spend any more time with our daughter.

"How bad does Sean look?" I asked, figuring Macon must've given it right back.

"I didn't hit him," he replied, his voice low and soft.

"What?" I asked, surprised.

"It wasn't worth it." He shrugged. "I didn't want to escalate the situation. Besides, fighting in a church parking lot is not on my bucket list." He gave me a crooked smile. Rolling my eyes, I huffed out a relieved laugh, secretly impressed by his show of restraint and maturity. It made me fall even more in love with him. It was on the tip of my tongue to say the words, but Harper's cries from her room stopped me. She'd crashed after the sugar high wore off and was fast asleep when we arrived back home. She apparently only needed a little power nap and was ready to enjoy her new toys.

SEAN WAS SUPPOSED TO MEET ME AT MY PARENTS' house the next afternoon to see Harper, but I texted him to let him know we needed to talk first. When he pulled open the door to his hotel room, my eyes widened at the sight before me. He stood there with low-slung jeans resting on his trim hips, his chest glistening, droplets of water sprinkled over his shoulders as he scrubbed a towel over his hair. It was the first time I'd seen his bare torso and arms in years, and boy had they changed. His muscles were well honed and defined. One side of his chest boasted an intricate tattoo that wrapped around his shoulder and disappeared out of sight.

I straightened my spine and lifted my gaze to his face, reminding myself of all the bad that came with this attractively wrapped package. He shook out his still damp hair and quickly brushed his fingers through the front. It fell perfectly into place across his forehead, making him look like a model.

"Hey, sorry. I wasn't expecting you so soon," he said, stepping aside to let me in. Grabbing the shirt draped over the desk chair, he slipped it on over his head. I watched as his rippling abs disappeared beneath the cotton.

Damn it, Brynlee, get it together. This was the man who broke me. I'd hated him for over three long years. I shouldn't have been admiring his rock-hard abs and broad, muscular chest.

He pulled the chair out and sank down onto it, motioning to the bed for me to sit. I perched on the edge, keeping my hands folded in my lap. I didn't want to get too comfortable on the bed where he slept and that smelled of his cologne.

His room was tidy, the bed neatly made. No wonder he hadn't been able to stay at his parents' house. After being in the military a few years, he'd become accustomed to having a clean space with no clutter. The home he grew up in was the exact opposite of that.

"I have a feeling I already know what you want to talk about," he began, lowering his eyes to the floor.

"Macon," I said, and he nodded morosely.

"I'm really sorry. There's no excuse for what I did. I lost my cool. He said some things that added salt to an already gaping wound, and I acted without thinking."

I took in everything he said, trying to remain objective about the situation. I knew what wound he spoke of. It was the fact Macon had said he'd been more of a father to Harper than Sean had, and although he was right, I didn't think it was a good idea to rub Sean's nose in it.

Regardless, I had to ensure that my daughter would be safe around him. She was my top priority, and if he was struggling with anger issues, he needed to get those under control.

"Has that happened before?"

"What do you mean?"

"Have you lost control like that and hit someone?"

"No." The word was drawn out, and he looked at me sideways, confusion knitting his brow. "Look, Bryn, I'm not going to hit him again. It was impulsive and imat—"

"That's not what I'm worried about." The crease in

his forehead deepened. "I'm worried about you losing control around our daughter." His eyes bugged out, and hurt flashed across his face.

"I would never hurt her. You have to know that," he pleaded. "I'm finally part of her life, and I would never do anything to jeopardize that." His words rang true, his voice filled with sincerity.

"And you have to understand that I don't know you anymore, and I have to think about my child."

He slid out of his seat and knelt in front of me. I tried to ignore the heat from his body as he planted his hands on each side of the mattress next to my hips, and his chest came within an inch of my knees. "It was an isolated incident and is in no way a reflection of the type of father I am. I know I haven't been around long, but that little girl has already become my entire world. She is safe with me. I promise you that."

I studied him for a long moment, taking in the desperation in his worried face. "Your visits will have to continue to be supervised for a while," I said finally, and he nodded in understanding, his tense shoulders relaxing.

"Thank you."

"Please don't make me regret this," I said, standing. He stood with me and when we were both vertical, there were only inches separating us.

"I won't," he promised, looking down at me. I froze as his gaze dropped to my lips. He looked like he thought about kissing me, but I wouldn't give him the opportunity to do something so stupid. Some sculpted muscles and piercing blue eyes weren't enough to make me forget how badly he'd hurt me. I stepped around him and went to the door.

"I'll see you later," I said, letting myself out. As soon as I was on the landing, I let out a pent-up breath and leaned my back against the stuccoed wall. What the hell was that? Had I imagined that look in his eyes? Surely he hadn't been planning to kiss me. I would've slapped him. Those days are long over. I never wanted Sean McEntire's lips on mine again.

He came over later that evening, sticking to our designated time. When my parents asked if he wanted to stay for dinner, he looked to me, silently asking if it was alright. I nodded, and he graciously accepted their invitation.

I hated to continue to put my parents in the middle, but their house felt like neutral ground, and my mom was almost always there. So even if I was at work or school, Sean could work in a visit so he didn't always interfere with my time with our daughter. Plus, I wasn't ready to have him in my space. My home was my sanctuary, and I wouldn't let his presence disturb my peace. I didn't want him back, but seeing him again reminded me of how heartbroken I was when he'd left.

"What's on your mind, kid?" My dad stepped up next to me and slung an arm over my shoulder as I watched Sean interact with Harper.

"Just wondering how long this will last," I replied, giving him a knowing look. He followed my gaze and studied my ex.

"I think he's in it for the long haul this time." My

eyes snapped to him in surprise. I hadn't expected that from my dad.

"Really?"

"Really," he assured me. "I should've seen the signs last time. He'd been antsy, like someone who was ready to run. I guess I was naive enough to believe I'd scared him into doing the right thing." His face twisted with regret, and I could see the guilt he lived with. "Maybe if I hadn't put so much pressure on the two of you, he would've stuck around and things would be different. I'm sorry for that."

"It's not your fault he ran. He had plenty of chances to call things off before that."

"I know, sweetheart, but I was still wrong. I think things would've turned out differently, though, if I hadn't been so damn worried about what everyone else thought of my baby girl."

"I think everything is turning out the way it's supposed to. If things had gone differently, Macon and I might not have ever gotten together."

"You really care about that boy, don't you?"

"I do." That was an understatement. I was head over heels in love with him and couldn't see spending the rest of my life with anyone else.

"He's a good man." That's all my father said before stepping away and disappearing into the kitchen, but those four little words were high praise coming from him.

Gathering our things, I went to the living room and crouched next to Harper. "We gotta get going soon. Let's get your jacket on." Sean's face fell. He didn't say anything, but I could tell he wasn't ready for his visit to be over. He met us at the door once I had Harper ready to go. "Tell Sean bye," I instructed, holding her on my hip.

"Bye, bye," she said, reaching for him. He froze for a second, taken off guard by her unexpected show of affection, but then his arms came around her. He closed his eyes as she squeezed his neck, and I could have sworn he let out a sigh. He walked us to my car and opened the rear door so I could settle Harper into her car seat. When I was finished, he opened my door and gave me a soft smile.

"See you later, Bryn."

I bid him goodbye and drove home, wondering if this new and improved version of Sean was here to stay.

Thirty-six

MACON

I<small>T WAS HARD TO FOCUS ON MY CLASSES WHEN ALL</small> I could think about was Brynlee. She seemed more at ease after her talk with Sean, but his presence still unnerved her. She'd spent a lot of years being angry with him, but she was trying to do the right thing for her daughter by letting him be a part of her life. It wasn't easy to let go of all that resentment, but she was working on it.

As we both geared up for finals, it got harder and harder to find time to talk. We managed to get in at least a quick conversation every day and were able to video chat one night just before Harper fell asleep. I got to see her for a few minutes while she snuggled against Bryn's chest. Once she was tucked into her bed, Brynlee slipped into her room, and the best part of our video call started.

She slowly undressed, propping her phone up so I had a front row ticket to the show. "Your turn," she said, her voice husky. My pants were off and my chest was bare in three seconds flat. She giggled, making her breasts bounce. "You're supposed to take your time. You know, draw it out a little for me."

"Huh uh. I wanna get straight to the action." She snickered and shifted in bed.

"Well, in that case…" Her voice trailed off as her hand ventured south, sliding over her stomach and down between her legs. She moaned when her fingers found her clit and started to rub slow circles over it. I palmed myself, stroking up and down as I watched.

"You're so beautiful." She was exquisite, lying there completely bare, her legs fallen open as she touched herself.

"I want to see you," she demanded, breathlessly. I obeyed, tilting my phone so it angled down onto my cock. I gripped it tightly, pumping slowly as my abdominal muscles clenched.

"Are you wet for me?"

"Yes," she panted, and the sound went straight to my balls. Stroking faster, I tried to match her pace. "Macon," she moaned, and I damn near lost it at the sound.

"Are you getting close?"

"Yes," she breathed again.

A moment later, I was ready to explode. "Come with me, baby," I demanded. She cried out as hot liquid hit my stomach, and I groaned.

"Damn, baby, that was hot."

"Mmm," she mumbled her agreement.

"I can't wait to see you again and replace those slick fingers with my tongue."

"I like that idea," she confessed, a devious grin curving her lips.

We talked for a little longer, but when she began to yawn every few minutes, I knew it was time to let her go.

On Thursday, I headed to the library to meet up with my study group. As soon as I came through the doors, I spotted Reece. Hoping to avoid any interaction with her, I ducked into the stairwell and headed to the second floor. I'd been able to avoid her for weeks and hoped to keep it that way.

I found my group and as people trickled in, my phone buzzed from my pocket. There was a message from an unknown number. Curious, I opened it and was stunned at what I found.

Hey, man, it's Sean. I know things have been weird between us since I came back, but I'd like to put that all behind us. Can we meet up when you're back in town?

I blinked twice and reread the message. He'd apologized to Bryn for his behavior but had never reached out to me after slamming his fist into my face. That day, it felt like years of friendship went down the drain. I said things I shouldn't have, and he checked me for it. In the heat of the moment, we both did things we regretted. I wasn't one to hold a grudge, so I sent him back a text agreeing to meet with him.

We settled on dinner Saturday after his visitation with Harper since Brynlee would still be at work. I met him at the diner in town and was ushered to a booth in the back corner where it was a little quieter.

"I think I owe you an apology," he said once we'd placed our drink orders. "It was childish and irresponsible of me to resort to hitting you."

"Apology accepted. I owe you one too. I shouldn't have said what I did. It was a low blow." He accepted my apology, and we agreed it was water under the bridge. We made small talk while we waited on our food to be delivered, but it wasn't until our plates were clean and our bellies were full that he started in with the heavy stuff.

He told me about his drug use our senior year of high school and how it spiraled out of control when Brynlee got pregnant. I sat in stunned silence as he recounted his experience detoxing and how he came to the decision to enlist. He knew his life depended on it and that if he didn't enter a controlled environment with a strict regimen, he would fall back on old habits. He still craved the high every now and then, but it wasn't as all-consuming as it had been.

"My whole life, I knew I never wanted to turn out like my parents, and I was slowly becoming what I vowed never to be. It had to stop, and I knew I had to do something drastic or I'd end up dead or hurting Bryn even more than I did."

Suddenly, I understood why he'd made the decision to leave, but there was something still bothering me about the whole situation.

"Why didn't you come to me? We could've told my parents, and they would've gotten you help. You didn't have to leave."

"I had to get out of this environment. I had to get away from the people who were feeding into it. I never would've stayed clean if I was home. I mean, shit, look at my parents." He huffed, shaking his head. "The people I was buying from and the ones I was using with would've dragged me back in. I couldn't risk it."

I nodded my understanding. Guilt gnawed at my insides, and I wondered how I hadn't noticed. I knew he drank and occasionally smoked weed, and I had my suspicions he dabbled in other things, but I had no idea the grip it had on him.

"Are you okay being back here now? You're not tempted to seek out those people and use again?"

"No," he replied adamantly. "I never want to go back to that. I want to go to school and establish a career and care for my family."

Something primal and possessive flared inside me at him referring to Brynlee and Harper as his family. I knew biologically Harper was his, but I'd been the one who was there from the moment she was born. I was the one who comforted Brynlee and held her when she was scared and worried. I was the one who supported her through her pregnancy and made sure she ate when she was too depressed to get out of bed. It was a slap in the face for him to claim them as his family when he hadn't done a damn thing for them.

I swallowed down my indignation and gritted my teeth. This meeting was to put the past behind us and move forward, not bring up old misdeeds.

"That brings me to the next reason I asked you here." My hackles rose, and I sat up a little straighter. I had a feeling I wouldn't like this next part. "You must know that I still have feelings for her, and I only left because I felt I had no other choice," he began, and I felt my jaw creak under the pressure of my gritted teeth. "She's still angry and hurt over what I did, but I think that's because deep down, she still loves me too." I nearly cracked and dove across the table at him but managed to keep my composure.

"We have a chance to be a family. To be happy. So, I'm asking you to step aside and let us try. Harper deserves to have her parents in one home and happy together. I know you and Bryn haven't been dating long, and I hope we can all remain friends, but I've loved her for years. And I could tell she still felt something for me when she came to my hotel room the other day." The way he said it insinuated that more had happened than actually did. Bryn told me about going to see him that day, and it pissed me off even more that he tried to make it sound like they did more than talk. My fists curled beneath the table as I fought the urge to deck him.

"If you truly care about her, you'll give us this chance to be a family."

No. Fucking. Way.

Was he serious? Did he really think I was just going to let him swoop in and try to win Brynlee back? Had that blast knocked something loose in his head?

"Over my dead, rotting corpse," I replied before I could think better of it. His eyes narrowed on me, and his jaw ticked.

"I thought we would be able to come to an agreement, you know, man to man. That you'd be willing to do the right thing."

"I *am* doing the right thing. Just because you lent your DNA doesn't make you the best man for the job." I stood and pulled some cash from my wallet. "And I'll be damned if I stand by and watch you destroy the woman I love again." It infuriated me that he acted like Bryn was an object to be passed between us and didn't have a say in the matter. Did he even consider her wants and feelings before he opened his mouth?

I tossed some bills onto the table and walked out. When he asked to meet up, I thought we'd be able to mend our friendship and move on with our lives. It didn't look like that was going to happen now.

Thirty-seven

BRYNLEE

MACON WAS QUIET, HIS SHOULDERS TENSE AS WE SAT on the couch watching a movie after my shift at the bookstore. I really should've been studying, but I was exhausted and just wanted to spend some time relaxing with him.

"What's on your mind?" I asked, running my hand up his arm and kneading the muscles on his upper back. He let out a sigh and turned to look at me.

"I had dinner with Sean this evening."

"That's great," I said, wondering why he seemed so stressed about it. I'd hoped they could retain some semblance of their friendship despite everything that had changed since Sean left, but judging by Macon's expression, that wasn't going to happen. My smile fell, and knots formed in my stomach. "What happened?" I asked softly.

"He wants you back." I winced as he confirmed something I'd begun to suspect in recent days. Our talks during his visits had been brief and mainly about Harper, but he said things every now and then that made me wonder if he still had feelings for me. My feelings for him were ... complicated, but I certainly wouldn't take him back now. "He wants me to step aside and give you guys a chance to get back together."

"He said that?" I croaked, surprised by Sean's boldness.

"Yeah. He wants you back and wants to be a family."

For once, I was speechless. I never dreamed he would do that.

"Is that what you want?" Macon asked, and my gaze snapped to his. His eyes filled with fear and pleading. Was he worried I would choose Sean over him? That would never happen.

"No," I answered, a little more sternly than I intended.

"I could understand if you still had feelings—"

"No," I repeated, interrupting him before he could finish that thought. "I only want you." His eyes searched mine, the hope in the warm honeyed depths causing my chest to tighten.

His mouth came down on mine, his tongue parting my lips. It was a desperate and needy kiss, one that we both threw all our energy into. It was a sigh of relief after a tense moment of uncertainty.

I climbed into Macon's lap and straddled his hips.

His growl reverberated in my chest, and I shuddered at the sensation, the deep rumble causing my core to tighten. His hands slid beneath my shirt, his fingers skimming over the sensitive skin of my lower back before dipping into the waistband of my lounge pants. My skin tingled everywhere he touched me, anticipation lighting every nerve ending on fire.

I was suddenly too hot and in desperate need of cooling down. Pulling away from his kiss, I yanked my shirt over my head, bringing my lips down on his. Our mouths crashed against each other's over and over like the punishing waves of an angry sea. I was desperate for his touch, desperate to taste every corner of his delicious mouth.

Suddenly, he stood, his strong hands cupping my ass. I wrapped my legs around his waist as he carried me to my bed. He laid me across the mattress, his body coming down on top of mine, his lips immediately going to my neck. He kissed his way down my throat and across my collarbone before finally pulling my nipple into his mouth. I cried out, my hips surging forward with the need for him to be inside me.

His kisses were urgent, his touch frenzied as he moved down my body. He was a man desperate to have me, and it stoked the flame of my desire. When his mouth came down on my clit, I moaned in relief. Tangling my fingers in his hair, I urged him on with an enthusiastic "yes" and "right there" peppered in with my low moans of satisfaction.

His fingers found my soaking wet entrance and slid inside, curling forward. They stroked my inner walls, pulling me closer to ecstasy as his tongue flicked and swirled over my swollen, sensitive bundle of nerves. My release exploded from within, and my back bowed off the bed. He always made sure I was taken care of every time we came together. I could never go back to a partner who only used me for their own needs, completely ignoring mine.

I pinched my eyes shut and shook those thoughts away. I wouldn't let thoughts of Sean and what he'd confessed to Macon spoil this moment.

Macon captured my lips in a punishing kiss, and I tasted my release on his tongue. The solid ridge of his erection pressed against the crease of my leg, and I fought the urge to wiggle beneath him until it lined up with my entrance. He reluctantly pulled away to grab a condom and once he was sheathed, he entered me without any resistance thanks to his earlier attentions. My body, still sensitive from my orgasm, clenched around his cock. He groaned, burying his face in my neck as I ran my hands up his muscular back.

My toes curled as he rocked into me, the pressure starting to slowly build once again. His teeth scraped gently over my skin as he worked his way back to my mouth. His kiss swallowed my moans as he drove into me again and again. He leaned back and gripped my hips, changing the angle of his entrance, and my orgasm detonated like a bomb. My legs shook with wave after wave of pleasure, until finally he collapsed beside me, both of us spent and satiated.

Nervous energy coursed through me as I awaited Sean's arrival. His visit with Harper today would take place at my house since my parents were out of town for Blake's cheerleading competition. He'd never been here before, and the thought of having him in my space had me all in a tizzy. With finals coming up, I desperately needed to study, but hadn't been able to concentrate. It was infuriating that he was still messing things up for me.

And that he had any kind of influence over my emotions.

I resorted to straightening up my already tidy house and reorganizing the ornaments on the tree. I didn't know why I bothered since Harper would just come through and play with them again, placing them wherever struck her fancy. Christmas was just around the corner so my house was decorated, and there was a sugar cookie scented candle burning in my kitchen almost all the time. Macon helped me hang lights on the outside last weekend when he was in town. I loved the way everything looked all lit up. Harper's joyous smile and contagious laughter were the best part.

My heart skipped a beat when there was a knock on my door, and I nearly dropped the bulb in my hand as I moved it from the cluster of ornaments gathered on the lowest branch. Thank goodness they were all shatter-proof.

I went to the door, heart pounding, and took a

steadying breath before opening it. Sean stood on the other side, a slow smile curving his lips. His teeth were perfectly straight and starkly white. He'd been lucky enough to have a naturally beautiful smile, unlike me who wore braces for nearly two years.

"Hey," I greeted, sounding breathless. "Come on in." I stepped aside and motioned for him to enter the house, my palms suddenly feeling clammy. Why was I so nervous for him to be here? It was like I felt the need to prove to him how well I'd done without him. That despite the fact he'd left me high and dry with a bun in the oven, I was doing just fine. I pushed down the bitterness threatening to claw its way up my throat. That was all in the past. It couldn't hurt me anymore. At least that was what I told myself.

Harper's eyes lit up when she saw who had just arrived, and she ran to Sean. He scooped her up and hugged her, placing a sweet kiss on her temple. It had taken her several visits to truly warm up to him, but once she did, their connection bloomed. He was so gentle and patient with her, even going so far as to let her brush his hair and pretend to put makeup on him. Every time they were together, I got a glimpse of the father he could've been, and the anger I tried to suppress boiled up again. She could've had this the whole time, but no, he'd abandoned us and waited until I was in love with someone else to come back.

Needing to put some distance between us, I stepped into the kitchen to grab a drink. I didn't need or want to hover while Sean bonded with our daughter. Besides, most of the living room was visible from where I stood leaning against the counter. I watched as he pulled a small box from his pocket and handed it to her. She squealed with excitement and bounced around on her tiptoes.

He helped her open whatever it was and took a moment to help her put it on. She turned and ran into the kitchen, seeking me out.

"Mommy, wook!" she exclaimed, holding up her arm for me to see. She wore a little digital watch decorated with princesses around her tiny wrist. Excitement glittered in her eyes as she pulled her arm back and admired the gift. I was a little surprised he'd come with yet another present for her considering how much he'd gotten her for her birthday and was going in half on a swing set with my parents for Christmas. I supposed he was making up for lost time. He had missed a lot of birthdays and holidays after all.

I sat at my kitchen table and forced myself to study while they watched movies and hung out. Sean read several books to her, and I couldn't help but laugh when he used silly voices for some of the characters.

An ache settled into my chest and the laughter died as the nagging sensation of regret and unfairness filled my soul. She'd deserved to have this from day one. She'd deserved a father who doted on her and read her stories and held her until she fell asleep from the moment she came into this world. And he'd robbed her of that. Maybe I understood more now why he left, but I'd never understand why it took him so long to come back. I also didn't trust that he wouldn't leave again. At least the first time, Harper didn't know any better, but if he left this time, she would feel his absence. She would know that he'd cared for her but that she hadn't been enough for him to stick around.

"Where is her room?" My head snapped up, and I hastily wiped at my cheeks at the sound of Sean's voice. He cradled our sleeping daughter in his arms and gently swayed from side to side.

"First door on the right," I replied, pointing down the hall. His concerned gaze settled on my face for a moment, but he didn't let it linger. I'd been caught up in my emotions and worries as I tried to read the same sentence in my textbook several times. It just wouldn't stick. None of the information was computing, and I certainly wasn't absorbing it.

Expecting him to head out soon, I stood from the table and walked to the living room so I could lock up behind him when he left. I glanced at the clock above the fireplace and noticed his time wasn't up yet. He'd miss out on the last twenty minutes of his visit, but when Harper needed a nap, you *did not* try to keep her awake.

"Are you okay?" I turned and found Sean standing at the threshold of the living room. His icy blue eyes glittered with the reflection of the white lights on my tree as he approached.

"I'm fine," I lied. He eyed me skeptically but didn't call my bluff

"There was something I wanted to talk to you

about," he began, and my heart sank. He was going to leave again, wasn't he?

"Okay," I choked out past the emotion clogging my throat.

"I know a lot has changed in the past few years, and I've made a lot of mistakes, but I hope you can forgive me, and we can move forward." I nodded, unable to speak. I wanted to forgive him. I truly did, but I wasn't there yet. The anger and sense of abandonment still welled up inside me every time I saw him. I needed more time to let the dust settle and truly let go of all the anger and resentment I'd felt toward him for so long.

"And if I'm being honest, seeing you again has reminded me of just how much I cared about you. I was an idiot to leave the way I did. I should've been honest with you about what was going on, but I was scared. You were so damn perfect, and I was a fuck up." He shook his head in an attempt to clear away the memories before he continued. "What I'm trying to say is I want another chance. I want a chance to show you that I've changed. I want a chance to be a family with you and Harper. She deserves to have that. She deserves to have a happy family with her parents together under one roof."

I blinked up at him in surprise, his unexpected declaration catching me completely off guard. When the shock wore off, indignation coursed through me, and my fists balled at my sides. How dare he pull this shit now! And to use Harper's happiness as a bargaining chip? He crossed a line. He didn't get what he wanted out of his conversation with Macon, so now he decided to go straight to the source. Well, he wasn't going to like what I had to say any more than he liked Macon's response.

"You son of a bitch," I gritted out, and then the flood gates opened, every grievance I'd ever held toward him pouring out. "For three long years, I've hated you," I proclaimed, and he flinched as though I'd slapped him. "You left me when I needed you most. You walked out on us. I was scared and vulnerable, and you just fucking left." Fury burned through my veins like a fire that couldn't be contained. Angry tears coursed down my cheeks as I pointed an accusatory finger at him.

"I loved you. Our situation wasn't perfect, but I'd planned to spend the rest of my life with you, through the good and the bad, in sickness and in health. I would've stuck by your side while you got help. Maybe if you'd trusted me to support you, you wouldn't have missed the first three years of your daughter's life." His face was pinched, his eyes full of pain as I continued unleashing everything I'd ever wanted to say to him.

"Then you have the audacity to come here and try to get me back when I've finally found happiness with someone else and use our daughter to convince me to take you back." With that last word, my hands found his chest and shoved. They curled into fists, ready to strike. I wasn't thinking clearly, my head and heart a mess. I'd loved this man once. For years, he'd been my everything, but those days were over. My heart belonged to another now.

His strong arms came around me as I struggled against him. I only managed to land one pitiful blow before I began crying in earnest. Violent sobs wracked my body as I pressed my face into his solid chest. I finally gave in and let him hold me.

"Shhh," he soothed into my hair, trying to calm me. He gently rocked me back and forth as I clung to his shirt, all the fight draining out of me. That release of emotion and pent-up rage felt good, but now exhaustion and defeat had me sagging against him. We stayed like that for a long moment, until I was all cried out, and he finally loosened his grip on me.

"I'm so sorry, Bryn." He swiped his thumbs over both my cheeks then dropped his hands to my arm. "I didn't realize you felt that way. I probably should've guessed, but I was blinded by my own feelings." His gaze fell to the floor, and he stepped back, releasing his hold on me.

"Do you love him?" he asked, watching me with concern, probably wondering if I would strike again. I nodded, chewing on the cuff of my sweater as shame washed over me. I pushed him and practically beat on his chest when I completely lost it. I apologized, feeling like a terrible person.

"It's okay," he offered, his voice calm and reassuring. "Besides, you really can't do much damage with those baby fists anyway." I looked up to find him watching me, a teasing grin curling his lips. I burst into laughter, and it felt good after releasing all that heavy emotion.

He chuckled, pulling me in for a hug, and I let him. "Friends?" he offered, and I nodded, relieved to have this conversation over with. I had a feeling, though, judging by the longing in his gaze, that it would take a while for him to come to terms with the lost prospect of us rekindling our relationship and being just friends.

I felt lighter when he left, having laid all our cards on the table and coming to an understanding. I hoped that if Sean and I could get past this and be friends, that he and Macon could do the same.

Macon would be here any minute, and I was anxious to tell him about what had happened. He would be upset that Sean tried to win me back, but he had to know that there was no chance for that. Minutes ticked by, and I checked the clock on the wall. He was running almost a half an hour late. He should've been here already. I checked my phone to make sure I hadn't missed any calls or texts from him, but there was nothing. Dialing his number, I pressed the phone to my ear and waited for him to pick up, but it just rang until his voicemail came on. I tried again and got the same thing. I sent him a text message, but nothing came back. Worry suffused me, and I began to pace. This wasn't like him. What if something happened to him? I kept trying to reach him, and each time his voicemail picked up, my heart sank lower and lower in my chest.

Thirty-eight

MACON

I PULLED INTO BRYNLEE'S DRIVEWAY AND PARKED ON the other side of Sean's car. He must've still been inside saying his goodbyes to Harper. It still surprised me how good he was with her considering he hadn't been in her life until very recently. For her sake, I hoped he stuck around and continued to be a good father.

I rounded the hood of my truck on my way to the front door when movement from inside caught my eye. The curtains were open on the big picture window in Brynlee's living room offering an unobstructed view of her Christmas tree. I froze in my tracks, pain spearing through my chest at what I saw.

Sean held Brynlee tight in his arms, his lips pressed to her hair, eyes closed with her face nestled against his chest. There wasn't a centimeter of space between them. My stomach churned, the coffee I'd drank on the way over souring. She told me she wanted me, not him. But the scene playing out in technicolor, backlit by strands of white lights told another story.

I momentarily considered rushing in there, pulling them apart and demanding answers, but I knew that would end badly. Turning on my heel, I went to the driver's side and yanked open the door, my heart pounding as it slowly shattered into a million pieces. The sting of betrayal felt like a knife ripping me to shreds. I'd been willing to fight for her when I thought Sean's desire to get her back was the only obstacle I was up against, but if she'd changed her mind and now chose him, I didn't stand a chance.

How could she do this to me? I thought we were on the same page. We spent the night pouring our hearts and souls into each other. It had been on the tip of my tongue to tell her I loved her.

Now I was glad I hadn't.

It wasn't long before my phone started to ring. Checking the caller ID, I saw it was Brynlee and placed it facedown on the seat next to me. I couldn't talk to her right now. I was too upset and risked saying something I'd regret later. She didn't stop there. She kept trying. A text message came through, and I fought the urge to look at it. I didn't think I could stomach anything she had to say. I couldn't stand to hear her speak the words I knew were coming. She'd tell me she was giving Sean another chance and wanted to be a family with him and Harper.

I drove back to school but left my heart on the pavement in front of Brynlee's house. I had a couple hours to let everything sink in and with each passing mile, my anger grew. Sure, I'd tried to think of a good reason for Sean to be holding my girlfriend like that, but nothing made sense. I was too blinded by my feelings for her to accept that she'd lied to me. She'd always been in love with Sean. I had just been a placeholder for when he came back.

When I reached the campus, I checked my phone and saw a missed call from my mom. Tapping on her number, I pressed the phone to my ear and waited for her to pick up.

"Thank goodness!" she breathed. "We were starting to get worried. Brynlee's been trying to reach you."

"I know," I admitted, unwilling to elaborate on why I hadn't answered her calls.

"What's going on?"

I let out a long sigh. "I don't want to talk about it, Mom."

"Well, you need to talk to someone, specifically Brynlee. She called here worried sick about you. She said you never showed up there, and she was afraid something happened to you."

"I'm fine. I just got back to campus. I'm gonna head inside and get some studying done before I go to bed." That was a lie. There was no way I'd be able to focus on studying tonight and probably wouldn't sleep a wink. I knew as soon as I closed my eyes, all I would see was Sean holding Brynlee and kissing her.

"I don't know what's going on with you two, but at least have the decency to let her know you're okay," she chided.

"Okay." We said our goodbyes, and I opened up my messages. There were three from Bryn.

Brynlee: Hey, where are you? I thought you'd be here by now.

Brynlee: Is everything okay? I'm starting to get worried.

Brynlee: Please call me.

I felt like an asshole for not answering, but part of me also felt vindicated. If she was so worried about me, why had she been all over Sean?

Me: I'm fine. Just got back to school.

I pressed send and not a minute later, her response came through.

Brynlee: Oh, I thought you were going to stop by and see me before you drove back.

Me: I did, but you seemed a little preoccupied with your other guest when I got there.

Seconds after I sent the message, my phone rang, and I realized there was no getting out of this. I couldn't avoid it any longer. It was best to get this over with quickly.

I answered the call, but words stuck in my throat. I couldn't say anything. Only the sound of my breathing could be heard over the line.

"Macon?"

"What?" I croaked out, finally finding my voice.

"I don't know what you saw." Guilt tinged her words, and anger slithered its way up my spine.

"Oh, I saw plenty," I informed her, squeezing my eyes shut against the mental image of Sean holding her like a long lost love he'd finally found again.

"It wasn't what it looked like," she declared, and I slammed my defenses into place.

"Really, because it looked like you were letting your ex hold you like you'd just gotten back together."

"Just let me explain!"

I couldn't take it anymore. I was going to lose my composure, and I didn't need to do that with her on the other end of the line. Despite how angry and hurt I was right now, I didn't want to say something to make her hate me. So I simply ended the call. It was best that way. Enough damage had been done. No use in adding to the rubble.

Thirty-nine

BRYNLEE

I FOUGHT THE URGE TO THROW MY PHONE ACROSS THE
room and let it shatter against the wall. Tears
streamed down my face, frustration and heartbreak
mixing in the salty droplets dampening my cheeks.

It was obvious now that Macon had seen Sean
hugging me after my meltdown and had greatly
misinterpreted the situation. From his perspective, I
knew it must've looked bad, but why wouldn't he let
me explain?

My hands shook as my fingers tightened around
my phone. I needed to calm down or I would upset
Harper. She'd awoken from her nap and had
demanded a snack. Absentmindedly opening a yogurt
and pack of crackers for her, I'd continued to try to
reach Macon. When he finally texted me back, my
legs nearly gave out with relief. I scrambled to open

his message and was initially confused by what he'd written. My stomach sank as the realization of what he must've witnessed smacked me in the face.

A deep ache settled in my chest at the thought of him believing I would ever betray him. How could he think I'd go behind his back to be with Sean? This was a clusterfuck of the highest order and would need to be rectified as soon as possible.

The next morning, I dropped Harper off to my mom. As soon as she opened the door and saw my tear-swollen eyes and red cheeks, she pulled me in for a hug and asked me what had happened. I recounted the events from last night to her as she held my hand.

"Oh, honey, I'm so sorry."

"What am I going to do? He won't be home again until Friday. I can't let this go on that long. I have to talk to him."

"Then you go to him," she stated calmly like it was the simplest thing in the world. And I supposed it was.

So that was what I did. I went into class, took my test, and once it was turned in, I hopped in my car and headed toward Macon's school.

My stomach clenched and my palms began to sweat as I thought of what I would say to Macon once I got there. Would he listen and give me a chance to explain or dismiss me like he had over the phone? I was a wreck by the time I parked outside of the house he rented with four of his college friends and took several minutes to settle my nerves. After a few deep calming breaths and a little pep talk to myself, I stepped out of the car and walked up the front steps. I knocked three times and waited. When the door finally swung open, a tall guy with dark, mussed hair in a hoodie stood before me, a basketball tucked under one arm. He eyed me up and down as he leaned casually against the doorjamb.

"Well, hello there. What can I do for you?"

Ignoring his flirtatious greeting, I wrung my hands together in front of me. "Is Macon here?"

Taking in my distressed expression and the scratchiness in my voice, he straightened and stepped aside. "Sure, come on in." He shut the door behind me and walked deeper into the house. "Macon, you've got a visitor," he called out. My heart rate picked up, and I began to shake again, my earlier attempts at keeping calm flying right out the window.

A moment later, Macon rounded the corner with a bottle of water pressed to his lips. He halted in his tracks when he saw me and lowered his drink, his jaw ticking.

"Brynlee." There was a warning in his voice, and I knew if I didn't act fast this trip would be for nothing.

"Where's your room?" His eyes widened in shock, but he stayed silent. I glanced over at the guy who'd answered the door, and his gaze flickered to the stairs. I didn't wait for permission or an invitation. I stalked up the steps, stopping halfway to look down at Macon. Motioning for him to follow, I lifted my brows in a "what the hell are you waiting for?" gesture. He finally began to move, trailing after me to the second floor. I stopped when I reached the top and awaited his direction. He pointed to one of the rooms to the left, and I went inside. He followed, shutting the door behind me.

"What are you doing here?" Traces of his surprise still lingered on his face, but exasperation was quickly replacing it.

"It was the only way I could get you to talk to me since you're not answering your phone." Until this moment, I'd been desperate to get to him and explain myself, but now that I was here in front of him, irritation was slowly starting to seep in. He treated me like I was the enemy when I'd done nothing wrong. I crossed my arms over my chest, waiting for him to respond.

He huffed out a ragged breath and settled his hands on his hips. "Look, Bryn, if you wanted to be with Sean, then you should've just to—"

"I don't want to be with Sean!" I snapped, uncrossing my arms and taking a step toward him. "If you would just listen for two seconds, you'd understand what's going on."

"I know what I saw." His gaze flashed to me, and the fire in his eyes glowed bright behind those amber depths. "You were in the arms of another man. His lips were on you," he ground out, his teeth clenched. "Tell me how I'm misinterpreting that."

I hadn't noticed Sean kissing me in my state of distress. It probably looked even worse than I had imagined. But that was no excuse for him to avoid me.

"When I saw those pictures of you and Reece

together, I at least gave you a chance to explain. You could extend me the same courtesy," I ground out.

His jaw ticked, and he scrubbed a hand over his face, a flicker of doubt flashing in his eyes. "Tell me how I'm not supposed to think you and Sean were getting back together right before my eyes. He was holding onto you for dear life, and you had your entire body plastered against his. You still love him, don't you?" His voice cracked on that last sentence, and I fought to keep my composure as tears stung the backs of my eyes.

"I don't love him, you big dummy. I love you!" I shouted, frustrated and ready to explode. "I had just told him everything I'd held back since the day he left, and I struck him. I fucking pounded on his chest like a lunatic." Shame burned across my cheeks as I recalled my actions, relaying the entire conversation to him so he'd understand. "He wrapped his arms around me to calm me down, and I broke. That's what you saw. It was the aftermath of me saying everything I'd wanted to say to him for three and a half years." He watched me with a mixture of trepidation and shock as I paced in front of him.

"He tried to get me to give him a second chance, and I gave him every reason I'd never take him back. I laid all my cards out on the table. He finally knows where I stand."

I sucked in a deep breath and faced him fully. His face was full of regret as he scrubbed a hand over his stubbled jaw.

"Fuck," he groaned and took a step toward me.

"Fuck," he repeated, a bit louder this time and shoved his fingers through his hair. "I don't even know what to say. I'm sorry." Head tilted down, he looked at me from beneath his lashes.

"Why wouldn't you talk to me?"

"I thought you chose him, and it felt like you'd stabbed me in the heart. I was hurt and so angry I couldn't see straight. And I was afraid of what I would do or say."

"Don't ever do that to me again," I commanded. "If there's a problem, we talk it out." He nodded.

"Did you mean it?" he asks after a long moment?

"Mean what?"

"You said you loved me?" In my rush to make Macon realize what had truly happened between Sean and me, I hadn't realized what I'd admitted. I'd told him I loved him.

"Yes," I replied, looking up into his hopeful eyes. He took another step toward me and then another until he was just inches away. His chest rose and fell, his breaths coming deeper and faster.

"Say it again." His gruff command curled my toes in my boots, and my lower belly coiled tightly as his warm breath swept over my lips. His eyes were suddenly heated for a different reason. My breath hitched as he closed the space between us.

"I love you." The words were whispered on an exhale.

His fingers speared into my hair and tangled into the locks at the nape of my neck as his mouth crashed down on mine. Tingles coursed through me as my body came alive. His hot, wet tongue swept over my lips, and I opened to him. He deepened the kiss, claiming my mouth as his. One arm wrapped around my waist, pulling me closer. His mesh shorts did little to cushion the hard ridge pressing into my belly.

I moaned into his mouth, and he released my hair, dropping both hands to my waist. He lifted me into the air, and I wrapped my legs around him as he carried me to his bed. Dropping me onto the mattress, he covered my body with his. He pulled back momentarily, his eyes finding mine.

"I love you too," he declared, his voice soft and low. His hand rose to cup my face, and his thumb gently brushed across my cheek. "I love you, and I'm sorry I didn't trust you. I just couldn't think straight." He hung his head, and I lost sight of those golden-brown eyes. I wanted them back. I wanted him to look at me like he had a moment ago, like I was the goddess of light and he was worshipping my rays.

I reached for him and slid my palm over his stubbled jaw, urging his face upward. His pained gaze met mine, and I leaned up, closing the distance between us. The kiss began softly, a promise of forgiveness. His mouth softened and yielded to mine as he returned the kiss. Soon our tempo changed, and our kiss became more frantic, more needy. His hips settled between my legs, and his hardened length pressed against my aching core.

I moaned, and he released my mouth to skim his lips over my jaw and down my neck. "Bryn," he breathed against my skin, sending shivers down my body. I arched into him, urging him on. He slid his hands under my shirt and up my sides before cupping my breasts. One nipple popped free as he tugged the cup of my bra down and latched onto me, his hot tongue flicking against the tender peak.

He leaned back and pulled his shirt over his head before ridding me of my top. His lips came back down on mine as he undid the clasp on my bra and slipped the straps down my arms. Warm, whiskey eyes roamed over my bare torso and face, and my skin heated under his gaze.

"Beautiful," he proclaimed, and I reached for him, pulling him back to me. My fingers danced over the solid muscles of his back, and he shuddered. When they reached his waistband, I pushed his shorts over his hips, and he lifted off me so I could free his erection. I stroked him several times, his silken heat thickening against my palm. His control snapped, and he wrapped his hand around mine, pumping a few times before pulling my hand away. My boots were yanked off, and my pants were tossed across the room in a matter of seconds. When he crawled back up my body, fire burning in his eyes, my breath stuttered in my chest.

My stomach tightened, anticipation coiling low in my belly as he hovered above me. He nudged my thighs apart with his knee, and I let them fall open. His finger slid down to the apex of my thighs, easily slipping down the center and dipping inside.

"You're already ready for me," his deep voice rumbled as he stroked the sensitive bundle of nerves, his fingers slick with arousal. With the other hand, he reached for his wallet on the nightstand and pulled out a condom.

"Yes," I breathed, squirming beneath him as he rolled it down his length. I needed him inside me. I couldn't wait another second.

He pushed into me with a groan and stilled as he tried to regain his composure. "You feel so fucking good." I flexed my internal muscles, urging him on, and a low curse left his mouth. Then he gave me what I was silently asking for.

He slammed into me, bringing my legs up so he could hit the spot deep inside that he knew would make me explode. I didn't think about anything as he increased his pace, bringing me closer and closer to release. Not the fact that his roommates could probably hear us or that the bookstore was short staffed because I was here instead of work. I didn't think about my responsibilities back home or my ex who'd nearly ruined my chance with the man I loved. In that moment, I was simply a college girl enjoying a midday romp with her boyfriend between classes.

Macon's mouth came down on mine as I tumbled over the edge, my cries muffled by his kiss. He slowed his thrusts as I drifted back to earth, then surprised me by flipping me over and gripping my hips. He slammed back into me. His fingers found the sensitive bundle of nerves above my entrance and circled them. Every muscle in my body tightened, another orgasm ready to shatter deep inside me.

I braced myself against his headboard with one

hand, my opposite elbow and forearm pressed against the mattress. I cried out as my next release consumed me, not bothering to conceal the sounds of pleasure floating from my lips. He leaned over me, his chest pressing against my back.

"I love those sounds you make when you come." I tightened around him, loving the words he whispered into my ear. He let out a low curse as he pumped in and out of my body a few more times before stilling.

He pulled out of me, and I collapsed on the mattress. After discarding the condom, he returned to the bed and fell atop the blanket next to me.

Forty

MACON

I PULLED BRYNLEE INTO MY ARMS, AND SHE RESTED HER head against my chest. We laid there quietly for several long minutes. I felt like a fucking idiot and the world's biggest asshole for how I'd reacted. I hadn't even given her the chance to explain what had happened and jumped to my own conclusions.

"Can you forgive me?" I asked, staring at my ceiling. She leaned up and looked at me, confusion knitting her brow.

"I thought we already established that," she replied, her eyes flicking between us suggestively, an impish smile curling her lips.

I turned to her, and her smile faltered as she took in my serious expression. "I don't assume I'm off the hook for being a royal prick just because we had sex. I kind of put you through hell. If you'd been the one not answering my calls, who took off without telling me, I'd have been out of my mind with worry. It was a dick move."

"It was," she agreed, biting the corner of her lip and glancing away. "But I think if we can agree to trust each other and promise to talk through these things in the future, we'll be okay."

"Deal," I said, offering my hand for a shake. When she took it, I pulled her on top of me and apologized again with another round of make-up sex.

THINGS WERE AWKWARD WHEN I RETURNED HOME FOR winter break. Brynlee and I were stronger after everything that had happened, but Sean's looming presence was a constant reminder that our lives were no longer the same. He was in our space, an ever-present figure in Harper's life and therefore ours. I was glad for Harper's sake that her father was present and involved, and if I was being honest, we were all relieved to know where Sean was and that he was safe. But I was constantly waiting for the other shoe to fall, looking over my shoulder to make sure he wasn't trying to move in on my girl when my back was turned.

After hearing that he was going to be alone for Christmas, Brynlee's parents invited Sean to their house. He was all smiles and full of cheer watching

Harper open presents and singing Christmas carols with her, but there was a sadness behind his eyes. Later, he confided to Brynlee that he couldn't go to his parents' house. The last time he'd been there, his father had thrown a beer bottle at his head when he suggested treatment, and his mom cussed him out. He left and never looked back.

I was trying hard to look past what he'd done and how he'd tried to get between Bryn and me. He'd been dealt a shitty hand in life and needed friends now more than ever. So, before he left that evening, I asked if he wanted to come over for dinner the next day and hang out. He'd eyed me wearily but agreed when I told him my parents had heard he was back in town and wanted to see him. It was the truth. They had asked after him, but everything had been so tense between us, I hadn't wanted him there.

When he arrived the next evening wielding a bouquet of flowers for my mom and a bottle of wine, she pulled him into a hug and held him for a long moment. His face filled with emotion, and his eyes fell closed as he reveled in her embrace. My mother had always been more of a mom to him than his own mother was, and I knew it hurt her that he'd stayed away once he was back in town. A pang of guilt speared through me knowing that was partially my fault.

Over the next few months, Sean and I began to mend our friendship. I didn't think we'd ever be as close as we once were, but it was still an improvement from when he first came back. In the beginning, I'd been skeptical about him sticking around, but he surprised us all by renting an apartment close by.

After that, Brynlee decided it was time to tell Harper who Sean really was. She sat her down one day and explained that Sean was her father and that he was going to be around a lot more. Contrasting emotions washed over me with the announcement. I was happy for Harper since she finally had her father in her life, but part of me felt like I'd lost something. I'd filled that void for the last three years, and now, it was like I was being replaced. But when her face lit up with excitement, all that faded away. She deserved to have all the love in the world, and now she had both of us. She was finally able to call someone Daddy, and she squealed it every time she saw him now. I was still Uncle Macon, and Harper having her father by her side wasn't going to change that.

Sean continued his physical therapy in the hopes of returning to active duty, but he hadn't fully recovered yet and wasn't sure he would ever be able to go back. He, of course, backed off Bryn now that he knew how she felt and that we were the real deal. He apologized for trying to break us up and win her back. There was no coming between us. He realized that now.

I started staying with Brynlee more and more when I was home from school. The transition began slowly with me leaving a toothbrush there. Then it was toiletries and a change of clothes. Eventually half my wardrobe filled her dresser and closet. Finally, one day she asked to make it official.

"I was wondering," she began, twisting her hands together as she chewed on the inside of her lip. "Since you've been staying with me a lot and most of your things are at my house now, if you wanted to move in with me?" She looked at me hopefully, her big green eyes blinking up at me.

"What do you mean? I thought I already did." Her mouth formed an "o," and her eyes grew wide. I laughed, gripping my stomach as her gaze narrowed on me, her mouth flattening into a thin line. She was not amused.

"You jerk. You ruined my moment," she chided, swatting my arm playfully.

"I'm sorry. I couldn't help myself," I proclaimed and pulled her against me. "But to answer your question, I'd be happy to move in with you."

"No, I don't want you to now." She jutted her chin out defiantly, and that fire I liked to stoke flickered inside her.

"I know exactly what you want," I said in a low tone, my voice full of gravel. My eyes dropped to her mouth, and she stilled. A current of desire rippled in the air between us, a palpable static charge that only had one solution.

I gripped her hips and pulled her into me, my growing erection pressing into her belly. Air hissed through her teeth as her fingers curled into my shirt, but she didn't say a word.

"Do you want me to take this off?" I asked, pinching the fabric between my fingers and holding it out from my body. She nodded once, and I shot her a crooked grin. I pulled the shirt over my head, and her hands were instantly on my torso. They glided up my abdomen and over the dusting of dark hair covering my chest. Her touch was soft and warm. I wanted to feel it everywhere.

Gripping her face in my hands, I brought my mouth to hers. She opened immediately, granting me access I took full advantage of. She moaned as our tongues met and glided against each other.

Shoving me backward, she pushed me toward her bedroom—our bedroom now—and guided me to the bed. Her hands moved to my belt and loosened it before flicking open the button. She dragged the zipper down agonizingly slow and shoved my jeans down my legs. My erection sprang free, and she licked her lips before staring up at me with a wicked gleam in her eye.

She planted her palms against my chest and gave me a gentle shove. I landed on my ass and scooted to the middle of the bed, sprawling out as I placed my hands behind my head. I'd come to learn that when I got her riled up like this and she got in one of these moods to just lie back and let her have her way with me.

She crawled up my body, prowling like a wild cat, and I caught sight of her in the mirror in the corner. I loved seeing her like this, and she knew it. I'd confessed to her one day that I could see everything in that mirror behind her when she put her back to it naked. She flushed, a little embarrassed at first, but when she realized how much I liked it, she began doing it on purpose.

And it was the hottest fucking thing I'd ever seen.

Her hand gripped my cock, and I sucked in a sharp breath as she stroked up and down. When her hot mouth descended on me, my head fell back despite my wish to watch her. She swirled her tongue over the sensitive head before wrapping her lips around my length and taking it to the back of her throat. She did it again and again, and I worried I'd lose it all before we got to the best part.

"I'm not going to last long," I warned. She pulled back, releasing me with an audible "pop."

Settling her knees on each side of my hips, she leaned over me and kissed me deeply as she teasingly rubbed herself on my erection. When she finally settled me at her entrance and sank down, we both let out sighs of relief. I cupped her breasts, rolling and pinching her nipples as she rode me. I let my hands drop to her waist and slid one to the apex of her thighs. My thumb found her clit, and she gasped. I circled it slowly at first, but when she begged me to do it faster, I gladly granted her request.

She came hard, grinding herself down on my dick, milking it with her tight channel until I found my own release.

We laid there next to each other panting, our sweat-dampened skin cooling in the tepid spring air. There were some things that were uncertain about our future—where we would find jobs when we graduated in a couple months, whether we'd stay in this house for a little while or find something new that we'd pick out together—but the one thing that was guaranteed was that our love would only grow stronger. Brynlee was and always would be my best friend, but now she was more. So much more.

Forty-one

Nine Months Later...

MACON

"TEN. NINE. EIGHT..." THE VOICES COUNTING DOWN to the new year drowned out all other sound around us. Our friends held drinks in their hands, some of them outstretched toward the jumbo-sized TV with the giant gleaming ball making its slow descent. Not me, though. I was frantically searching the crowd for the only person I wanted to see when the clock struck midnight.

"Five. Four." There! I spotted her at the same time she spotted me as she pushed through the throng of people crowding around the bar. She reached me at the very last second, and I pulled her into my arms, burying one hand in the soft blonde curls cascading down her back. Her lips met mine as we ushered in the new year, cheers and whoops erupting all around us.

I slipped my hand into my pocket, my fingers finding the cool band I managed to keep hidden from Brynlee and our friends all evening. Sliding my hand down her left arm, I released her mouth and brought her fingers to my lips, brushing them over her knuckles. I lifted the ring to our joined hands and waited for her to shift her gaze to it. When her eyes landed on the white gold band, they went wide with surprise before snapping back to me.

"Marry me." My voice was low and gruff, emotion coating my throat. It was meant to be a question, but I was so desperate for her to say yes, that it came out as a pleading command instead.

Her eyes misted over, and her chin wobbled ever so slightly. I momentarily worried that I'd upset her. Either by asking or by asking the way I had. But then she nodded emphatically, a huge smile spreading over her gorgeous face. My breath left me on a relieved sigh, and I gripped her trembling hand. I slid the band with the oval diamond Blake helped me pick out onto her finger. One singular tear spilled over and ran down her cheek.

Brynlee threw her arms around my neck and captured my lips in a hungry, desperate kiss. I pulled her close to me, our bodies flush and vibrating with joyous laughter and tears.

"I love you," she proclaimed against my lips.

"I can't wait to spend the rest of my life with you." Our kisses outlasted the cacophony around us as the high of ringing in the new year waned. Our friends slowly trickled back to our table, some of them bumping us as they passed.

"Okay, guys, the ball drop is over. It's like 12:05. You can stop kissing now," Jonah proclaimed. Brynlee and I reluctantly pulled away from each other with wide grins plastered over our faces.

Brynlee shot me a look as if to say, "should we tell them?" I simply shrugged. They'd figure it out eventually. We took our seats and not a minute later, Shayla gasped on the other side of my new fiancée.

"What is *that*?" she demanded, pointing to Brynlee's ring finger. All eyes landed on her, and she held her hand up to show our friends. The girls squealed and the guys hooted, lifting their hands for high fives. We were peppered with congratulations, well wishes, and excited hugs. I watched Brynlee with wonder in my eyes as she beamed, the broad smile never leaving her lips. This amazing woman would be my wife one day. And I would make sure she always knew just how much I loved her.

Epilogue

BRYNLEE

I PACED THE SMALL ROOM, THE SKIRT OF MY GOWN swishing with the frantic movements. My anxiety was unwarranted. I knew that. Still, I couldn't keep the old memories at bay as worry gnawed at my gut. *What if he doesn't show up? What if he changed his mind?*

Shayla crossed to me from where she'd been adding the finishing touches to her makeup, and I halted. She slid her hands into mine and offered me a reassuring smile.

"It's going to be okay." Her eyes were soft and understanding, and her words rang with truth. I knew Macon would show and that he'd be standing at the end of the aisle, waiting to say his vows, to promise his everlasting love to me. He was a good man, a man of his word. I needed to let go of the fears and insecurities that he was never responsible for.

"The way he looks at you," she began, her eyes filling with affection. "That man adores you. He won't let you down today. You're his entire world."

"Thank you." I gave her a weak smile as I fought the tears burning the backs of my eyes. She was right. I knew Macon's heart. I just needed to listen to my own and stop letting my head get in the way.

My pulse thundered in my veins as footsteps approached. Would it be him? He knew he wasn't allowed to see me before the ceremony, but if I knew my groom, he would bend the rules as far as he could just to be near me.

A tentative knock rapped against the wooden door, and my photographer's voice sounded from the other side.

"Brynlee, it's Marsha." I opened the door and met her smiling face. "I have someone out here who's dying to see you, but he knows I won't let him." She smirked as her eyes cut to the hallway just outside the room where my bridesmaids and I were getting ready. "But, I know of a way I can get some photos of the two of you together without him seeing you."

Marsha positioned us on either side of the open door, keeping me shielded from his sight the entire time. We found each other's hands and held on as she snapped photos of us. He lifted my hand to his mouth and pressed a tender kiss to the backs of my fingers and the inside of my wrist. The camera clicked and shuttered as I blindly brought a hand to his face and cupped his cheek.

"I love you," he proclaimed through the door,

covering my hand with his. He held it there, basking in my touch as I savored the feel of his skin against mine. It was as though he'd sensed my earlier dismay and was there to offer me any comfort he could.

"I love you too," I whispered back, pressing my hand to the wood panels, yearning to hold him, to press my lips to his.

"I'll meet you at the altar."

His words settled into my chest, and I covered my mouth to stifle the sob that threatened to break loose. This was really happening. He was really here and dedicated to spending the rest of his life with me. No hesitation. No doubts. Just unwavering certainty and dedication. He made me feel whole and loved and like I was everything he'd ever dreamed of.

When it was time for the ceremony to begin, we all lined up, my little girl with a basket full of rose petals stationed in front of me. "You look so pretty, Mommy," Harper said as I knelt to straighten the bow on her dress."

"Thank you, but I don't think anyone is going to notice me at all when they see how beautiful you are," I crooned, pressing a kiss to her cheek. The gesture left a tiny smear of pink on her skin that I wiped away with my thumb. She beamed, scrunching her shoulders up to her ears and swaying side to side like little girls did when they received a compliment.

The doors opened and I stood, smoothing my hands over the front of my gown. They shook as a swarm of butterflies took flight in my stomach. My father's large mitts covered mine, stilling them against the onslaught of nerves. I looked up into his moss green eyes, so much like my own, and found his comforting strength, and it steadied me.

The music changed, and the wedding march began to play. I turned to find Macon waiting at the other end, and our gazes locked. His hand went to his mouth, and even from this distance, I could see the awe written across his face.

Everything else fell away as I drew closer to him. Sound was drowned out, and everyone disappeared from my line of sight. Only he and I existed in that moment. His eyes never left me as I approached, and my lips trembled as I noticed the tears he fought to contain.

When my father finally released me, I slid my hands into Macon's and never once looked away until it was time to retrieve his ring from Blake. My sister handed over the simple band with our names and wedding date engraved on the inside, and I slid it onto his finger. His eyes glittered, the golden flecks shining brightly as we pledged our lives to each other. The only thing left now was to seal the deal.

Macon stepped closer to me, one hand going to my waist and the other to my cheek, his warm palm sliding against my skin. I braced my hands on his shoulders as he kissed me. It was a sweet but determined kiss, a promise of what was to come later.

As we lay in the dark, his promise fulfilled, I nuzzled into his side as he gently stroked my bare arm. "How are you feeling, Mrs. Lewis?" he asked, grinning down at me.

"Like the luckiest woman in the world."

"No way," he countered, pulling me closer. "I'm the lucky one."

THANK YOU SO MUCH FOR READING RECKLESS Abandon! Want more Brynlee & Macon? Subscribe to my newsletter using the QR code to unlock the bonus epilogue.

NEXT UP IN THE WILLOW BROOK FALLS SERIES IS Twisted Fate. One click Delilah's story today!

Download Here

IF YOU LIKE STEAMY, BROTHER'S BEST FRIEND ROMANCES and enjoyed Brynlee and Macon's story, then you'll love Taylor and Dalton! Check out Six Nights in Paradise today.

"ONE OF THE HOTTEST STORIES I'VE READ THIS YEAR."
   -USA Today Bestselling Author Amy Stephens

"THIS BOOK IS ROMANTIC, HOT, STEAMY, SEXY...UGH SIMPLY perfect!!"
   -Lenor, Goodreads reviewer

TURN THE PAGE FOR AN EXCERPT OF SIX NIGHTS IN Paradise>>

EXCERPT FROM SIX NIGHTS IN
PARADISE

"Hungry?" he asked.

"Depends," I responded playfully, and his lips quirked.

"On what?"

"Whatcha got in the bag?" I swung my legs around and sat up on the side of my chair. He opened it, the paper crinkling between his hands, and pulled out a beignet.

"Oooh, gimme!" I reached for it and he gave it up easily. "Mmm," I moaned, devouring the powdered sugar covered ball of fluffy fried dough. Beignets were my favorite. Did he know that somehow, or was this a happy coincidence?

"Chocolate milk?" he asked as he held out a small sealed plastic bottle.

"Thank you." It was like he read my mind.

We ate our sugar laden breakfast — my second breakfast — in silence. Once all the pastries and chocolate milk were gone, I offered to take all our trash inside and dispose of it. When I came back out, Dalton was spraying himself with sunscreen on the patio. I turned to shut the door behind me and heard him let out a low curse. Assuming he must have gotten some of the spray in his eyes, I turned quickly, ready to retrieve some water for him to flush it out. I wasn't prepared for what greeted me instead. Dalton's dark gaze seared into me, heating my skin. I shrank back into the corner of the patio as he stalked toward me.

"What the fuck are you wearing?" he growled, stopping only inches from me.

"What?"

"Don't play dumb with me. Ninety percent of your ass is on display for anyone to see."

His chest was heaving and so was mine, but his breath was coming hard and fast from anger, mine from arousal. Or maybe it was the other way around. He looked at me like he wanted to spank my ass and send me to bed for being defiant. *Or so he could ravage me.* The heated look in his eyes had my thighs clamping together, but his words made me spitting mad. *Who the fuck does he think he is?*

"It's a bathing suit," I seethed.

"It's a thong," he snapped.

"Wrong," I countered. "They're Brazilian cut," I corrected him.

His eyes flashed down my body and I knew what he was thinking. Was there anything else on my lower body that was *Brazilian*?

"You're practically naked," he growled, and the

sound sent a pulse of arousal straight to my core. He leaned in closer, bracing his palm against the wall behind me. My heartbeat skyrocketed, the anticipation of a kiss stealing my already panting breath. "The only thing I *can't* see is your ass crack."

His crass statement should have smothered the flames of my lust, but all it did was fan them. I had to bite my tongue so I wouldn't ask if he wanted to see that, too.

Want more? Grab your copy of Six Nights in Paradise now!

ALSO BY ASHLEY CADE

Wild Hearts Series

Something That Could Last

Everything We Left Unsaid

Anything For this Love

Willow Brook Falls Series

Twisted Fate

Other Books

Six Nights in Paradise

Desperation

ACKNOWLEDGMENTS

Thank you to everyone who helped bring Brynlee and Macon's story to life. To Tiffany, my PA, beta reader, proofreader, cheerleader and motivator, I couldn't do this without you.

To my alphas and betas, Kelly, Katelyn, Autumn, Jennifer, and Amanda, thank you for taking the time to read the earliest drafts of this book. As always, your feedback has been invaluable.

Thank you to my amazing editor Silla. You are a freaking rockstar!

To Kate at Y'all That Graphic, thank you for this gorgeous cover! It is perfection.

To all the readers who picked up Reckless Abandon, that you for giving this book (and me) a chance! I hope you enjoyed Brynlee and Macon's story.

ABOUT THE AUTHOR

Ashley is a USA Today Bestselling author who likes her small town romance extra spicy with a touch of angst and a splash of humor. Her swoon worthy heroes will melt your kindles (along with your under-garments). She resides in Ohio with her husband and two sons where she pens emotionally gripping love stories about imperfect people who find their happily ever after.

Connect with Ashley

Newsletter • Facebook • Instagram • TikTok
Goodreads • Bookbub • Pinterest • Website

Made in the USA
Las Vegas, NV
27 April 2024